SORCERESS HUNTING

LISA BLACKWOOD

SORCERESS HUNTING

A Gargoyle & Sorceress Tale / Book 3

LISA BLACKWOOD

Sorceress Hunting

Gargoyle & Sorceress Book 3

COVER DESIGNED BY: Heather Hamilton-Senter

EDITED BY: Perry Constantine

PROOFREAD BY: Tracy Vandervliet

Special Thanks to Stan H for his eagle eyes.

EBOOK ISBN: 978-1-990608-49-0

EDITION: 10/27/2021

❧ Created with Vellum

BOOKS BY LISA BLACKWOOD

Gargoyle & Sorceress

Dawn of the Sorceress

Sorceress Awakening

Sorceress Rising

Sorceress Hunting

Sorceress at War

Sorceress Enraged

Legacy of the Sorceress

Sorcery & Firedrakes

Scion of the Sorceress

Sorceress Eternal

In Deception's Shadow Series (Epic Fantasy Romance)

Betrayal's Price

Herd Mistress

Maiden's Wolf

Death's Queen

The Prince's Gryphon (forthcoming)

Ishtar's Legacy Series (Epic Fantasy Romance)

Ishtar's Blade

The Blade's Beginning (short story)

Blade's Honor

Blade's Destiny

The Blade's Shadow

First Queen of the Gryphons

The King of the Anunnaki (forthcoming)

The Anunnaki's Blade (forthcoming)

Huntress vs Huntsman (Epic Fantasy Romance)

Master of the Hunt

Night Huntress

Dragon Archer

Soul Mage (forthcoming)

FREE BOOKS

GET TWO FREE STORIES FROM MY BESTSELLING SERIES WHEN YOU SIGN UP FOR MY NEWSLETTER.

I send regular monthly newsletters with details about new releases,
special offers, freebies, and other bookish news.
If that's something you'd be interested in, just follow the link below.

http://lisablackwood.com/join-the-newsletter-here/

ABOUT THE BOOK

Some victories feel more like defeat.

Lillian and Gregory may have defeated the demonic Riven, but human authorities are now aware that something equally as intelligent but far more deadly shares their world. To the Avatars' dismay, this is not just a guns in the woods, boots on the ground kind of hunt. Scientists are spearheading this pursuit, and Lillian and Gregory are their intended targets.

If that wasn't complication enough, Lillian's little brother, Shadowlight, saves the life of a female soldier and now he must hide his pet human from the other fae for her own safety.

Corporal Anna Mackenzie is no pet, but she'll be the first to admit she feels fiercely protective toward the lonely young gargoyle, and if anyone messes with the kid, she'll go full metal bitch all over their ass.

Long after the Avatars had left the glade, a lanky figure shrouded from head to toe in black and crimson armor dropped from his perch two-thirds of the way up the hamadryad. He landed lightly, only the slightest rattle from his armor and weapons betrayed his presence.

He straightened and looked around the clearing, which was protected on all sides by a manicured, evergreen maze. After another quick glance around, he turned his attention to the ground beneath his boots. Giving it a prod, he dug a furrow in the soft earth.

The Mortal Realm—the one place he'd never thought he'd step. Yet, here he was, for good or ill. Distaste twisted his lips, exposing his fangs. Already, he could feel this realm plucking at his magic, wanting to drag it from him and render him as helpless as the other fae he sensed guarding the maze.

That wasn't something he would allow. Weakness of any

kind was abhorrent, and he had eliminated any personal soft-ness at an earlier age.

One didn't survive to rule over the Battle Goddess's armies by being weak.

Commander Gryton took another look around before moving out of the hamadryad's shadow. He was still mildly shocked the Gargoyle Protector had not sensed his arrival.

But then again, the male half of the Avatar pairing was still exhausted in mind, body, and spirit from recent events. Events which the Sorceress's hamadryad had willingly shown Gryton as she transported him here.

Another perplexing mystery in need of resolution. He didn't know why the hamadryad had shared knowledge with him, or so willingly brought him to this realm. However, that particular mystery would keep. He'd come to this cursed land for another reason—his collars. He'd known the moment the warded collars had left the Battle Goddess's domain, had in fact been working on the other set when the theft had occurred. He'd acted immediately but still hadn't been fast enough to stop the thieves from vanishing with his collars into the abyss of the Mortal Realm. It hadn't taken long to discover the identities of the thieves. And, oh, how the Battle Goddess would rage when she learned the truth.

That Stalks the Darkness would take his newborn child and run wasn't a great surprise, but Gryton had soon discov-ered the gargoyle hadn't been alone.

The truth was a greater shock. The gargoyle's dryad keeper, the Battle Goddess's own confidant, had fled willingly.

With that act, his path had been set—follow Darkness and River to the Mortal Realm and bring them back to the Battle Goddess or, at the very least, retrieve the collars.

To go before the Lady of Battles with only an explanation would have ended badly for all concerned.

So here he found himself in the Mortal Realm with a most unusual set of circumstances arrayed before him. He'd assumed Darkness and River were simply defecting and had taken the collars as a goodwill gesture to show the Gargoyle Protector what the Battle Goddess had planned.

Had that happened, it would have been disastrous for the Lady's plans. Given a little time with the collars, the Protector would have studied them and taken steps to neutralize the spells and then adapt his personal protections to become impervious to such an attack in the future.

But that wasn't what had happened at all. No, a siren from an ancient time had unbalanced the male half of the Avatars, and her act of interference had opened other unforeseen possibilities.

The hamadryad had shown that in a moment of panic over the lives of humans, her young and very foolish dryad mistress had collared herself and her other half.

Well, in truth, the tree's version of events showed the protector collaring himself, but that must be incorrect, surely?

Fate was not usually so kind to him, Gryton reflected, but whether it came about because of an idiotic young dryad or a befuddled Gargoyle Protector, he would happily benefit from their mistakes.

Now all he need do was capture one of them and return to the Magic Realm. The collars would force the other half to follow.

With the Avatars' return, the Battle Goddess would be content, and Gryton could keep his head and his immortality intact.

He merely had to avoid detection until he could set traps. Though it might not be the most straightforward task to complete with the number of fae he sensed lurking around this maze and surrounding land. There was also the matter of the other two gargoyles who would require a healthy dose of caution.

But the greatest danger should have been the Avatars themselves.

When he'd arrived in this realm, the Avatars had still been in the glade, learning from the hamadryad that the ancient siren had sacrificed herself and in so doing defeated the Riven army.

The Protector's attention was diverted, but not so much he should have wholly missed Gryton's arrival.

Luck?

Or the hamadryad's meddling?

Neither idea was appealing as both scenarios placed events out of his control.

Though he might also credit it to the Protector having his natural senses dulled by the new collar around his throat as well as years trapped in this realm.

That was a much happier explanation than the Sorceress's hamadryad manipulating events to her liking.

Whatever the cause, it led to a rare set of occurrences he couldn't pass up, not if he wanted to remain free of Lord Death's clutches. That one knew what Gryton was. Another thought slipped through his mind. None in this realm knew what he truly was. Here, he would be safe after a fashion—at least as safe as any being could be from the Lord of the Underworld.

Even the Avatars didn't remember what he was.

Perhaps he might have a use for the Mortal Realm after all?

When fate handed out her gifts, it was always best to accept them graciously.

With a final glance at the hamadryad, he eased out from between her branches and traversed the open center of the glade, past a ring of broken ward stones and into the maze's shadowy corridors.

All the time, he felt the hamadryad and the enchanted cedars of the maze watching him with an awareness not based in the physical world. He didn't care what she had planned, he would not be manipulated by a tree, no matter if she was the Mother's Sorceress.

He had his own agenda.

One which might take days or moons to complete, but he was nothing if not patient. Besides, the Avatars had already shown themselves to be less than they used to be.

A flicker of a hunter's bloodlust stirred in his core, his magic awakening at the thought of a challenge.

He reined in his emotions, and his magic soon returned to its slumber. With a final glance back at the watchful tree, Commander Gryton made his way out of the maze and into the gardens beyond, heading for the dark canopy of the forest in the distance.

There he would hide until he'd learned more about this realm, and just how compromised the Avatars had become.

CHAPTER ONE

*L*illian sat curled on the couch and stared at the television, a cup of tea growing cold in her hands. Every few seconds, her attention switched between the media's special presentation covering the events of the night before and the messenger spells her grandmother was weaving where she sat on the opposite end of the couch.

The powerful spell Gregory had summoned to heal the fae injured during the Rivens' attack had also knocked out the power grid, cell phone service, radio, internet, and most other modern conveniences.

Only after the battle's subsequent cleanup had they learned those services were down. The power grid came back online first, followed by radio and television. Unfortunately, cell service was still down.

Hence why Gran was using messenger spells to relay orders and news among the Clan and Coven. Gran whispered the ending incantations of the spell. The letter she held flared with light as magic transformed it into the shape of a hummingbird. It hovered above Gran's open palm for a moment more before zipping out the open patio doors.

Lillian stared at where it had been, still mesmerized by the whimsical, though presently useful, bit of magic. It was the fifth one Gran had made, and Lillian still marveled at it.

In her defense, she was operating on only three hours of sleep. Which was nowhere near enough time to recover or process all that had happened. Her other half was doing a better job of focusing. Currently, he'd stopped pacing to study the television.

She wasn't sure how much he understood—he was very intelligent and knowledgeable about all things magical and the universe, in general, but she didn't know if he grasped the subtler points of modern human culture.

Up until this point, her gargoyle protector had done his level best to avoid and ignore the humans, but by the way he focused on the news, with his ears flat against his mane and his tail flicking in agitation, she imagined he was starting to rethink his opinion of humans and how he viewed them.

'Yes, my beloved gargoyle,' she thought to herself, *'the humans are a force to be reckoned with. You can't just continue to pretend they are unimportant and of no consequence.'*

It was close to noon, and the last of the fae search parties were straggling back to the cottage a few at a time.

They were using cloaking magic to hide. The whole area was under military lockdown, and any suspicious movement would bring a storm of trouble down upon all their heads.

The word among the humans was that a suspected terrorist attack was still being investigated, but nothing had been confirmed. The news switched between images of scared people being herded back to their houses, grim-faced police, grimmer-faced military, and clips of an earlier riot caused by some hotheads.

Though unknown to the humans, the minor act of civil unrest had been squelched by several Coven members weaving spells to pacify the worst of the fear.

Gran had said there had been enough bloodshed in the last twenty-four hours to suffice. They didn't need more. Besides, the spells were easy enough to cast with the plentiful magic Gregory had summoned while battling the Riven. More magic was saturating the Mortal Realm than it had seen in hundreds, if not thousands, of years. Of course, the magic would soon diffuse across the globe so the local concentrations would diminish. For now, the Coven and Clan seemed to be enjoying the bounty, even if the situation requiring it was less than ideal.

It should have been enough her loved ones had all survived, and the Riven had been exterminated, but Lillian couldn't relax.

Of course disaster might come from a completely different quarter.

Her hands strayed to her flat belly. She prayed it would stay that way. Her mind was in the process of conjuring up all the possible disastrous complications a pregnancy might invoke when the news anchorwoman informed the viewers a press conference had just been announced and would start in a few minutes.

Lillian's cynical side wondered if whatever the press conference revealed would make the possibility of a baby seem less dire in comparison.

From the corner of her eye, she caught Gregory shifting a wing out of his way to squint over his shoulder at her.

Oh, shit. Mr. Hyperaware was picking up on her worry. Maybe he'd think it was the news and the humans.

She gestured first at Gregory and then at the couch beside her, hoping he'd think she just wanted comfort, and not guess she was actually trying to hide something from him.

As he was prone to do, he didn't respond the way she thought he would. Instead of sitting on the couch next to her —which wasn't really big enough for an eight-foot-tall gargoyle, she admitted—he settled on his haunches and leaned against her legs.

"What do you think about how the humans are responding to this new crisis?" Gregory's deep voice soothed her nerves even if he asked a question she didn't know how to answer.

"Honestly, I thought they'd have stormed our walls already." Lillian shrugged and then narrowed her eyes. "We know from what we've overheard that the human authorities —at least the military—suspects our family of some involvement in the strange occurrences. And that we just *happened* to plan a masquerade on the night the Riven attacked? They'll find it too much of a coincidence not to investigate."

"I would hunt out the truth, were I them," Gregory acknowledged.

"Exactly." Lillian sipped at her cold tea as she glanced back at the television. An official was introducing someone in uniform. "But then, what if they found something more interesting to study than us?"

Gran and Gregory turned their gazes fully upon her.

"Surely you've both had the same thought by now?"

They glanced at each other in silence.

"Oh, come on. I can't be the only one to worry the

humans might have caught one of the Riven. Gran, you said before they had found Riven bodies. What if this time they found live ones?"

Gregory rumbled an unhappy sound. "We will infiltrate their ranks and learn if they have managed to capture one of the beasts. It's possible one may have evaded our search spells. If that is the case, we must dispose of it before it has a chance to infect others."

Gran raised her hand and pointed at the television while at the same time turning up the volume. "We may have other concerns."

Lillian followed Gran's direction. Undaunted by the flash of cameras and the shouts of reporters, a group of military brass had gathered in front of the town hall, using the first landing of its stairs as an impromptu stage.

The speaker on screen, a man Lillian would guess to be in his late forties, was saying no one had claimed responsibility for the attack. He went on to say the as yet unknown gaseous substance, which had rendered its victims unconscious or caused them to have mild hallucinations, seemed to have no other long-term side effects. However, the local residents would all be screened to rule out further danger.

"Gas attack, my ass," Lillian muttered under her breath. "I told you that's what they'd call the Siren's enchantment."

"In this instance, a lie serves us much better than the truth," Gran countered.

"True."

Gregory made a deep huffing sound. "They have something else planned. You can read it in their expressions even over that strange device." He gestured at the television with a vague motion.

Lillian realized Gregory was correct.

"Screenings," she muttered. "Blood tests! They are going to go door to door collecting samples. I doubt it will be voluntary."

"Indeed," Gran muttered a curse under her breath. "Since they were shooting at the Riven too, they damn well know it wasn't a gas attack. They'll be looking for a way to ferret out non-humans with their tests."

"And any kind of blood test will likely involve DNA tests."

"Yes." Gran's expression turned distant, meaning she was deep in planning mode.

CHAPTER TWO

Gregory swiveled his ears in the direction of the kitchen, and more specifically, the back entrance to the cottage. The sound of approaching footsteps reached his ears. A moment later, Lillian's older brother, Jason, entered the house and made for the main living area.

Gregory didn't bother to summon concealing magic as the coven member was alone. Though he was tempted to merely for a reason to use magic. It and the ability to speak mind to mind were the only powers he still had sole discretion over not requiring a direct command from Lillian. He fingered the tattoo collar circling his neck.

Even that meager power was his to call only because she had already made it a command. They hadn't had time to study the full limitations his tattoo imposed upon his magic, not yet. But they would need to learn and explore how greatly he was crippled. At least, with Lillian's order, he was able to access his defensive magic to protect her.

Earlier, they'd discovered Lillian couldn't give him

complete access to all his magic in a broad sweeping command. The tattoo didn't allow such. His skin still felt raw from the tattoo's blistering warning.

When she would have issued a dozen different ones, he'd cautioned her against it. Being decapitated by the tattoo-like slave collar was not how he wished to return to the Spirit Realm.

For the time being, the magic under his command was limited to the ability to hide in shadow, track his prey, and detect evil should it venture within range. He didn't even know what that 'range' was yet.

But he would learn and overcome these new disabilities.

He watched Lillian as she came to her feet at the arrival of her brother. After brief hugs, they exchanged stories.

"The whole town has been asked to remain in their homes," Jason was saying, "until such a time as it is deemed safe for residents to venture out again."

Gran cleared her throat, "In other words, we're in lock-down until they have poked, tagged, and categorized everyone to their heart's content."

"Exactly," Jason agreed with a nod, not a hint of his usual jovial attitude in attendance. "That begs the question of when, where, and how are we getting out of Dodge with the lockdown in place?"

"We're not." Gran's voice held a dangerous edge, one Gregory admired.

She knew the reasons they couldn't leave. Not that Gregory was going to be run off by a pack of misinformed mortals.

"We can update our disguises and cover stories, and start over elsewhere," Jason continued doggedly. "It's not like the

Coven hasn't done it before. It's a damn better option than getting tagged and bagged for some scientist to dissect in a lab."

"Jason has a point," Lillian said. "It's going to get a little tense around here. There's no way we can avoid the medical teams they will send house to house, not without shouting we've got something to hide."

"Doesn't matter." Gran folded her arms. "We can't run. Not this time. Your hamadryad is here. If it was a regular hamadryad, you could take a cutting and start over somewhere else. However, this hamadryad is presently also the Mother's Sorceress. I do not feel comfortable leaving such power undefended within easy reach of the humans. Perhaps the humans will never guess she is more than a tree, and she'll be safe, but I won't risk all the remaining magic in this realm on wishful thinking."

Gregory stretched and shook out his wings and then dropped to all fours. He walked to Gran's side and gave her a playful headbutt. "Both wise and beautiful. No, I won't leave Lillian's hamadryad, nor will I abandon my other fae allies. Many of the Clan are tied to the land and their territories and cannot move easily."

"Flattery will get you everywhere," Gran said with a twinkle in her eye. "We're going to stay and give the humans exactly what they think they want."

Lillian's curiosity washed over him, resembling a turbulent wave. As he expected, she jumped into the conversation. "You plan to use magic on the humans, to somehow make them think they've tested us already."

"A good guess, but no," Gran said with a grin. "While that would work, it would take a huge amount of magic and planning. No, I plan on giving the samples, but then later following them back to their lab where we will switch them with samples of human blood. We already have some in storage for just such a need, but we didn't plan on such a large-scale situation. To be safe, we'll require enough for the entire Coven membership. For that amount, we'll immediately start canvassing neighboring towns for unsuspecting humans matching Coven members' appearances. With luck, we should be able to trick the human scientists without having to use magic upon them."

"Still, it isn't going to be easy sneaking in and switching samples." Lillian pursed her lips as she was prone to doing when she was planning. He found it an endearing trait and merely let the conversation flow around him. They'd eventually come to the same conclusion he already had.

Reaching out with a tendril of magic, he sought the other two gargoyles in this realm. The first he brushed against was a bright, young magic, flashes of excitement and curiosity bleeding across the link. Shadowlight, then. Lillian's newly discovered younger brother. The sense of happiness and willingness increased when the other realized it was Gregory.

"Sorry, young one. It is your father I need."

With a mental acknowledgment, Shadowlight vanished from Gregory's thoughts to be replaced by the more disciplined mind of Stalks the Darkness.

"Avatar, how may I be of assistance?"

"We have learned the humans plan to study the blood of all the townsfolk, hunting for differences which will allow them to track the magic users."

There was mental silence followed by a hesitant, *"You wish for me to seek out the humans behind the threat and deal with them before they can unearth something you would prefer remained hidden?"*

Gregory missed working with others of his kind. Life was so much easier viewed through a gargoyle's viewpoint. Innocents were protected. Threats were dispatched. Evil wasn't tolerated. Life was good.

Gregory sighed deeply. *"Alas, no. This is not our realm, and so we must abide by the Clan and Coven's wishes in this. At present, they are a touch divided, but it looks like they will allow the samples to be taken to offset suspicion and later we'll replace those same samples with human blood they have collected from other sources."*

"I see," Darkness said and then launched into his own report. *"The leshii, Greenborrow, warns of another development. Several of our patrols have found human soldiers among the Riven dead. Those already infected by the Riven were dispatched. Those deemed uninfected have been taken to the healers to have their wounds treated and their memories wiped."* Darkness paused before continuing, *"I have more disturbing news. When last I spoke with Greenborrow, he was looking for the fae leader, Whitethorn and a sprite by the name of Goswin. I believe I may have found what became of them. During the last leg of my patrol, I caught the scent of Whitethorn. I followed it and came upon a large group of humans in a meadow. They were studying the area. By the smell of blood and the gore splattered around the meadow, a vicious battle had been waged there. There were no bodies present. Either other members of the Clan had been there before me and started cleanup but had been interrupted before they could finish, or they hadn't been there yet, and the humans had already removed the bodies."*

"Can you tell if Whitethorn and Goswin survived the battle?"

"No, not after the humans had trampled all over everything."

There was another pause, and Gregory sensed the older

gargoyle was talking with his son. *I'm sending Shadowlight on ahead to meet up with Greenborrow. I don't want my son near these humans.*

"Agreed," Gregory said, belatedly feeling a little uneasy for allowing the gargoyle child out in the field at all. *The leshii can watch over Shadowlight. Once he's safe, return to the cottage as soon as you're able. By then, the Coven should have collected all the human blood they will need. In the meantime, I'll see what I can learn.*

Gregory released the other gargoyle's mind and returned to his body, becoming aware of the stone cottage and the warm, homey smells of the kitchen.

The other conversation had run its course. Lillian, Gran, and Jason all watched him with silent patience. He touched Lillian's mind.

Ah, they'd come to the same conclusion as he had earlier.

"I've spoken with Darkness, and he will aid us in sneaking into the humans' domain when it's time. However, we have a new development. Greenborrow and Darkness have found human soldiers, some wounded and others infected by the Riven. Darkness also reports he found signs of Whitethorn and Goswin." Gregory flared out his wings, stretching and limbering up tense muscles. "It looks like they may have been found by the humans. We have no way of knowing their condition until I've had a chance to investigate."

Stepping into his path, Gran blocked him as he made for the back door. "You and Lillian will need to be here when the humans come. I can't imagine we will be last on their list, more likely among the first wave. Whitethorn and Goswin will have to wait for their rescue until the rest of the Clan and Coven are safe." Gran frowned unhappily. Though he didn't know if it was because she hated to make her friends wait, or if she doubted they were alive.

Gran braced one hand on her hip while the fingers of the other hand drummed out a rhythm on her thigh. "You'll have to be human when they come and be docile while they take your blood." Gran looked thoughtful and added, "At least it's a mostly human looking red. Can you spell it to look identical to human blood?"

"Easily," he rumbled as he stepped around her. "Do not fear. I will be on my best behavior."

He chuckled at Gran's disbelieving look and then turned to Lillian.

Her expression showed determination. "Tonight, after we've switched out the blood samples, we'll look for Whitethorn and Goswin. Obviously, we'll have to hunt up whatever other evidence the humans have found and destroy it."

"Yes."

He knew what Lillian hadn't said. They would reclaim the bodies of Whitethorn and the sprite if they hadn't escaped the battle alive. Which, he was coming to think, was very likely.

Whitethorn was powerful and old. If he lived, he would have found a way to communicate with them or escape. That he hadn't done either meant he was likely already dead.

CHAPTER THREE

*S*hadowlight bounded down the path, the afternoon shadows already growing long behind him. He was alone for the first time in his life and found the experience exciting and a little lonely. Though he was proud his father had given him a mission. He was supposed to join Greenborrow while his parents prepared to aid Gregory and Lillian.

When he'd first learned his sister and her guardian needed help, he'd wanted to go with them. Infiltrating the humans' territory and switching samples had sounded fun, and it would have given him the opportunity to practice his invisibility weaving. However, he also liked the leshii, making his present assignment tolerable.

There would be time to sneak up on mortals later. He had an important job to do by helping Greenborrow determine if other members of the fae were missing and how many. He really was on his way to do that. He just happened also to be finishing the patrol his parents had started. He'd watched as they had cleaned the sites they'd found. He'd even helped at the last two, so he knew he was more than capable if he should run into a battle site in need of cleaning.

It didn't make sense to him why all the fae viewed the humans the way they did, not when they had other creatures to fear. Hmmm, he *was* young and had never met a human in person. Perhaps it wasn't right to judge.

Shadowlight turned down a new game trail, and the scent of Riven and old battle hit him full across all his senses. He skidded to a halt, scenting the air, seeking the direction of the highest concentration. Ah. There. To the left of the track he was presently following. He took his time studying the immediate area for dangers and ambushes. His mother's hamadryad had shown him a great many survival skills while he gestated inside her. He saw no reason not to trust to her teachings.

Even with his concealment magic shrouding him from view, he prowled along on all fours, making as little noise as possible. When he'd taken in the scene thoroughly, he studied it a few moments more to be sure.

Scattered across the ground, like boulders left by a retreating glacier, several broken bodies of human and Riven origin lay in a haphazard circle around the base of a balsam fir. Even the evergreen's pungent fragrance couldn't hide the breath-stealing scent of violent death and the stomach-souring stench of Riven taint.

The stench burned his nose, tongue, and throat, but he ignored those senses and focused on others as he eased into the immediate area. He called his magic and rid the earth of the demon-tainted corpses first, and then the human bodies next. He added a prayer to speed their souls into the next life.

He noted some of the humans had died from mortal wounds inflicted by the attacking Riven, while others showed apparent signs of Riven infection. The sharp fangs and claws were some of the earliest signs of contamination. Interestingly, a few of the humans must have swiftly come to understand what their companions were turning into and ended them before the change made them harder to kill.

He continued to cleanse the land, following a trail of broken underbrush and trampled greenery.

Here, there were fresher signs. He came upon another Riven body where it had crawled away from the battle. He glanced at the signs on the ground again. No, it hadn't been crawling away, it had been creeping in pursuit of something else. A second blood trail led away from the battle.

The Riven, its mad hunger driving it ever onward, had managed to crawl quite a distance with only one leg. The other looked to have been sheared off by one of the human weapons his sister had warned him about. During last night's battle with the Riven, he'd heard the terrible noise the guns made, and he'd already seen the damage many times while he aided his parents purifying the forest. But that hadn't been what killed the Riven.

Shadowlight glanced down at the body once more before summoning magic to dispose of it. Had this one not been driven to continue the hunt for its prey, it might have survived the night.

But judging by how the head had been severed from its neck, he guessed its intended 'prey' had gotten tired of being hunted and had set an ambush for the Riven. He continued his search with more caution than earlier. This battle's participants might not all be as dead as he'd first thought. Easing into deeper shadows, he continued his hunt. When he reached the blood trail's end, he found two more Riven and a human soldier. The human lay propped against an old giant of a tree, his body wedged between two of its massive roots.

Braced against the soldier's drawn up legs, the long metal device, which he'd learned was what made the fierce sounds and tore the flesh of its victims to shreds by using many tiny projectiles, lay dormant.

Of the two Riven, one was still alive, but impaled on a trap. The other one to the left side of the soldier was dead. Its body torn with ragged tears. This one had also been decapitated, and not with the swift, clean stroke of a sword. It looked more like it had been hacked at repeatedly with a smaller blade. The wounds spoke of desperation, or perhaps the last fierce strength of one knowing his own end was at hand but was determined to take another of the enemy with him.

Surprise and respect stirred in Shadowlight's heart. Here was one of Light's champions, found among the humans, but a hero all the same. The human's heart still beat, as weak and labored as his breathing, but it would not for much longer, not with the wounds he had suffered.

And the soldier had also sustained several Riven bites, and their taint was already infiltrating his body. He would grant the soldier a merciful death once he'd dealt with the other remaining Riven.

This Riven squirmed and thrashed as it tried to free itself from where it was impaled on a broken sapling. Clever human to have set the trap and used himself as bait.

Even with the terrible wounds, including one which had taken most of one arm, the Riven continued its slow, painful struggle toward the human.

Shadowlight didn't know what it planned to do once it

reached its destination. It wasn't as if the human could become anymore tainted. One of his father's memories surfaced and slid along his consciousness. Ah, that was the Riven's plan. The demon soul within had concluded its host body was too damaged to repair and the human only a few strides away was a better option to act as host until another was found. Together the old Riven spirit and the new one developing within the human's soul would find a place to hide for a time, and then start infecting others to rebuild their numbers.

Shadowlight growled softly and released his concealment spell, wanting the Riven to know what was going to send it back to the dark. When the beast became aware of something other than its human target, the Riven glanced up at Shadowlight, flashing its fangs in a mix of surprise and defiance.

Shadowlight unleashed a lance of destroying shadow magic and sent it cascading deep into the heart of the misbegotten beast. The Riven opened its mouth wide in a silent scream and then blew apart into a hundred thousand wisps of shadow and light. With its destruction, the forest around Shadowlight already felt cleaner. He turned his attention to the human-killed Riven next, vanishing its taint with the same purifying spell.

He scanned the immediate area looking for other Riven but sensed only the taint of their spilled blood. He went to work on that, wanting to postpone the other grisly task for a few moments more.

"Enemy of my enemy is my friend. Or some shit like that," a voice gasped close at hand. Shadowlight swung his attention back to where the soldier lay. He'd thought the soldier was unconscious, but he was wrong. A set of dark brown eyes studied him under thick dark lashes.

"Do a girl a favor and do to me what you just did to those things." She coughed and then gasped in pain.

Shadowlight paced closer until he was almost on top of the soldier. This close he could scent the soldier's female essence over all the blood, gore, and taint. Not a male like he'd first thought.

"Don't know what you are," she choked out, and then dragged the back of her hand across her bloody lips, "and don't really care as long as you kill me before I turn into one of those evil bastards. I can feel it growing inside. But it fears you."

Curious, Shadowlight hunched down next to the human.

She studied him in turn, her gaze lacking fear. His mother's memories showed that for some, when death came for them, it was a relief, and they did not fear the end. While others cried and begged and pleaded, fighting against what came next until their last breath.

"I am a gargoyle," he said into the silence.

"Gargoyle, eh?" She seemed to think his words over for a moment. "Well, Gargoyle, since you're no friend of those things..."

"Riven," he supplied and then added, "They serve the endless void, not the Light."

"Riven. Suits them. Can I count on you...?" She held a knife in one hand, likely the one she'd used to kill the Riven, and gave it a little shake. "Can't seem to do it myself."

No, she wouldn't. The Riven taint wouldn't let her. It needed a viable host to anchor it to this realm.

Shadowlight took the blade from her. He didn't need it to

finish her off, but he wanted something to postpone what he'd have to do next. He'd seen his mother and father do what needed doing several times this night. As for himself, he'd yet to end any life not already a Riven. Those ones were already dead in one sense. This human watching him with her pain-filled eyes was something else altogether, and he feared the act of ending her would change him in some way. He suddenly felt his age. He wanted his mother or father at his side.

But they weren't here. And the human was.

She was young. Although several years older than him. From what he'd seen and sensed, she was brave and as honorable as a gargoyle. He couldn't leave her bright spirit to be overtaken and enslaved by the Riven tainting it.

Yet, he found himself reluctant to end her life even though it was required.

The Riven taint was too deeply embedded to be routed out by normal magical means. While he had powerful healing abilities and could fight off Riven taint with little effort, the human had no such reserves left.

His dryad mother was a healer, and her knowledge and memories told him his magic could heal the human's injuries, but the Riven taint was not something that could be healed. It had to be hunted down and eradicated first.

By its very nature, his magic-laced gargoyle blood was designed for hunting and eradicating evil. A blood exchange would kill the Riven taint, but there was a good chance the human wouldn't survive it either. If she did, what then? She'd be tied to him for life, just like the unicorn was to Gregory.

And that was just with one sip of blood. He feared this would take much more. All his knowledge came from his parents' memories, but neither of them had ever had reason to heal a human in such a way. He wasn't even sure it would work.

A brave human was dying at his feet, worse than dying actually. He had to help, or at least try.

"Little human, can you still hear me?"

She blinked her eyes open and then took a moment to focus on him. "Yes. Just do it. You're running out of time. It's growing stronger."

"You are brave. Stronger, I think, than many of your kind. There may be another way to help you." Shadowlight dropped down onto his haunches and mantled his wings around himself. He really didn't want to kill her, sensing it might darken a part of his soul if he did. "Gargoyle blood contains powerful healing and purifying magic. If I share my blood with you, it will hunt down the Riven taint in yours and destroy it. However, it might also kill you along with the taint."

She laughed, and it turned into a groan. "God, this is the strangest conversation I've ever had. I'm worse than dead without your help. So what if your blood kills me?"

"Yes, but it would be a painful death." Shadowlight gave a little shrug. "I could grant you a quicker death with my talons. However, if you are not afraid of pain, I would prefer to attempt to heal you."

"Can't believe I'm talking to a hallucination. On the off chance this is real, I'd be stupid to say no. Besides, I really want to get revenge on the bastards who did this."

Her voice drifted into silence, and he realized she'd just blacked out again. She'd given consent, though, hadn't she?

Shadowlight gave another little shrug. He understood her reasoning. If he'd been in a similar circumstance, he'd want a second chance to live, to hunt down his enemies, to avenge his family. Because that's what he sensed when she'd talked of revenge. The men who had died here with her were like family.

He brought his wrist up to his muzzle. A swift, sharp nip and his fangs sliced through his skin and his own blood coated his lips. Scanning the human, he sought the locations of the Riven bites. Finding five in total, he dripped his own blood upon them.

With a strangled hiss of pain, she gasped. Her eyes snapped open. He used the opportunity to press his bleeding wrist to her lips. She choked and sputtered at first, trying to spit out his blood, but he merely pushed his wrist harder against her lips.

"Drink, it's your only chance at life, and even then, a slim one."

The human's wide-eyed stare didn't change at first, but after a moment his words must have sunk in because she forced herself to swallow.

Her fingers wrapped around his forearm with a desperate strength as the muscles along her neck tensed and flexed as she fought past her natural gag reflex. The hard-fought battle drained away the last of her strength, and her fingers loosened their grip, but her iron will won the fight, conquering her aversion to his blood. Though, by her deep grimace and occasional muffled gag, she didn't like it. To be honest, he took no joy in the act either. It simply hurt.

She jerked her head to the side.

"Enough." She held up a hand, which trembled with near violence. "If you force me to drink more, I swear, I'll throw up all over you."

Shadowlight didn't know how much blood was required but took her at her word and instead held his wrist over her bite marks again.

"Dammit all to hell, that hurts!"

He nodded. "It's working then."

"Fuck. You don't say!" She curled into a fetal position and buried her face in her forearms. It did little to muffle her pained sounds.

"There is no one else near," he offered helpfully. "You can scream if you want."

"Good to know," she gasped and shuddered. "Might take you up on your offer later."

"Or I can knock you unconscious, though it might be better if you remain alert enough to tell me how you feel." He paused and lapped at his bleeding wrist so his saliva would aid in healing the small wound. After a brief internal debate, he decided to tell her the truth. "I've never done a blood exchange or healing before. I'm too young and have never had the chance. Although, I know how it is done."

She looked up, her expression etched with pain, her brown skin sweat-covered and taking on an ashen, greyish tint. "Seriously?"

If she would have said more, it was stolen by a convulsion gripping her body.

He sat next to her and then gathered her up against his side so she wouldn't beat herself black and blue against the tree's gnarled old roots. The Riven taint was putting up a good fight, but he sensed his blood was winning. Soon, there would be nowhere in her body it could hide.

"Distract me," she managed after the first wave of convulsions past. "Young. How young?"

He didn't see any point in lying. The truth couldn't harm her.

Besides, he wanted to make friends. The few fae he'd interacted with treated him with the greatest respect but were aloof and cold. Well, perhaps not Greenborrow. The leshii seem genuinely interested in offering friendship. Something about this human's boldness and quick mouth reminded him of the leshii.

"I'm eight."

"Eight?" She eyed him from the tips of his horns all the way down to where his talons dug into the soft loam. "Eight what? Eight years?!"

He stopped lapping at his wrist. "Yes."

"Are you fully grown?"

"No."

"Lord," she choked. "If you're a child of your kind, I don't want to meet any adults."

"My father is only a little taller. Hmmm...it's probably best if you don't meet him just yet."

Shadowlight decided his parents probably wouldn't be happy about what he'd done.

Perhaps not Lillian or Gregory either. Gran? She seemed the most open. Maybe he could confide in her once the human was healed. Yes, that sounded like a good idea.

Decision made, he looked back down at the human. She was unconscious again, but she breathed. A quick survey of her wounds showed they were still grievous. However, he thought she might live.

For now, he would have to find a place to hide her from the other fae. Once she was healed, there wasn't anything the others could do. They'd eventually see the good in her.

They wouldn't harm another of Light's warriors, after all.

With a happy snort, he scooped up the human and headed back toward home. After he stashed the human somewhere safe and wove a spell of protection, he'd find Greenborrow as his father had ordered. Later, when no one would miss him, he'd come back and tend to the human's wounds and then find a more permanent place to stash her.

CHAPTER FOUR

"Come on," Lillian held out what she called a polo shirt and gave it a vigorous shake. "Put. The. Shirt. On. Now. They're almost here."

Gregory stood across from her and returned her frown. It wasn't actually cold, even though a rain shower had moved in while they'd discussed plans.

Lillian worried and fretted he wouldn't be dressed in time before the human soldiers arrived. He scrounged for what the healers were called, something uniquely complicated only they would come up with. Oh, yes, medical technicians. He still couldn't get particularly worked up about humans. Besides, he was now in human form, dressed in human fashion—which he hated. It was a passably warm day even with the rain shower. He saw no reason to wear the unnecessary layer the shirt represented. Even his fragile human hide could maintain enough heat without it.

"Do I have to get Gran in here?" Lillian asked, one fist

planting itself against her hip, while the other one held the shirt in a white-knuckled grip.

Gregory huffed, finding the situation humorous. He stepped up to Lillian, closed one hand around the shirt, and the other around the back of her head and pressed their lips together.

Being in human form had some benefits. He deepened the kiss and was rewarded by Lillian softening into his touch. She relaxed against him. Both hands came up to caress the muscles of his chest, the shirt long forgotten. He debated dropping it on the floor to free his other hand to roam. Unfortunately, his ears picked up the sound of a sharp rapping at the front door.

A pity, he would have liked to have seen where the kissing would have led. He liked the new relationship he'd been building with his Sorceress. Alas, the humans were at the gates, and he needed to be on his best behavior. He'd promised, after all.

He broke the kiss, and Lillian made a little sound of protest. Giving her a lazy grin and a quick peck on the cheek, he said, "That's the going rate for me to play at human and suffering the full regalia that goes with it."

Gregory admitted a touch sheepishly that he liked using a few of the human terms—they needed so little added explanation. Lillian didn't seem to see the humor and huffed like a quail disturbed from its daytime roost.

"Now..."

"Is not the time to argue," he said and pulled the shirt over his head. "The humans are at the front door and impatient to get in if that's what the repeated, heavy-handed pounding means.

Lillian grumbled something less than delicate under her breath, and then grabbed his hand and tugged him toward the door.

"Do you remember the details of your cover story if someone attempts small talk?" Lillian asked as she started down the stairs.

"Every word."

Gregory allowed himself to be steered toward the big armchair and then be pushed down into it. A moment later a cup of something hot was shoved in one hand and a couple of cookies in the other. The television was still on, and the coffee table was loaded with food and what Lillian called a board game.

Gran had clearly engineered the scene to look as natural as possible.

Gregory ate the cookies and reached for the nearest plate with his favorite type—the ones with the warm, chewy dark substance called chocolate. It was regrettable they were entirely bad for one's body. He scooped up another handful. If he was going to sit through this episode, which involved willingly shedding blood for one's enemy, he'd take his reward first.

Still wearing an apron coated with a fine layer of flour from all her baking efforts, Gran walked past him on her way to the front door, seemingly unconcerned with the newcomers' arrival. Lillian, on the other hand, was fussing nervously with plates, saucers, and teacups.

While the door swung inward, Gregory studied Lillian's expression and body language—which was supposed to reflect mild surprise but was in fact so false anyone who looked upon her would surely become suspicious. He reached out and slung an arm around her waist and dragged her into his lap.

Her yelp of surprise sounded far more genuine than any act.

He took a sip from his mug and nearly spat it back out. Black coffee, hot enough to burn three layers of skin off the roof of his mouth. With a deep grimace, he forced himself to swallow the offensive liquid while he glanced toward the door with natural curiosity. A medical technician and three other soldiers stomped through the front entrance.

Gran dusted the flour off her hands and held one out in greeting, but the human in the lead merely looked for a place to set down his equipment.

One of the other soldiers, not one Gregory had seen before, addressed Gran. "I assume you've been keeping up with the news and know about giving samples for testing. It's voluntary, but we strongly suggest everyone get tested to rule out possible health complications."

Gran gestured the newcomer in farther and closed the door. "By all means. Anything we can do to help. Although, I have to say I'm confused by one thing. Wouldn't it make more sense to have people report to a hospital if they start to feel sick?"

The medical technician spoke up, his response sounding like something he'd already said several times in the last hour. "If there is any chance of illness, we want to quarantine it early to stop any possible spread."

"Ah, that's the first bit of wisdom I've heard since all this began." Gran smiled as she rolled up her shirt sleeves until she'd exposed a good bit of her forearm.

Gregory watched, a touch curious, as the human sat on a chair next to the one Gran had dropped down on.

The procedure was over quickly though he didn't think Gran liked to see the small vial sticking out of her arm. She'd gone a little pale and looked away. Once it was over, and she was holding a small bit of cotton to the tiny injury, she looked up and met Gregory's eyes with a little shudder. "I hate needles. Never could stand the sight of my own blood."

Jason took his turn in the chair, and the procedure was repeated just as painlessly. Lillian struggled out of his lap, and he let her take the chair next. He stood a moment later and made his way over to her side, attempting to appear bored and unconcerned.

And he was—about giving blood. But he didn't have to like how the human soldier in charge wandered over to hover at Lillian's shoulder. This wasn't a random male interested in a pretty female.

Gregory smiled. Clever humans. This male was hoping his mere presence would cause Lillian's family to make a mistake. He also gathered from the male's mind that there were others nearby with some kind of device which allowed them to see and hear what was going on within. He squelched the urge to wave at them in the human way to see how they would react.

"Your turn," Lillian said in a falsely cheery voice. Gregory grunted and sat down. He exposed his arm like he'd seen the others do. There was a poke, and then he caught a faint whiff of his magic-laced blood. Had he been in gargoyle form, the tiny blood drawing device would not even have penetrated his skin.

This had to be the first time in all his existence he'd allowed an enemy to claim first blood without a fight.

The Mortal Realm offered him new delights every day. He was turning toward the medical person to see if he could intimidate him out of annoyance and sheer boredom, when a sharp knock sounded at the door.

Gran was already halfway there by the time Gregory transferred his attention from the medical technician to the door. He stretched his senses outward and already had the newest arrival identified before he'd even entered.

Gran opened the door and Major Resnick stepped in, a greeting already on his lips.

"Vivian, always nice to see you," he shook her hand and then stepped around her after a moment and made straight for Lillian.

The human at Gregory's elbow removed the needle and put a small bit of cotton and a tiny bandage over the site. Gregory managed not to sneer. The tiny wound had already healed as soon as the metal was removed from his arm.

"Lillian, good to see you again," Resnick continued in his disarming small talk. "I take it the equine escape artists haven't run off into the woods lately?"

Eyes narrowing, Gregory studied the human warrior. Something was off.

Resnick was a capable, astute leader. The type to take in a situation, study it from different angles, and then come to a tactical decision. Sociable, he was not. He'd probably prefer to take a bullet rather than make small talk.

Lillian frowned and then gave a truthful, "I hope not. If they have, I'm sure they'll be found."

"Always glad to help." Resnick turned his attention fully to Gregory. "And you must be Lillian's mysterious fiancé, which no one in town has met."

Gregory straightened from the chair and towered over the other humans in the room.

Even in human form, he didn't see the need to cram himself down into a smaller form than absolutely required. Of course magic and shapeshifting didn't have size limits—matter simply had to be compressed. However, Gregory was just more comfortable seeing things from a particular vantage point.

Making Major Resnick crane his head to look him in the eyes...that was an added benefit. Rather juvenile, but mildly rewarding all the same.

"Name's Gregory." He mimicked what he'd seen on television and held out his hand to the human. "Nice to meet you, Major. Lillian told me about your meeting in the woods."

"Ah, as I told her, I'm always glad to be a help. Besides, it was nice meeting another of Vivian's delightful clan."

Gregory chuckled at the human's far from a subtle inquiry. He stared down at the human, allowing a touch of challenge and his millenniums-old gargoyle nature to rouse and show in his eyes.

To the human's credit, he held his gaze and returned Gregory's unvoiced challenge.

Gran came up to them before anything more interesting developed.

"Major Resnick, can I interest you and your friends in some refreshments? There's a pot of coffee in the kitchen, and the cookies are still warm."

A couple of the humans showed mild interest, but Resnick merely shook his head.

"Another time. We still have several stops to make." He gave Gran a smile which held a hint of true warmth before glancing back at Gregory. "Don't worry. As soon as everything settles, I'm sure I'll find a reason to stop by."

With that less than subtle remark, Resnick, followed by his men, departed without so much as a goodbye or a glance behind. Then again, they hadn't come to exchange human niceties.

Curiously, Lillian had grabbed a pen and pad of paper off the end table and was furiously scrawling some message.

When she was finished, she tore off the top sheet and slapped it to his chest and began again.

He read her messy writing. 'Way to blend in! Ever heard of the word subtle? It's a concept you really need to work on.'

A grin stretched across Gregory's lips.

Gran folded her arms under her breasts and directed a deep frown at him, and then jerked her chin in the direction of the kitchen.

Ah, he was about to get an ear full from more than one female. Lovely. Only in the Mortal Realm did he receive scoldings.

He followed Gran and Lillian into the kitchen and then down the stairs to the basement. They continued past the wine cellar and on into the secret rooms and tunnels where the magic-forged weapons were being stored.

Their presence reminded him that he would need to solve this human dilemma quickly so the Clan and Coven could continue with the preparations for war with the Lady of Battles.

"It's safe to talk," Gran said when Lillian motioned at her own lips in question.

"Good, because we need to be ready to move. They aren't going to waste time getting that blood analyzed."

Gran nodded her head at Lillian's words. "Exactly right. Gregory, your magic allows you to hide, but your ability to shapeshift might be more useful to us at this point."

"You wish to change our plans?" Gregory, still in human form, quirked an eyebrow and rather enjoyed the novelty. "What did you have in mind?"

"I think it would be safer to swap out our samples while they are still en route. Certainly, easier than trying to get inside the military's HQ afterward. If you can impersonate one of those medical technicians, you might be able to switch the samples with no one the wiser. Unlike one of the other coven members, if you're caught, you can extract yourself far more quickly and easily. Though dear, try not to vanish before their very eyes. That's likely to do more harm than good."

Lillian's brother came in carrying a box which looked exactly like the type the humans had put the blood samples in.

He didn't smell a hint of magic upon it, so Jason or another Coven member had done what Lillian would have called a little 'sleight of hand.' Gregory smiled. He'd always been fond of efficiency.

"Do you think you can impersonate one of the humans and switch the samples in time?" Stress thickened Lillian's voice. It was cute how she still worried about him.

"Yes, but I'll have Darkness shadow me in case I get into trouble I can't get out of without a distraction."

Lillian's expression darkened. When he touched her thoughts, he picked up that she worried two gargoyles could muck up far more quickly than one alone.

He smiled. She might be right.

He'd definitely bring the other gargoyle along. Then he

frowned, realizing something else. "You'll have to come, too. The collars won't allow us to be apart."

Lillian nodded. "You're right. Unfortunately, I don't know how to take on another human appearance."

"You won't need to. You'll merely be maintaining your gargoyle form and shadow magic."

"Never was very good at that, in case you didn't notice."

"I'll help. Besides, you'll find it easier now with the abundance of magic in this Realm."

"Yeah, about that." Lillian fingered her own tattoo. "After that last big healing spell you did, I couldn't stay gargoyle and shifted back to dryad me. How do we know I'll fare any better this time?"

"We don't know." He shrugged. "But we'll consider this the first test."

"That's so not reassuring."

Gregory huffed with humor and then allowed Gran to hustle him from the room. She continued to direct them outside and into a waiting vehicle. Lillian gave him a little shove when he balked at getting in. He'd never been inside one of the little boxy things.

Lillian strapped him in and then hopped in the back unable to contain her laughter. His human face was probably more expressive than he'd intended, but he hadn't realized he'd be using the human's mode of travel.

Gran grinned at him and then the vehicle bumped and jolted into motion in such a way he was sure a few internal organs were still trying to catch up.

To distract himself from the unpleasantness of his present situation, he called to Darkness and River.

"We may need you both. Come to me as swiftly as you can."

"Yes, Lord Protector," Darkness answered with his respectful tones. *"We will come at once."*

Not that now was the time for an idle chat, but he would have appreciated it if the other gargoyle could have been a longer distraction.

Gran took another corner at high speed, and he found himself gripping the part of the vehicle Lillian's memories had labeled 'the dash.'

As if the thought of her was enough to catch her attention, she tapped him on the shoulder and then gave him a look of sympathy. "Hey, Gran. We need to be alive to switch the samples. If we're all killed in an accident, it's not going to help the other Clan or Coven members."

"Oh, please." Gran huffed loud enough to make any gargoyle proud. "I'm barely speeding. Besides, we need to get you to the rendezvous point with all haste."

Gregory dug the fingers of one hand into the dashboard and braced his other against the roof of the vehicle as the car jerked forward with greater speed.

He dared to send a glower in Gran's direction but held his silence.

Gran took another hard turn. The vehicle shuddered as one wheel caught the gravel at the side of the road. Vivian didn't even flinch. Gregory couldn't say the same thing about his stomach. He locked his jaws and sent a silent prayer to the Father with the hope he'd live to see the Magic Realm again. Preferably, before the Mortal Realm and its citizens killed him.

CHAPTER FIVE

Gregory survived the trip though he did wonder if a few of his organs were still somewhere back at the crossroads where Gran had taken a hard left without slowing. She'd eventually stomped on the brakes and pulled over. From there, they'd continued on foot, much to his immense pleasure. If they'd remained in the car much longer, Gregory might have thrown up all over the dash like his stomach had been urging. Riding in a truck's bed was much preferable. Inside a car? Never again.

Movement flashed between the trees ahead, but Gregory wasn't worried, he'd sensed the messenger spell's approach long before it came close. The tiny hummingbird spell zipped over and landed in Gran's outstretched hand. It glowed brightly for a few seconds and then the spell dissolved into mist.

"Greenborrow and Russet report they found a dying tree willing to sacrifice itself for our needs," Gran said. "They say it landed nicely across the road. Major Resnick's group has discovered the problem and are on their radios calling for equipment to remove the tree."

Lillian cleared her throat. "Resnick and company won't stay and watch the tree being cleared. They'll likely commandeer the newcomers' vehicles."

"Exactly," Gran said with an accompanying nod. "And you and Gregory need to insert yourselves with them before that. Now would be a good time to do a little physical remodeling."

After a quick search through Lillian's memories for the meaning, Gregory grinned belatedly. Yes, that was a good description of what he was about to do.

He reached for his magic instinctively, only to have it remain dormant. He touched his throat. How had he forgotten the damned tattoo?

"Oh," Lillian muttered. "Sorry. Gregory, you have my permission to shapeshift."

When he called his magic a second time, it answered, flooding him with its abundance. As the frosty chill spread through him, he focused on the mental image and essence of the human who had drawn his blood. His magic spiked, a wave raced over his body and sank its chill bone-deep. His body accepted the new form between one heartbeat and the next.

Lillian blinked at him. "Damn, that's fast. When will I be able to manage that kind of speed?"

Gregory laughed, the tone different than usual due to the changes in his body. "A few millennium's worth of practice helps."

"I suppose it would." Lillian glanced down at her body. "You think I should be in gargoyle form? You're certain?"

Certain? No. Yet he didn't want her playing a female

soldier. If she were found out, she'd be an easy target. He didn't like the idea of her ghosting him in gargoyle form much better, but at least this way she could remain invisible and run or fight much more efficiently. He would have left her behind, guarded by the other fae if it wasn't for the cursed brand around his throat.

"I'm certain. Gargoyle form is your best defense."

"Yeah, knew you were going to say that." Lillian didn't waste time, though. She stripped off her outer clothing down to her loincloth and crisscrossing breast band, both of which he'd spelled so they would shapeshift with her.

Gran stepped back and turned her attention out into the forest as if to watch for danger. Gregory didn't bother with the same ruse, more concerned about how her tattoo might react to her shapeshifting.

Lillian dropped to her knees and bowed her head. After three slow even breaths, magic flowed along her skin, and black wings with a hint of crimson at the edges sprang out of her back. She made a small hissing growl as her body continued its change.

When it was over, Lillian looked up at him, her wings drooping along her sides. Then with a full body shake, she folded them tight to her back and stepped up to him. After a quick glance down at her limbs and tail, where she was clearly counting body parts, she looked back at him.

"Well, I'm all here. Guess that went well." She stepped closer and then her expression morphed into a toothy grin. "I'm taller than you. How's that for novelty?"

She came to stand nearly toe to toe with him and proceeded to sniff at his hair, leaving his face until last. He stood stoic, waiting for what was coming next.

Lillian didn't disappoint. Her rumbling laugh filled his senses a moment before her warm, wet tongue licked him from chin to hairline.

He refused to rise to her baiting or wipe a forearm across his face. When she didn't get a reaction, she huffed and dropped to all fours. "You're no fun."

"I try not to be," he answered with half his attention focused on the forest track. They would need to move quickly if he was to infiltrate the human ranks. He set a brisk pace and Lillian trotted at his side, quickly outpacing him.

She rolled an eye and then an ear at him. Changing directions, she galloped back to his side.

She was having far too much fun at his expense, Gregory decided.

"You're too slow. We'll never make it in time." She dipped her one wing as she sidled up next to him. "Get on. It'll be faster."

Gregory frowned. He was supposed to carry her—that was the natural order of things. He grunted unhappily. Nothing about this life was normal. Why should this be any different? Besides, she was right. They were running out of time.

With an annoyed huff, he swung a leg over her back and mounted. He'd barely settled in place before she set off down a game trail which led in the general direction they needed.

Every time she leaped over a fallen tree or swerved around a broad trunk in their path, he thought his human-formed body would fail him, and he'd find himself sprawled on the ground in an ungraceful heap.

⁓

Ahead, flashes of light glimmered through the trees, marking the road and the site where the tree had come down to block it.

Even with his dulled senses, he could see and hear the humans as they organized themselves. Some were examining the tree—yes, that was Major Resnick studying its base. His suspicious little heart wouldn't find anything more than a rot-hollowed trunk. The dryad and leshii required nothing as mundane as an axe to fell a tree.

Lillian rolled an eye at him. "I hear the other vehicles approaching from the east. They will be here within minutes."

"We have time enough. Besides, I think the leshii already has the humans in hand."

Lillian slowed and then came to a stop ten feet from the road's edge, where the shadows were still thick enough to hide them even without the use of magic.

Gregory reached for her thoughts, merging with a little affectionate caress of his mind against hers. *"Call your conceal-ment spell and then follow my lead. You'll have to run alongside the road and shadow the vehicles the whole way. You can't allow more than twenty feet between us during the journey or the collars will activate."*

"I'll stay close. I promise." She sounded determined.

"Your gargoyle body can reach speeds greater than even I can run, but I don't think you'll have to test your limits today." He jerked his chin to the left where the leshii was making his way to their location. *"I have a feeling Greenborrow might have some surprises for the humans if his grin is anything to go by."*

Lillian flicked an ear in the leshii's direction. *"He knows we're not here to hurt the humans, right?"*

Gregory started to nod and then changed his mind.

"*Greenborrow*," he warned. "*The humans are not game for you to hunt.*"

The leshii snorted. "*My dear boy, the humans are always game but don't worry. You can tell your lovely lady her humans are safe from harm. I only plan to have a little fun at their expense.*"

"*Do nothing to expose us and endanger Lillian.*"

"*Never, you two are far more fun than the humans.*"

Gregory huffed. "*How reassuring. What other plans do you have to distract the humans?*"

"*A few, but unfortunately nothing that will occupy them long enough to allow you time to sort the samples here.*" The leshii shrugged. "*You'll have to do the switching once you're deep in their lair.*"

"*I'll manage.*"

"*If you're caught trying to switch out the Coven's samples, it will be an admission of guilt as surely as if you signed a written confession.*"

Gregory nodded in agreement. Really, how hard could it be to switch a few small samples of blood?

CHAPTER SIX

*L*illian had merely bobbed her head and agreed to their plans. Which was how she found herself hunched down behind the substantial body of the last military vehicle in line. The leshii was some distance ahead, herding a mother bear and her cub closer to the line of vehicles. As far as distractions went, what he had planned was creative. She just didn't know if it would be useful or bloodless. She didn't like the idea of some poor bear accidentally getting shot.

Gregory waited in the shadows to the left of her position. With her shoulder pressed against the armored vehicle's back end, the vials in question only mere feet from her, she was sorely tempted to snatch the vials and run if it would save Gregory from having to brave the dragon's den.

Unfortunately, her concealment spell couldn't hide the vehicle without causing a stir so she couldn't switch the samples even if she had the substitutes in her hand.

Still, it was tempting.

Lillian buried the impulse and waited, looking instead at the spell Greenborrow had given her. It glowed softly between the fingers of her right hand. The leshii had instructed her not to touch herself with it and to make sure when she captured her target, she got good skin contact. The leshii promised the human would be asleep before he hit the ground.

Simple. Clean. Effective.

Lillian studied the four-inch span of glowing magic suspended above the tips of her talons. The spell resembled a spider's web, but the filaments shifted and swirled to her sight in a way no spider could manage.

A sudden snapping of twigs and the shaking of under-brush near at hand had her switching her attention back to the forest just as a waist-high ball of fur burst onto the road.

Several flashlights tracked the noise and homed in on the bear cub within seconds. The half-grown cub squalled in alarm at the bright light and then bolted for the second vehicle in line, where its back-passenger door was still hanging open. The cub made for what it likely mistook as a dark cave-like interior and vanished within.

A holler came from inside the vehicle, followed by an 'oh shit' and both front doors burst open. The soldiers inside jumped out, their guns already trained on the armored vehi-cle's dark interior as they slowly backed away.

Major Resnick's familiar voice rose over the other surprised exclamations. "Turner. Winslow. Grab the tran-quilizers."

Lillian divided her attention between the two soldiers making their way toward the back of the first armored vehicle, and Resnick, where he stood facing the patch of forest which had first spat out the cub.

He held his big-ass gun at the ready, Lillian noted.

From the darkness about thirty feet to the left of the road, she heard the mother bear's approach. The bear let out a huffing growl, which the cub answered with a loud distress call. At the sound, the mother's lumbering walk changed into a rolling, powerful run.

"And here comes momma." Resnick's voice held a hint of 'you've got to be kidding me,' but he was otherwise nonchalant about the charging, angry mother bear. He calmly gestured everyone to move behind the vehicles. "Turner. Winslow," he added without taking his eyes off the forest.

"Ready, sir," they echoed each other.

"As soon as you see the first hint of her black hide."

Lillian's attention swung back to her own target only to find he'd moved. Now he was flanked by two other soldiers, his gun trained on the forest.

Gregory wasn't going to be happy, but they didn't have time for a new plan. With luck, she could snatch the human and vanish before the other two soldiers noticed.

With her concealment spell firmly around her body, she stalked her target and was in position at the exact moment the bear ran onto the road. It was a smallish black bear, Lillian noticed as she slapped one hand over the human's mouth and wrapped the other around his wrist. The soldier went limp in her arms, and miracle of miracles, his badass gun didn't go off.

She dragged him a short distance from the road and realized the dryad, Russet, had joined her. Together, they began stripping the soldier.

Gregory joined them a moment later and motioned them off. "Order me to use my magic," he whispered in her ear. "It will be faster."

Lillian's tail flicked in mild agitation. Now that was an ambiguous command, but she was in a potentially dangerous situation which might give Gregory more freedom over his magic.

After uttering the command softly, she sat back on her haunches.

There wasn't much to see, actually. A flickering of the shadows and then Gregory was wearing the soldier's uniform.

He made a sour face and then tugged and pulled at the clothing for a moment before reaching down for the gun. He swung the strap over his shoulder and adjusted it like he knew what he was doing.

She wondered if he did. When he'd scanned the soldier earlier, he might have gained more than just his likeness.

Gregory took up position like the soldier had held earlier. None of the other humans seemed aware of the switch.

Lillian sought out what had transpired with the leshii's little bear drama. The bear in question was lumbering around still, but completely unfocused and lacking coordination. After a quick scan, she spotted the tranquilizer dart embedded in the bear's shoulder. The cub had rejoined its mother. Neither man nor beast looked harmed.

Mission accomplished.

Lillian eased back into deeper shadows as the mother bear and cub lumbered into the forest to sleep off the drugs.

By the look of things, the bears wouldn't make it far, but Lillian knew the leshii would watch over them and see to their safety.

The growing rumble of approaching vehicles announced the next part of the plan was about to commence, and this one would be far more dangerous.

The new vehicles and their tree-removal detail arrived. Lillian watched with misgivings as Gregory took his place inside one of the vehicles. When the first vehicle pulled away, Lillian ghosted behind.

She was only able to keep up with the convoy because of a few of the leshii's other well-placed distractions, such as a herd of deer that ran up the road ahead of the vehicles for a short time, and later, a belligerent-looking moose no one was stupid enough to antagonize.

Resnick didn't strike her as a suspicious man, but his bullshit meter had to be going off by now.

No matter how hard he looked, there would be nothing concrete he could point out to his superiors.

Shadowlight stood over the unconscious medical technician hoping the male would wake up.

Surely one that was awake would prove much more interesting. He gave the human a nudge with his muzzle.

Nothing.

Greenborrow had ordered him to stay and watch the human so the leshii, Darkness, and River could track Major Resnick's convoy and provide distractions to slow it so Lillian could keep pace.

Shadowlight would have loved to have taken part, but he was also pleased the leshii trusted him enough to have him watch this unconscious human.

The duty was one he'd gladly fulfill any other day. Unfortunately, it was keeping him from other commitments today.

It had been some hours since he'd given his blood to the female warrior he'd found in the forest. By now, his gargoyle blood would have finished ridding her of the Riven taint, or it would have killed her. She was a fighter. He thought she'd survive his blood, but in her present weakened condition, the elements might be enough to kill her.

Worry gnawed at his belly. He glanced down at the unconscious male at his feet.

By the look of it, this human would sleep for some hours yet. Shadowlight knew he was not overly far from where he'd stashed his rescued human. If he sprinted, he could be there and back in a relatively short time. The male human at his feet would be safe enough for now. He scented no predator nearby. All the activity on the road had driven everything else off long since.

Yes, he was sure it was for the best to check on his pet human. The one at his feet didn't need him.

CHAPTER SEVEN

The vehicle Gregory rode in came to an abrupt halt. The other passengers exited, and he followed their example, allowing himself a swift glance around at the other vehicles, military personnel, tall fences, and numerous buildings. All the above looked to have doubled or tripled in numbers since he'd last laid eyes on this place.

A sense of alert wariness hung in the air. The deceptive calm was like a banked fire just waiting for more fuel to burst into life once again.

Gregory silently admired their readiness. They couldn't have had much in the way of peaceful rest in the day since the Siren and the Riven had clashed here in this land.

The humans had lost a number of their own in the battle —a battle the humans wouldn't have understood because to them magic, be it good or evil, was nothing more than myth and legend.

But now they knew something dangerous was in the woods with them.

He could only imagine their confusion. Many of their patrols had come back, the signs of battle clear upon their bodies and uniforms, but with no memory of what had transpired, because he and the other fae had taken that from them.

Not for the first time, he wondered if he might have made a mistake with that decision.

However, there was no time to dwell on it now—the others were dispersing to their assigned tasks. So too must he.

Gregory sought the bundle of memories he'd borrowed from the human whose likeness he now wore. He sifted through them until he found what he needed. The way to the labs.

He reached his destination—some kind of portable building complex—without incident. Inside he found three other humans already crammed into the tight work areas. He made his way over to the only open workstation. Relying on his borrowed memories, he quickly popped open the two cases he'd brought with him.

The blood belonging to the magic wielders was easy enough to spot—it possessed a slight glow. One he could see, but not something a human could discern with the naked eye. Once he located the ones he wanted, a small touch of magic mirrored the markings from each vial onto the corresponding Coven-collected samples.

With Lillian's immediate family done, he moved on to other Coven members, finding them in the sea of blood samples by the trace of magic present in them. This part took longer since some of these ones were at the other technicians' stations.

A touch of concealment magic and skills a pickpocket would envy solved that particular hurdle.

But the speed with which he was accomplishing his task did nothing to sooth Lillian's growing anxiety. He could smell the tang of her fear even inside the building.

"Do not worry," he sent using their mental link. *"I am almost finished here. Just. One. More. Ah, there. See, no epic disaster."*

"Well good for you! Now hurry up and get out here. I just smelled a hint of Riven."

Gregory paused, the last vial he'd switched halfway back to its case. *"I'm on my way."*

He placed the vial back with its brethren, the human at the workstation none the wiser. With that done, he made his way out into the cooling evening air.

Lillian waited for him next to the building, concealed within the highest concentration of shadows she could find. He joined her after a quick scan of his surroundings. As he dragged in a deep breath, he caught the faint whiff she had noted.

"Most definitely Riven. Though very faint. As we speculated, they captured or found Riven remains." Gregory's protective instincts flared to life.

He needed to hunt out the source of that scent and destroy every last trace so its evil couldn't find a new host. Yet he needed to keep Lillian safe, too.

"They may have Whitethorn and Goswin. We need to rescue them if they do," Lillian said, adding another complication to an already complex situation.

But she was correct.

"I'll remain in this form for now and see how far I can get. I imagine wherever the scent leads will be as brightly lit as the place I

just left. Shadows will not be plentiful, so don't risk exposing yourself. We can send your father back here later to rescue Whitethorn and the sprite, should we find them."

Without the collar limiting him, Gregory knew he could be in and out with no humans the wiser. He didn't want to say as much to Lillian. He'd hurt her enough with his accusations about her failure in judgment concerning the Siren and the collars created by the Battle Goddess. That wound didn't need picking at.

"Very well." Lillian's whisper drifted to him from the shadows to his immediate left. "Let's do some recon."

Her excitement at the thought of finding news of Whitethorn and Goswin washed over him in a fresh wave. As he started in the direction of what had been the town's community center and arena complex, but was now the military's main headquarters, he realized he felt better with a task to perform. Freeing himself from the collar might be beyond him at the moment, but friends, those were within his ability to save, or at least locate.

"You've got a plan?" she asked as they approached a closed gate with guards standing off to either side.

"Yes, banter around the names of the two top scientists I plucked from the human's memories."

"Handy that."

He didn't bother with a reply and stopped smartly before the gate. After saluting an officer who was exiting, he turned his attention back to the gate guards. One seemed familiar from his borrowed memories.

"Are Doctors Fleming or Rogers still inside? Major Resnick found something interesting, and he wants them to have a look."

"Something more interesting than what is inside?" the guard questioned, a hint of surprise in his expression.

"No idea," Gregory bluffed, "Major Resnick didn't tell me, just ordered me to find Fleming and Rogers ASAP."

"I saw Rogers return fifteen minutes ago, and Fleming hasn't taken a break in hours. Whether you can pull them away from their labs long enough to come with you is another question altogether." The guard shook his head. "It's like the fucking Twilight Zone around here."

"Tell me about it." Gregory gave the guard a somber nod of agreement as they ushered him through the gate, Lillian an invisible ghost at his heels.

He made his way deeper into enemy territory. It was busier here, with many personnel going about their business with the discipline all soldiers adopted if they wished to survive long on a battlefield.

Gregory studied the immediate area outside the building's main entrance.

"Do you see those five vehicles parked in the front? They are being loaded, not unloaded."

Lillian stopped dead, and Gregory had to sidestep at the last moment so he wouldn't run into her.

"Oh shit. You seeing what I'm seeing?" Her tail flicked in agitation. *"They are packing up supplies, or more likely shipping samples elsewhere for more in-depth study. By the size and number of vehicles, they must be planning to move something they deem important. Look at that firepower."*

"Indeed, they are well armed," he acknowledged. *"And we may not have much time. If they have a Riven or have captured Whitethorn and Goswin, then we can only assume they will not waste time in moving them to a more secure location."*

illian's stomach tied itself in knots. If Whitethorn and Goswin were still alive, they needed rescuing. She wanted to help accomplish that. Yet, handicapped by the collars as they were, she feared for Gregory's safety, too.

He looked vulnerable with no natural weapons or protective spells at the ready, just the fragile covering of his uniform. Was this how Gregory viewed her when she was merely a dryad?

"You worry too much," he sent with another mental command to relax. *"The Divine Ones have always protected us."*

"Yeah, when they aren't demanding we die for the cause, or while having their baby."

"Lillian!"

"Sorry," she mumbled, but she wasn't feeling very repentant.

She still thought it was grossly unfair they demanded their Avatars not know physical love and yet allowed them to crave it. Damn double standards. Or something along those lines. But that discussion was a fight for another day.

When they reached the community center's main entrance, Gregory uttered a similar statement about Resnick a second time. They were again granted entry into the facility.

Lillian squeezed herself between the four guards and on into the building, being careful to stay close to Gregory. *"Not to concern you, but I'm fast running out of shadows to hide in."*

"Easy, love," Gregory said with humor clear in his mind. *"I've been cloaking you for the last five minutes. I saw your growing wariness. You've done very well up until now, but if I could have left you outside, I would have."*

Gregory bypassed the elevators and opted for the stairs.

"Of course they'd keep the damn Riven below ground, far from any useful windows we could use as an escape."

"A prison should not make escape easy."

They arrived in the basement. Lillian's first look inspired the words clean, bright, and downright sterile. She no longer smelled the Riven taint as strongly as before either.

It took her a moment to pinpoint what was different. Ah, there was no more rumble of the A/C units on the roof. The night was cold enough they'd shut down. Without the ventilation system circulating the Riven scent, it grew fainter in their part of the building.

"The Riven, or its body, isn't here. It must be somewhere else. The only way to find it might be to search room by room."

"Or," Gregory added. *"They already moved it onto one of those transports we noted when we first came in."*

"We can't let them transport it elsewhere. We have to destroy it now before its evil contaminates someone else."

Gregory rumbled agreement.

She scouted farther down the hallway. The long corridor had several side branches, but short, exploratory trips only revealed temporary offices. This late at night, some were empty, but more than a few were occupied by military brass.

"Gregory, my nose tells me no magic wielders are down here. Let's go back up. Maybe I will scent something as we cover more ground."

"We should go," he agreed. *"Remind me to send another of our allies to spy on the humans. This place looks to be a good location to overhear what they don't want to be overheard."*

Lillian had to agree. You didn't bury your top brass below ground unless you wanted to maintain a few hard-to-keep secrets.

Gregory huffed. *"Shadowlight would love to explore down here."*

"No way is my baby brother coming anywhere near the humans."

"I don't disagree. However, keeping that one out of trouble will be most difficult. He's an explorer by nature."

"I'm just glad Greenborrow has taken him under his wing."

Chuckling openly, he countered, *"Greenborrow will be beside him every step of the way, if not leading, as they seek out trouble together."*

Lillian glared.

Gregory wisely refrained from further discussion on the subject as she doggedly followed him back up the stairs to scout the next floor up.

Lillian estimated they were one floor from the surface. She could almost taste freedom and its damp night air—not this already recycled ten times an hour stuff. They had scouted each of the lower floors, trusting their noses to tell them if there was anything of interest. So far, their search had turned up a lot of nothing.

Together, they headed back to the stairwell, both agreeing that putting two gargoyles in an elevator—a small, enclosed space with no easy out—was a terrible idea.

Gregory was just reaching for the door's push bar when the elevator hummed and creaked into motion. In the time it took to glance over her shoulder at the noise, the lights went out.

Crouching, Lillian flared her wings out around Gregory as she pulled him to her side. He didn't fight her, holding perfectly still.

The emergency lights cast the hallway in a dull yellowish glow until they, too, blinked out.

Any hope it was a random innocent power outage flashed out with them.

Every instinct screamed 'trap' and clamored for her to bolt for the stairwell.

"Gregory, we've been discovered." She didn't know how or when. Maybe security had seen him as he'd made his way through the corridors and reported his activity as suspicious.

The elevator reached their floor within seconds.

With a smooth precision, which did nothing for Lillian's peace of mind, a team of scarily quiet humans emerged from the elevator, guns first.

From one of the offices, a mere ten feet from the elevator, a man carrying a flashlight emerged into the hallway.

He took one look at them, pointed his flashlight to the ground and backed against the wall.

Lillian counted six soldiers in the hallway now. Two peeled

off and made for the man with the flashlight. They checked his office and then herded him back inside.

So, it wasn't some random security thing they'd tripped. The soldiers were specifically looking for Gregory.

Damn. So much for making their way to the surface and walking out peacefully.

Five more soldiers were heading in her direction. If she and Gregory bolted for the stairwell, the soldiers would see the door open. Their best chance to remain undetected might be to sneak past the soldiers and hide in one of the offices until the furor died down.

That might take until long past dawn. Or never.

The soldiers moved closer to their position. She eyed the space between them. No way could she squeeze past without betraying her location.

Now she heard something else distressing—the sound of heavy boots on the stair treads. Lots more boots.

"Fight or flight?" she whispered into his mind. *"It's your call, but I hear more on the stairs, too. We may not have a choice."*

"We fight our way free." He jerked his chin toward the stair-well. *"Go."*

She bolted into motion, Gregory so close behind, he brushed against her tail and right wing as they ran. Flashes of light, radio chatter, and shouted commands chased them into the stairwell.

Gregory darted ahead, taking the steps three at a time. He was still mostly in human form, but dark talons tipped each finger now instead of blunt human nails. Behind, she heard the soldiers pursuing while ahead Gregory had run into the other team on the stairs.

There was a sudden flurry of sounds—the smack of flesh on flesh, grunts of pain, startled shouts, and cursing.

Gregory slammed two soldiers together with enough force to stun them and then he leaped clear to engage four more coming down the stairwell from above. At that moment, Lillian realized Gregory was sharing. A large gargoyle grin spread across her face. She knew just where to put the two soldiers Gregory had left at her feet.

She grabbed the nearest by his jacket as he struggled up. She helped him to his feet, and then on over her shoulder where his weight and momentum carried him down the flight of stairs and into the path of the other soldiers coming up from the level below.

"Sorry," she whispered to the second soldier at her feet and tossed him down to join his friends.

Above, Gregory had cleared a path. She leaped over or around the unconscious or barely conscious bodies left in his wake.

Ahead, the stairwell door was propped wide, a rectangle of blinding light prevented her from seeing much beyond that point.

Tears streamed down her face, but she forged on because Gregory had disappeared into that light.

She had enough sense to remain at the stairwell's threshold where the shadows could still hide her. In seconds, her eyesight blinked back into focus. What she saw didn't inspire much hope of escaping without gathering a few bullet holes.

Gregory stood just outside the stairwell, mere feet into the community center's lobby. He was encircled by a good two dozen soldiers.

Rage and fear stirred in Lillian's heart at the number of guns pointed at Gregory's body.

illian scanned faces and spotted a familiar one—Major Resnick.

He held a tranquilizer gun pointed at Gregory. Somehow, that wasn't reassuring.

"Normally," Resnick said in a cold voice, "if someone came this far without clearance, they'd be shot on sight. However, I have a few questions for you and dead men are much harder to question."

Gregory tilted his head in acknowledgment, and Lillian could visualize the familiar glint of humor in his eyes. Only her irrational guardian would find thirty guns pointed at his chest amusing.

Major Resnick's expression remained stony though he did lift one eyebrow a fraction of an inch. "Were I in your place, I wouldn't be finding it humorous. I know Corporal Jenkins, and that fancy face job might have fooled us had the real Jenkins not just crawled out of the forest and reported how he was ambushed. Now, hands behind your head and face down on the floor."

Lillian tensed as Gregory reached out and touched her mind. *"My Sorceress, grant me my defensive magic and be ready to follow close on my tail."*

"Use your magic, but don't get yourself shot. And if we kill a bunch of soldiers to escape, they'll just hunt us and our allies all the harder."

"I know, but my defensive magic can do more than kill on a large scale." He gave the equivalent of a mental shrug and added, *"I've just never had a reason not to simply kill my enemies, until now. I'll have to teach you this part of your gargoyle magic at some point."*

"Down, now. Or we'll shoot you down." Resnick sounded like he was losing patience.

Gregory rolled his shoulders and slowly placed his hands on the back of his head. He went down on one knee like he was going to do as they demanded. "It's not a mask."

Resnick's eyes narrowed at Gregory's words. "I'm sure we'll get to that during the interrogation."

"Another time, perhaps." At Gregory's words, his shadow magic swirled up from the ground and its chilled currents washed against Lillian's body. It had no effect on her, but when it touched the first human, it exploded outward in an ever-enlarging circle, carrying with it any hapless humans it had captured.

Gregory bolted into motion as the soldiers landed hard, a good twenty feet away.

Lillian followed him so close she bumped him once when he slowed to turn a corner.

On the plus side of things, his defensive magic had also taken out most of the lights, and she was no longer blinded by all that vicious brightness.

Gregory's shadow magic continued to hide and protect them from the startled humans. The distraction would only last moments at best. Some of the downed soldiers were already picking themselves off the floor, as other newcomers came to their aid.

Lillian didn't care. They were swiftly through the last checkpoints. Shoving surprised guards out of their path, they were soon surrounded by glorious night air and freedom.

Ahead, Gregory shifted into his gargoyle form and dropped to all four so he could run faster. She lengthened her stride to come alongside him.

All around them, the terrain was suddenly torn up by bullets biting into the ground. Dirt and tall stalks of grass were mowed down as a continual rain of deadly projectiles pelted the ground less than ten feet from her present path.

Gregory snarled in pain or anger; she couldn't tell the cause from her position two strides behind him. The roar of an engine drowned out all other sounds. A helicopter was taking off. Possibly more than one, she concluded, as a greater noise rose up from the military camp behind them.

Two armored vehicles with manned guns on the back were racing across the field she and Gregory were presently running through.

"That was too damn close. Can they see us?" Lillian asked.

"No, but they can guess."

Gregory veered to the side and slowed enough she shot right past him. At which point she realized the move was intentional on his part. He was protecting her, putting himself bodily between her and the enemy closing in behind them.

His maneuvering also allowed her to see the bloody

furrows running along his flank where more than one bullet had found its mark.

"You're hurt," she uttered. The stupid remark exited her mouth before she could stop it.

Gregory merely rolled his eyes at her. "They are flesh wounds. A lucky round which made it past my defensive magic."

Lillian instantly knew what he hadn't said. The bullet had only made it through because he'd concentrated the vast majority of his magic around her. The shadow spells were still coiling around them, but they were fading. Either Gregory was weakening, which she doubted, or he had another idea.

"My magic hides us from view. Unfortunately, this long grass still shows where we've been. In my haste, I didn't weave a spell to conceal the evidence of our passage until too late. Now they know the rough area where to concentrate their attention and fire."

She glanced over her shoulder as she ran. Their mad dash for freedom was creating a trail through the tall grass even a toddler could follow. Ahead a marshy bog was meandering its way around the back acreage of the community center. There'd be no easy way to hide their path. Even with magic.

More gunfire and a small explosion of grass and dirt erupted alongside Gregory, forcing him to leap sideways. He shouldered her in the side, steering her into a new trajectory. For once Lillian was not complaining about his overprotective tendencies.

"I think it's time for your first flying lesson."

"What?"

"Our shadow magic will be much more effective against the dark sky. There will be no trail for them...."

Again, Gregory drove her into a sharp turn. A half second later the land where they would have been exploded in a cloud of debris.

"Damn, I think that was an RPG. They mean business."

Gregory didn't even miss a beat. "Ahead, when we reach that small rise, spread your wings and allow your stride to power you more upward than forward. Jump like you mean to clear a fallen tree trunk and spread your wings. Ride the air. It will come naturally to you."

"Like hell!"

But the rise—not much more than an anthill really—was upon them and when Gregory jumped into the air, she did too, squealing in terror. Yes, she learned, a gargoyle could squeal.

Her wings, true to Gregory's word, stretched wide instinctively, capturing the air and propelled her body up higher into the sky with each stroke. Her wings might know what to do, but her legs churned and thrashed like they were still hoping to find something with more traction than the air.

Gregory maneuvered under her, putting himself between her and the ground as they gained more altitude.

For another whole ten seconds of pure panic, she thought she'd entangle their wings and send them both spiraling to their deaths. Blessedly that didn't happen. Instead, her body and wings began to mimic his motions in the air.

He'd been firmly in her mind the entire time, but her blind panic had kept her from detecting him.

"That's it. Follow my lead." His confidence washed over her senses. "You're doing fine. We will be able to land soon, but not here. We are over solid forest at the moment. There's a road a little distance ahead, which should be empty this time of night. We'll land there and make our way home through the forest."

Home sounded good. The shelter of the forest sounded nice too.

She'd settle for either at this point.

"I just want to say this was an absolutely terrible time for my first flight lesson."

Gregory chuckled. "All in all, I thought it went rather well. We are free. We don't have too many holes in our hides, and you did actually make it into the air under your own power." He pulled ahead and then performed an aerial maneuver that would make a stunt pilot hold his breath.

"Show off."

In a blink, he was flying next to her again.

She concentrated on beating her wings and not falling out of the sky. They flew what she thought was another two kilometers before she saw the road ahead.

"Oh, thank heavens," she hissed, feeling a strain in her wings and shoulders. "I'm so not in shape for flying, but this has got to have been my best cardio workout ever."

"You're tiring?"

Lillian held back a sharp retort and instead said, "I'm a little tired."

"We're almost there, but landing is more dangerous. I'll carry you to the ground this time. We'll practice landing over shallow water the first few times. Trust me, it's a much safer practice."

Lillian wasn't at all sure about having him help her to the ground. It summoned visions of tangled wings and broken bodies.

Gregory curled the edge of one wing a fraction and was

suddenly right over top of her. He flew so close she could feel his heat.

"Get ready to fold your wings tight to your body at my command. Don't struggle or try to unfurl your wings until we are safely on the ground. Understand?"

The road was almost under them, and she didn't have time to argue. Besides, she trusted him with her life. "I understand."

"Fold your wings now."

She did, and his tail snaked around her waist and hips as his arms snapped forward to lock in a firm embrace around her chest.

A squeak of surprise escaped her as his wings fanned out to slow them, and the combined forces of gravity and momentum threatened to peel her from his hold and leave her broken on the ground below.

But Gregory didn't fail her. With a few more violent beats of his wings, they landed in the middle of a tree-shrouded road.

She panted harshly but dug her talons into the road's gravel surface, mindlessly happy to be on the ground and to be in one piece.

Slowly she came to recognize the area. They weren't far from the old sawmill the Clan and Coven used during their lunar Wild Hunts. Well, the one they used to use before all the reporters, scientists, and military arrived. The sawmill should still be a safe place to hole up for a couple of hours until she had her breath back.

Gregory didn't immediately release her, although his grip loosened to allow his hands to skim along her arms as if he searched for wounds. He, too, still panted, his chest pressed against her back and wings, his warm breath puffing against her neck and right side of her face.

"Are you alright?" His voice rumbled in her ear, and she detected a note of worry there.

"I'm fine. A little shaken up, but no lasting scars." She turned in his arms and touched her muzzle along the underside of his jaw while she simultaneously wrapped her arms around his waist. Her horns framed the sides of his face, but he seemed not to care. As for her tail, it seemed to seek out Gregory's lower legs like it was trying to prevent him from going anywhere.

Tonight, Gregory could have been badly hurt. She didn't know if he could have survived being riddled with as many rounds as were aimed at him if his magic hadn't been there. What if in the future he was unable to call upon his magic because she didn't give an order in time?

Gregory gave an affronted huff. "I would never have allowed them to land that many blows. Even if they caught me asleep and unaware, these weapons wouldn't kill me. I'd heal. Sometimes I think you forget what I am. What I am capable of doing to protect you."

Lillian knew his words were true, but she had seen her beloved brought low before, and he had died defending her in past lives. She might not have those memories at the moment, but he'd alluded to such.

Gregory nuzzled her, and then dragged her as close as two bodies could be. "Silly little dryad, those times we faced off against creatures far deadlier than a few humans—some of those creatures could kill even a demigod such as the Lady of Battles."

"Oh my god."

He held a finger up to her lips to silence her. "And other times I lost you first, not because I couldn't protect you but because you would throw all you were into destroying an enemy before it could decimate other worlds. In so doing, you sacrificed your mortal body to call upon the full force of your Avatar magic. I don't like to remember the times I lost you first. So, my little dryad, feel free to make me forget those unpleasant thoughts."

"I'm a gargoyle, at the moment, not a dryad if you couldn't tell."

Gregory laughed with genuine humor. "Like I could forget it with you wrapped around me like a towel."

Lillian pretended insult and tried to extract herself. The slight flaring of her wings stirred the air and brought a fresh wave of blood scent to her nostrils, reminding her Gregory was still bleeding.

"If you are so invincible, why the hell are you dripping blood on the road? Eh?"

Gregory snorted and then waved a hand at the few drops of blood. They shimmered for a moment and then misted away.

"You were able to do that without an order." It was more of a question than a statement.

"It is part of my defensive magic. Your earlier order is still in effect."

Lillian sighed and nuzzled him. Then another unhappy thought caused her stomach to tighten. "How much blood did you leave in that field? They will scour every blade of grass for evidence."

Gregory stretched out his injured wing to show it had stopped bleeding and was already healing. "And they will find nothing of interest. I ordered my magic to eradicate any drops left behind no matter how far away."

Not surprising. Her guardian gargoyle always seemed to have every contingency covered.

Lillian broke away from Gregory's warmth.

"Come, we're not far from the sawmill where the Wild Hunt gathers. We can rest there for a short time before we make a run for home.

Gregory agreed distractedly, his faraway look saying he was already thinking up further contingency plans.

Lillian's right hand drifted to her belly for a moment before she dropped to all fours and broke into a trot, leading Gregory into the forest.

There was one event, should it come to pass, which even Gregory might not know how to handle. She hoped she never had to find out.

CHAPTER TEN

Commander Gryton watched the unfolding spectacle with what might have been a spark of humor, had he possessed such a weakness. His lips compressing, he unfolded his arms and pushed off from the brick wall at his back. He'd watched the Avatars, both in gargoyle forms, lead the soldiers of the human army on a merry chase.

Clearly, the female half of the pair was not yet familiar with her gargoyle body. He was sure what he'd just witnessed was her first attempt at flight.

The Avatars were not what he was expecting. He knew their reputations, the past feats which would give even the most powerful of beings pause. Yet, he saw little of the awe-inspiring personality apparent.

As a child the Sorceress had been a somber little thing. Obedient to her dryad mother and the Battle Goddess's edicts. At the time, the Battle Goddess had falsely assumed the demon seed sufficient to keep her docile. The seeming obedience proved an illusion. She'd only been biding her time until her protector matured enough to rescue her.

During that time, Gryton had kept his magic leashed so the Sorceress wouldn't see the full strength of his power and start speculating what he truly was.

His continued survival hinged upon the Avatars' ignorance. Yet, many times, he'd wondered almost hopefully if the female half would recognize him for what he was.

But she never had.

What the Divine Ones deemed a violation of their rules was dealt with swiftly and with no compassion. Even their Avatars were not immune to their judgment. It wasn't a surprise the Avatars did not know him.

The Divine Ones had stripped that knowledge—a whole lifetime—from their Avatars.

Lillian and Gregory didn't remember one moment of their last incarnation. Certainly not the one fatal moment of weakness which nearly cost them everything. A mistake which had changed the path of all three realms.

That was the start of Gryton's own personal misery. He didn't serve the Battle Goddess because he wanted to. He suffered her rule to survive. Only her powerful army protected Gryton from her Twin's gargoyle legion.

Oh yes. Never could he forget, not for one moment, that Lord Death had been ordered to destroy him. And Death never gave up the hunt.

So Gryton served the Battle Goddess—for now, and he would remain loyal until she got from the Avatars what she needed to bring about her own Twin's downfall. Once Lord Death was out of the way, she planned to challenge the

Divine Ones with the help of an army of creatures possessing god-like powers bred from their Avatars.

It was an ambitious plan. One he personally thought had no hope of success. Surely the Avatars wouldn't repeat the same mistake which had earned the Divine Ones' infinite wrath a second time?

Yet, to judge by recent events transpiring in this realm, it seemed they would. How foolish the Avatars were made by their love for each other. Now there was an emotion he vowed never to feel—and be brought low by.

Fate was drawing him forward, and he would consent to be the instrument that helped the Avatars find their doom if it would ensure his own survival.

First, he had a little clean-up to do.

Gryton walked through the middle of the human's military camp, concealed by his magic. The last thing he needed was to be discovered by any of the Avatars' allies that might be spying on the mortal's camp.

In truth, he merely wanted to accomplish what he'd come to this realm to do in the first place, and then leave it behind. Regrettably, something here in the human's encampment needed his attention first, a loose end in need of tying.

Gryton made his way deeper into the camp as it buzzed with activity.

None saw him. His power was different than a gargoyle's shadow magic, more mind than body. As he continued to direct the mortals' attention away from his location, he felt the slight drain on his magic reserves.

He strolled into their main building, past two guards, and several devices. The devices noted his passage and set up a racket, beeping and wailing loud enough to be heard even in the Spirit Realm. Without a glance behind, he hastened his step. His instincts focused solely on the bit of blighted, rotting darkness that masqueraded as a Riven's soul.

Mindless slaughter was always an affront. If one was going to kill, there should be some purpose behind the effort.

He would do this Realm a single service.

Following the taint to its source, he found himself in an open area. Oval in shape, a transparent barrier about twice his height encircled the entire area. Situated just outside that odd barrier, rows of seats marched up the sides of the building, halfway to its ceiling.

He didn't know what the building had been before the human military had repurposed it—an amphitheater perhaps? Not that it mattered.

Before him, in one of the transparent square cages was what he'd come for. The last Riven still in existence.

He approached the three cages in the center of the floor and bypassed the first two with their sleeping occupants.

The Riven hissed at Gryton. He ignored the creature's act of bravado and came closer. When he was a body length away, the beast launched itself at the back wall, clawing madly at the surface as panic set in, but the substance was too hard and thick, and the creature merely damaged itself in its escape attempt.

Gryton tapped a finger against the transparent surface, the metal talons of his gauntlets sounding loud in the silence. When that failed to penetrate the Riven's panic maddened mind, he cleared his throat.

"Turn and face judgment, unworthy one."

The Riven froze but didn't turn around.

Well, at least he had its attention. Gryton's lips pulled back in a smile, though the beast couldn't see the expression.

"Were it not for your kind's interference, the Battle Goddess's plans may well have borne fruit. But your greed—the attempt to sacrifice the female half of the Avatars for your own gain—led to her being placed in her accursed hamadryad to heal."

The Riven hissed.

Gryton narrowed his eyes. He should just kill the creature now, but the days of torture he'd endured when the Battle Goddess first learned the Avatars had escaped her again required payment in kind.

He drew a knife from his belt and drove it into the surface with all his strength. The blade embedded itself in the clear substance hilt deep. Small cracks and fissures spread out from the center, enlarging as he fed the smallest trickle of his magic into it.

"I devised a new way to enslave the Avatars. Before I finished, they came under attack again. This time, the Sorceress's biological parents came to her aid and brought with them my collars and used them in an unforeseen way. Again, all because of a threat created by the Rivens' mindless greed." Gryton raised his gloved hand and pressed it to the cage's surface, feeding more power into the damaged area. "And so, for a second time, the actions of the Riven allowed the Avatars to triumph over their adversaries. At least this time, I may be able to salvage this somewhat. However, you, the last of your kind, will not be around to witness it."

He slammed his hand into the glass-like cage and worked

more of his magic into the strange substance. His power ate away at the hard, clear surface, and when the hole was large enough for him to step through, he did and grasped the Riven in tendrils of burning light.

Flames leaped up from the Riven's body, quickly eating inward. Within moments, the Riven was no more.

Gryton stepped from the cage and brushed ash and energy residue from his armor. The kill held no satisfaction, but at least those unnatural monsters the blood witch had created were now gone from the universe.

Why she hadn't exterminated them herself, he never knew. Likely because she couldn't admit to having created such a failure in the first place.

Pride. Something he endeavored never to allow to take hold. Pride, too, was a weakness if it blinded a being so much, they could no longer see the truth before their eyes.

Pride and arrogance and love. They were all mind-corrupting weaknesses.

He walked past the other two cages with barely a glance. The deaths of a sidhe and a little sprite were generally of no importance. He slowed and glanced at them a second time. Still, he'd also seen too many plans disintegrate recently. Perhaps these two fae might prove useful one day. With an offhanded wave of one hand, he sent his magic to mark the two fae with his power. Both species were long-lived, intelligent, resourceful, and would make capable servants.

It only took a moment for his power to burrow deep and vanish from his sight. The spell would remain dormant until he called it forth. That done, Gryton started back the way he'd come only to halt again before a wide gate-like door.

Sending out small scouting spells, he sighed at what he learned.

Beyond the gate, three lines of humans waited, their weapons ready and aimed at him. There were no shouted orders like they'd given the Avatars. He sidestepped behind the solid support wall to one side of the gate as they loosed their weapons upon him. Loud riotous noise heralded a storm of tiny projectiles. They tore through the gate and impacted the wall he was sheltering behind.

It was doubtful if such tiny weapons could penetrate his magic-warded armor. Yet, a cautious nature had always served him well.

The onslaught only lasted moments and then it was over. He doubted if they had exhausted their weapons. More likely they were waiting to outflank him. Fighting his way free would draw too much attention. Especially since he wanted to maintain a low profile until he had one of the Avatars in his possession.

There were too many humans to use his mind control on effectively, so he summoned a transportation spell—one he'd already prepared earlier and stored for later use. Now seemed a good time.

He heard the soft scuff of their boots as they prepared to flank him. When the first of their number surged forward into his line of sight, he initiated a secondary spell. His fiery magic raced forward in greeting. Their screams reached out to assault his ears just as he triggered the transportation spell. It grabbed on to his essence and then with a jarring sensation and a moment of vertigo, he was once again in the forest. The echoes of dying humans faded from his hearing. The small circle of river rocks he'd attached this end of the spell to smoked slightly as they gave off their excess heat.

He would plan better in the future. Something as inconsequential as a pack of humans should not have forced him into using one of his escape spells.

CHAPTER ELEVEN

*S*hadowlight ran over the ground, jumping, weaving and darting through the forest with all possible speed. He followed a shallow stream for another quarter hour until he came to two familiar trees fallen crosswise against each other. The way they'd landed had created a slightly sheltered area in the 'vee' where the two trunks overlapped.

He'd dragged over some vines from where they'd been growing along one trunk to create a ceiling of sorts. His little shelter blended into the surrounding forest well enough. It had the added benefit of being close to a water source. The small stream held a few fish within its depths.

Secretly, he was rather proud of the shelter he'd found.

He stalked up to the shelter, ears scanning for sounds of movement within. He ducked and squeezed under the vines. Inside semi-darkness ruled, but his eyes adjusted quickly, and he could make out the form of the human warrior. She lay curled on her side, knees drawn up to her chest.

He couldn't see her face, but her sides still shifted slightly with each breath. Now that he was inside the shelter, he could hear the feeble beat of her heart. She had survived the night up until this point, but she was very weak. If he didn't do something soon, he doubted she would live to see another day. A shiver shook her frame, but she didn't wake.

Scouring his mother's memories, he learned cold and shock could kill as quickly as the wounds themselves. He also learned multiple blood exchanges might be required some hours apart. That seemed odd to his gargoyle instincts he'd inherited from his father. However, his mother was a healer so she might know more even though she wasn't a gargoyle.

He sat on his haunches and studied the human a long moment and then, his decision made, he used one fang to slash open the skin on his left forearm, following the pale scar from that earlier injury. The second time hurt just as much as the first.

He rolled the human to her back and then used one hand to pry open her jaws while he held his injured wrist over her mouth. The human choked and sputtered weakly on his blood. He hastily shifted her onto her side until her airway was clear again.

Frowning, he debated his options and settled for just dripping his blood over her still healing wounds. At least it would help heal those. A quick inventory showed all but the greatest injuries, three on her torso and two on her lower extremities, had already repaired themselves.

He was just finishing up with the last wound when another shiver wracked the human's frame. She twitched and mumbled something in her sleep.

While the muttering might mean she was regaining consciousness, the shivering couldn't be good. If she grew more chilled, it might not matter how much blood he gave her. She would still die. He needed a fire. Yes, it might draw attention, but he didn't have a choice.

Anna awoke with a groan. Moving caused every muscle in her body to twinge with remembered pain. Not good, so not good. She must have been hurt. It wasn't the first time, but whatever happened this time must have been bad enough to require morphine. Only morphine caused the weird-ass kinds of dreams she'd been having.

"You're strong for a little human soldier. I wasn't sure if you would survive."

Little human soldier?

"Oh, you've got to be fucking kidding me."

One of her morphine-inspired dream denizens sat across from her, feeding a stick into a small campfire. It was the gargoyle child, complete with wings, horns, and a tail. Yep. A tail. He was using the deadly looking tip of said tail to push a large flat stone closer to the fire pit. A camp kettle of some unknown design sat on top of the stone.

It looked old, but the etched design didn't appear to be from any culture she'd seen.

"It belongs to my father," the gargoyle said. "I borrowed it. I think you might have a greater need for it. Most of your belongings were destroyed in the battle, or too contaminated to keep."

The battle. Right. Nasty vampire-like monsters. Members of her unit dead. It hadn't been a morphine-inspired nightmare, not unless she was hallucinating still. She pushed back the panic and grief and focused on survival. She needed to keep her shit together for the next few hours and get back to base.

The gargoyle pulled a pack from a shadowy recess she hadn't noticed and rummaged around until he pulled out a large item that was unmistakably a canteen.

Seeing it triggered a ravenous thirst. The gargoyle held it out to her. When she didn't immediately take it, he gave it a little wiggle. The sound of sloshing water had her fingers tightening into a fist.

"You've lost a lot of blood. You need the water to help recover your strength." He held it closer to her and gave it another shake.

Suspicion stayed her hand, but he was correct. If she was going to survive to report back, she needed the water. When he held it out a third time, she took it. The weight was nearly too much for her trembling arms. Damn, she was weak as a kitten.

Her second attempt to lift the canteen met with success. Cold water bathed her mouth and lips, washing away the taste of old blood.

She took three more swallows and then forced the canteen away. Thirst demanded she drain the damn thing, but she didn't and carefully screwed the ornate cap back on.

With mild curiosity, her fingertips skimmed over it, feeling the jewels embedded on the sides.

On the scale of fucking weird shit she'd seen tonight—the gargoyle across from her was way higher on the list than a strange canteen.

She started to wipe her hand across her lips and stopped. Gore from the battle still coated her skin.

"It's alright. My blood and magic neutralized any taint upon your skin or uniform. It's just old, dried blood now, nothing more sinister."

Right.

A shower was a luxury she wasn't likely to see for a while, even if she managed to escape her new friend and report back to base. Hell, did she ever want to get back to base and report to her CO. Then this whole mess could be someone else's problem.

"You've lost a lot of blood. What I gave you would have gone to healing the wounds and ridding you of Riven taint, as such it didn't replace what you lost. Your body will need to do that on its own."

Her stomach tightened into knots. Just like that, he blasted her naïve thought to bits. Right. She'd gone mad and drank his blood. That was some fucked-up shit. This was never going to be someone else's problem. She had gargoyle blood and god knows what else running through her veins, soaking into her cells.

She'd seen some bad shit before, but nothing in her military training had readied her for this circus freak show.

The gargoyle's mobile ears drooped, plastering themselves against his mane, his expression one of hurt.

"I'm not a circus freak." His tone said he didn't know what that was exactly.

Tension rippled through her body anew. She hadn't spoken out loud. She knew she hadn't.

"Hmmm." She forced her breathing to calm. Her pulse still sped, but her training took over. "You know what I'm thinking." She didn't phrase it as a question, so added, "How?"

"I told you my blood would link us for life."

Oh hell, that did sound familiar. When she'd been infected, those monstrous Riven bites leaking their evil into her mind and soul, she'd been able to feel what that taint wanted to shape her into. Her mind kept wanting to shy away, partly in horror but more in disbelief.

Anna remembered the gargoyle. He'd given her a choice. A chance at life.

She couldn't deny she was healing, and herself once more. Logically, she was glad it was this juvenile and not a fully-grown adult who had found her. Somehow, she doubted she'd still be alive to question this mental link he spoke of if an adult gargoyle had found her first. Maybe she should cut the kid some slack and see what kind of intel she might learn.

"Sorry I lumped you in there with the circus freak thing. I was thinking more about those Riven beasts."

The gargoyle's ears swung forward, and he gave her one of the toothiest grins she'd ever seen.

Lord, those weapons, and this one was just a child.

"Thank you for saving me." Now, how to go about asking the next part? "And because of this blood sharing thing, you can read my thoughts?" There had to be a scientific explanation for all the crap that had happened in the last few hours.

He came around the fire and bumped his muzzle under her hand. "No, but we can talk to each other mind to mind. That's what you did. I just picked up on it. With training, you'll be able to control it better."

"Seriously?"

"*Yes,*" he said into her mind by way of demonstration.

Anna held her breath, her mind whirling with all the possible implications and applications that could arise from his ability. The ability to communicate mind-to-mind—now that was one tactical advantage the military needed to know about.

"And this ability is something all gargoyles share?"

"Yes. Most magically-gifted races have the ability to varying degrees."

Magical races? Oh boy, once she made it back to base, this was going to be the debriefing of a lifetime. Or a medical discharge and a few visits with a head shrink. "I think we're getting ahead of ourselves," she said and held her hand out. "Corporal Anna Mackenzie, Infantryman CFB Petawawa."

"I am Shadowlight, son of Stalks the Darkness and Born at the Mountain's Foot Where the River Runs Cold—but mother says I can just call her River."

She committed the names to memory. "Well, Shadowlight, I will admit I'm interested in what else you can do besides this mind-to-mind communication."

Shadowlight launched into the topic, seemingly all too pleased to have someone to teach.

Whereas she was all too happy to collect intel.

Shadowlight answered her every question and offered more on subjects she didn't even know to ask about. He knew he shared more than he should and that she thought she was plying him for her so-called intel. But in turn, he was studying and learning about her. Her loyalty and innate goodness. She was devotedly loyal to her people, but he also knew she hadn't yet figured out she was now as much Clan and Coven as she was human. He didn't know how to tell her she wasn't entirely human anymore.

Already, there were a few changes he could see. Her skin had lost its earlier sickly greyish tint, and now glowed a healthier brown tone which was probably her natural color. Her eyes, once the strange cream and brown bicolor of a human's, were now as black as his. Her nails, too, had darkened like his talons.

He'd bet one of Gran's cookies the human hadn't noticed those changes yet since the gore from last night's battle disguised her new retractable talons rather conveniently.

He decided not to enlighten her. There would be time for that later. As it was, dawn was approaching, and he really should go back and check on the medical technician Greenborrow had ordered him to watch. Guilt assaulted him. He should have left quite some time ago, but he'd gotten distracted.

"I must go," he stated as he extracted himself from the small confines of the shelter. "I have been away too long. My parents will come looking for me soon." Or mind call him, and he didn't want to be near the human if they should contact him. They might be able to sense her proximity to him. Out loud he added. "And you do not want to be found by them or the other fae yet. They would consider you a threat."

The human nodded. "A security risk. Those I understand."

"Good," he said, happy she was so compliant. "I'll leave you then, but I will return at nightfall to move you to a safer shelter. In the meantime, I've erected a dome around this site. The magic barrier will protect you from the elements and predators. You'll be safe. There is some food in the pack. Gran made it for everyone. The...trail mix is rather good, as are the granola bars, and I especially like the peanut butter cookies. Goodbye, Corporal Anna Mackenzie."

"What? Wait, but we're just…"

He didn't wait to hear the rest and was already darting into the surrounding forest, summoning his shadow magic as he ran so as not to give away her location to any other fae that might be nearby.

All in all, he thought his first meeting with his pet human had gone well. She seemed reasonably intelligent, and he had high hopes she could provide the other fae with valuable insight into the minds of their human enemies. And he rather hoped she might become his friend. He would like that.

CHAPTER TWELVE

*L*illian dropped the armful of wood she'd taken from the shed out back and placed it off to the side as she knelt before the cold fireplace. The night was chilled, cold enough for a fire. She hoped it didn't signal an early fall and subsequent winter. It felt like she'd already missed most of the summer. Healing in a hamadryad for three months tended to do that.

The fire was for Gregory. Not that he was ever cold. He was his own heat source, but she sensed he missed things from his world. While she didn't know what kind of accommodations the Magic Realm boasted, she figured fire was probably something both Realms shared. Hence, she was crouched before the fireplace in their master bedroom.

Old ashes still dusted the bottom from the last time she'd built a fire—months before when she'd still led a normal life, completely oblivious to the fact she wasn't human, or that magic was real.

She swept out the ashes more by routine than focused

effort, her mind on other, greater, problems than a few ashes. Gregory craved closeness. Yet after what had happened the night the Siren enchanted Gregory, Lillian wasn't sure how to maintain their previous closeness without accidentally revealing what had happened between them. She felt her stomach tighten with nerves just thinking about the lies and how she'd stripped Gregory of the memory.

Sex. It's called sex. Grow up and deal with it, she mentally scolded herself. *If nothing comes of it, then nothing comes of it, and Gregory certainly doesn't need to beat himself up for breaking some archaic vow.*

At least that was her reasoning for using the collars to make him forget. Though she wondered in a small part of her mind if she wasn't just using that excuse so Gregory wouldn't realize how foolish she'd been. She'd done a few embarrassing things in her life, but she also knew if Gregory looked at her with betrayal dulling his gaze, a part of her would die. She wanted to be his equal, to make him proud, to earn his respect, but she also knew nothing she'd done that night was worthy. The greater shame was that, in her heart, she knew the Sorceress of old would have found another way.

Yes, she'd done what she'd thought was best under the circumstances to save as many human lives as possible. But if Gregory lost respect for her because of it?

Well then, she'd just have to be strong and keep her secret because there was no way she wanted to lose Gregory's respect or have him loathe himself.

Given a choice, she'd make sure neither outcome came to pass. Which brought her to her first relationship hurdle. How to provide Gregory with what he needed without revealing something forbidden had already occurred. If she tried to guard against him intruding on her thoughts, he'd just get more suspicious, and then sniff out what had happened. He could read her far too well—knew some of her thoughts when they were touching.

Her only hope was to make certain her thoughts were clear and distinct, and not give him reason to dig deeper.

She hoped her plan with the fire was a good start. She'd know pretty quickly if it failed. Subtle Gregory wasn't.

She had the fire burning merrily by the time Gregory exited the bathroom with his customary two towels tied around his waist. His ebony mane was hanging around his shoulders and still dripping water.

A smile tugged at her lips. Gregory, predictable as always, made straight toward her with another towel in one hand and a large comb in the other.

He stopped next to her, still towering over her in his silent way as he stared down at the top of her head. The mat she'd set out by the fire was big enough even for Gregory to stretch full length on. She patted the mat. "I know we should get some rest since we have to be up again in a few hours, but I'm still wound too tight to sleep. I thought we could help each other relax."

Gregory made a deep huffing sound in humor but dropped down next to her.

"Here," she held her hand out for the comb, "I'll start with your mane. The fire's heat will help it dry."

She knelt behind him, with her knees to either side of his broad hips and began working loose the tangles in his mane.

His wings spread out to the sides to allow her in closer to his back, so it wasn't such a reach. She quickly fell into a routine. The rhythmic brushing relaxed her nearly as much as it did him. She took her time until every tangle was out, and his mane flowed smoothly down his back.

When she was finished at last, she stretched up and laced her arms around his neck in a backward hug.

Their nightly routine brought her a deep sense of peace. They remained silent; words were not needed between them. He brought her palms up to his lips and planted warm kisses on each while he curled his muscular tail across her hips and along her back. The tip curled around her shoulder and under her chin. She'd grown familiar with his way of returning her hug. With her cheek pressed against his damp mane, she closed her eyes and inhaled his pleasant scent, made stronger by his shower.

With another slow, easy smile, she pressed a kiss to the bulky muscle of one shoulder. Gregory rumbled happily and twisted toward her.

"Hah! No, you don't. Tonight is for you. You're the one who dodged bullets." She slowly ran her fingers over the healed grazes on his shoulder, flank, and wing. "Well, mostly dodged."

"I'd have taken worse to protect you."

"I know." Lillian ran her hands down his back, skimming them between his powerful wing joints, where they merged smoothly with his flight muscles. His wings shifted at her touch as if the light caress tickled. "You've really got to stop trying to martyr yourself."

"Never."

She huffed out a good imitation of his annoyance. "Well then, I'll just have to keep making it up to you, I suppose."

Gregory turned to her, a hint of wicked humor in his gaze.

"Subtle, Gregory, really subtle." She smiled and made a gesture encompassing the entire mat. "Lie down."

With another of his contented rumbles, he did as she instructed. She noted he completed the task with far more grace than she could have managed. When his head was resting comfortably on one of his folded forearms, he rolled his eyes in her direction, still not saying anything, just waiting for her to make the next move.

Lillian needed to fill the silence with something more than tension. "Did you know I was supposed to start college this fall? I was so pleased I got accepted—I didn't think I would, because I was homeschooled. At twenty, I'd already be a couple of years older than most other students going in. I figured what the hell, so what if I was twenty and not eighteen. I wanted to become a massage therapist."

She reached across him to snatch up the massage oil where she'd left it warming close to the fire. His ears lifted from his mane to track her movements, but he didn't otherwise move. "I knew Gran wasn't happy about my decision to attend college. I didn't know why since I planned to come back and practice at the Spa once I was finished school." Pouring a little oil into the palm of her hand, she started on the muscles between his wings, working her way slowly upward to his shoulders. He shifted slightly and sighed deeply, tension flowing out of him as she worked.

"In truth, I'm not sure if I could have left you. I didn't understand it at the time, but I was becoming more and more drawn to you," she laughed self-consciously, "a stone statue.

Now it also makes sense why Gran didn't want me to leave. She was protecting me like you'd asked. What would you have done if the Riven hadn't attacked me back in the spring? What if you hadn't awoken early from your healing sleep?"

"You wouldn't have left me, not for long." He huffed softly, his ears swiveling in her direction again. "But had you somehow managed to fight the draw between us long enough to have traveled any great distance, I would have sensed it and followed you. Although, I wouldn't have been thrilled to find you'd left me behind."

Lillian laughed. "I can imagine how our first meeting would have gone under those circumstances."

The idle talk had calmed her nerves, and she continued, much more relaxed.

Unhurried, she made her way lower, paying particular attention to the joints of his wings, which made him practically squirm, and then his sides. To her delight, she found he was ticklish there, too. When she moved on to his lower back, he sighed again, relaxing now that she was away from the ticklish zone. As she worked her way down, she hit the upper edge of his towel. She traced along the terrycloth's edges, a delicate caress, and then she reached for the knot at the side, where he'd tied the two together.

Gregory held himself perfectly still as she worked at the knot—he seemed calm and relaxed outwardly, but she felt the line of tension run through his muscles in what could only be anticipation. When she glanced toward his face, she found him watching her with half-closed eyes, their dark depths giving nothing away.

She got the knot untied and tapped him on the hip. "Up," she ordered as she grabbed another towel warming by the fire.

He came to his knees, and she took the damp towels from his bath and tossed them off to the side. He lowered himself back down to the mat with another contented sigh, and she laid one of the fire warmed towels across his hips.

Starting at his flanks, she alternately worked her palm into his warm muscles and then used her fingers to work out any knots of tension she found. Once she'd conquered those, she skimmed her fingers down one powerful thigh. A sudden spike of wickedness had her switching from his thighs to the more sensitive base of his tail.

At the first touch, he hissed something unintelligible, and the tip of his tail thumped almost violently against the floor. His wings threatened to unfurl and knock away her tormenting touch.

Taking pity on him, she moved on down his nearest leg, going slow and thorough until she reached his foot. After lovingly working on it for some time, she switched to the other and then worked her way back up his leg.

Then she eyed the great tail where it rested loosely coiled next to her, its bladed tip still twitching gently. Well, why not? It's a part of him too.

After pouring another generous dollop of oil in her palm, she started working on his tail. Repeatedly, the appendage escaped her grasp and wrapped itself around some part of her instead. Gregory's playful side was rearing up, and she knew she was in for trouble if she didn't finish up soon.

As she fully expected, his tail got harder to hold as she neared the tip. Gregory, now more interested in play than a massage, continually tried to snatch it away from her. Being slippery with massage oil made it an almost impossible task on her part. Predictably, his third attempt met with success, and the tip escaped her and got inside her defenses, where it curled around her waist and up under her shirt. He then proceeded to tickle her in retaliation.

Lillian admitted defeat as she burst into giggles. He rose up and tackled her. Completely taken by surprise, she was knocked off balance, but he rolled and caught her in his arms before she hit the ground. She'd barely registered he'd shifted into his more human looking hybrid form before warm lips were pressing kisses along her neck. While he was alternately nuzzling and nibbling, his tail was flicking caresses up and down her sides.

While she was still unbalanced, he shifted positions, coming to his knees with her pinned against his chest. Once she knew which way was up, she wrapped her arms around his neck and pressed soft kisses along the line of his jaw. A large hand was suddenly under her backside, and she was hoisted up higher until she could easily brush her lips to his.

"Hmmm," Gregory rumbled under his breath between kisses. "I might actually like playing at being human. Although, I think we need to work more on this first." His lips stroked against hers before breaking away again to brush kisses along her cheeks and brow. "To be certain, of course."

"Of course." Lillian nodded sagely.

He shifted slightly, his knees edging outward for better balance and she suddenly found her own legs straddling his broad thighs. The new position combined with the thin material of her nightgown left no doubt he liked holding her close. She leaned back and put some distance between them, enough so she could meet his gaze. He drew in a sharp breath and held it. Something struck her as very vulnerable about his body language just then.

Leaning forward, she placed another lingering caress upon his lips and then said, "You're the most beautiful being I know, both inside and out. No matter what the coming days may bring, I am honored to have you at my side. None could ask for a better protector."

She dropped her gaze and stroked her fingertips down his chest, and then added, "Or lover, I imagine."

Gregory made a soft sound, a wordless promise as he reached for the hem of her nightgown. She wiggled out of it as he helped to drag it over her head. Under it she was bare, and her nipples beaded as his knuckles brushed across them.

He dropped the nightgown in a pile next to them and turned his attention back to her. Finding herself growing shy under his gaze, she ducked her head and her hair swung forward to shield her breasts.

Gregory seemed unconcerned by the development and began kneading her hips with his strong fingers.

"Mmm," Lillian arched her back, shyness retreating before the heat rising within her. She pressed against him and simply allowed him to move her how he liked. The undeniable evidence of his arousal trapped between her thighs gave her pause and at the same time did something to fire the heat in her blood to new levels.

After a few more moments, he released his grip on her hips and glided his fingers up her sides and then cupped the heavy weight of her breasts. He cupped her gently before leaning down to taste first one then the other.

"Tonight was supposed to be about you," she said as she clung to his shoulders, needing something to hold on to. While he was lavishing attention on her breasts, his one hand had been trailing south.

Smug male laughter wrapped around her. "We are one being."

She gasped out a surprised moan at his touch and simply let him have his way. After several more minutes of his skillful attentions, intense waves of pleasure had her eyes drifting closed. He continued to guide her movements, and she sighed out another sound of pleasure. The building waves rolled over her before she'd expected it and Lillian called out his name as she came apart cocooned in his wings.

Gregory kissed her down from the peak, and she slumped against him, all her bones suddenly mush. Slowly, reason returned, but she wasn't displeased by events.

A voice tinged with male pride brushed against her senses. "I take it I did that well?"

"Gloriously," she replied, though she also knew he hadn't reached the same end yet himself. "Would you like me to return the favor?"

"Anything you decide will give me pleasure, my beautiful dryad."

She smiled and then returned to kissing him while she, in turn, allowed her hands to roam lower. The wood had burned to embers in the fireplace by the time they drifted to sleep much, much later.

CHAPTER THIRTEEN

Major Resnick led his team through the woods with an outwardly calm exterior, pretending there was nothing unusual about hunting invisible monsters. Inwardly, his mind was awhirl with all he'd seen in the last twenty-four, no make that thirty-six hours. Now the damn days were blurring together.

When he'd first been assigned to the mission, he'd thought alpha site was some kind of hoax—although, even he couldn't hazard a guess as to what force had snapped trees like they were toothpicks in a one-kilometer radius around the site but had otherwise left no evidence behind.

Things got stranger when the results from the samples taken at the crater came back. Everything in the immediate area was dead. It wasn't just the trees and the animals either. Every blade of grass and patch of moss, they were all dead. Everything. Even the microbes. Nothing survived.

Some of the men had renamed Alpha site to Armageddon site.

He wasn't superstitious or an overly religious man, but somehow, he couldn't blame them. After a brief hesitation, he'd started calling it Armageddon site in the privacy of his own mind.

That event had happened three months back, heralded by a towering pillar of light. Some of the locals had snapped pictures of the event and then came the media frenzy. What the general public didn't know was that it had even been seen in space.

The government spin doctors made it out to be a particularly intense solar storm and the northern lights. Yeah, the locals didn't buy into that story either, but the rest of the world did.

Resnick's own world was far from peaceful, but he'd stuck to his personal mantra: do his job and let the scientists figure out what happened at the bloody Armageddon site.

But then a local farmer found a mutated body near the town, and top brass ordered the search farther afield for more clues. The scientists couldn't link the two sites together beyond the presence of unexplainable anomalies. They had no idea how the body had gotten there or what had killed it.

Clearly, the specimen had looked like it had been in a battle and then crawled away to die. Nothing had touched its remains, not even insects according to the report. They'd had a damp spring and summer so far, cooler than average. Yet the body was mostly mummified, which made no sense.

Then just two days ago they'd found a live one, and two other...as yet undiscovered species.

Still, his mind had trouble accepting the truth—that humans were not the only intelligent predator on the planet.

All such information was need-to-know. Secretly, he

wished his mission hadn't required him to need to know to do his job.

Ignorance truly was bliss. At least it helped one sleep peacefully at night.

He hadn't slept since the town-wide masquerade, which was likely a blessing. He didn't know what kind of nightmares would haunt his dreams now.

But what had happened was no dream. It was a very real battle. Many of the patrols out that night hadn't returned at all, but anyone with ears had heard the firefight that ensued.

At the time, Resnick was passed out in the center of town like most everyone else. By the time he came to and reached the location of the battle, the fighting was over. There were signs of struggle, but no bodies. The survivors remembered nothing, just like all the town's folk.

But search dogs were able to run three different specimens to ground.

One creature—a mad beast with pale skin and sharp fangs—Resnick had wanted to put down on the spot. Brass had ordered it brought in for study.

The other two specimens were caught because they were trying to kill the vampire-like creature. The tall elfish one had managed to put two arrows in the vampire. In turn, Resnick and his men nailed the big guy with three tranquilizer darts.

Their new target had escaped back into the forest. They were tracking him when they found a tiny four-foot tall female...something...trying to hide her unconscious friend from the search dogs.

Weird shit happened.

Resnick just wished it would stop happening on his watch.

And just last night he'd returned to base to find an

intruder impersonating one of his men. Clearly, this one was an infiltrator of some kind and had planted himself with Resnick's convoy to get inside the base.

His superiors claimed the decoy Corporal Jenkins was there to execute the vampire-like specimen but had been discovered before he was able to complete his mission, and the one in the suit of armor had been sent to finish the job.

Something didn't sit right with Resnick.

Why would the one in full armor kill the vampire-like specimen but not free the other two prisoners? He'd had plenty of time to release the other two while he'd been down on the rink, but he hadn't bothered. It didn't add up. Could the imposter Corporal Jenkins and Armor Suit represent two different warring factions?

When he'd brought his concerns to his superior, he'd been assigned patrol detail.

As if it was his fault the newcomer had vanished before all their eyes. None of it made sense.

"Major, I found something that might prove interesting."

Resnick made his way over to Lieutenant Landry, still scanning the area for nasty surprises. "Interesting is a forbidden word. The science geeks have killed it for me. Permitted words are 'dangerous' or 'what-the-fuck-is-this.' Understand?"

"Yes, sir." The lieutenant eyed him dubiously. "They're the cameras Corporal Mackenzie set up last week before she went MIA."

Anger and guilt warred within Resnick before he could push it back.

Mackenzie wasn't much more than a kid. She was what, twenty-four? Bright, brave, foolhardy, third generation military. How the hell was he going to face her father? Brigadier General Samuel Mackenzie had been Resnick's CO during his first tour. Despite a decade difference in their ages, they had maintained a close friendship for the last twenty years.

In part, that's why Corporal Mackenzie had landed in Resnick's unit. The day of the masquerade, he and his team had been out on patrol when the ridge they'd been exploring gave way. Mackenzie, Griffith, and Jones had all gotten a rough ride to the base of the ridge. He'd ordered them all back to get checked out.

By the time all hell had broken loose later that night, his three injured team members had been released from medical. He'd only learned after he'd come stumbling back to HQ that they had gone back out to help once they'd heard gunfire. No one had seen or heard from them since.

"Sir?"

"Do you have something to view the data on?"

"No, but Ruthven does," Lieutenant Landry said and jerked his chin in Master Corporal Ruthven's direction where he was already shouldering off his pack. He passed a tablet to Landry.

"Good. Let me know if you see something more dangerous than deer." To the others, he motioned for them to fan out and do another quick scout of the area. Enemies that could pop in and out without leaving a trace made even him paranoid.

When they couldn't find so much as a leaf out of place, he ordered a short rest.

Resnick took a drag on his water as he looked at the trees around him, and then up into the thick canopy overhead.

"You know," he said more to the trees above than any one

of his men. "I think I know how our Robin Hood and the pixie Marion managed to avoid detection for so long."

He remembered how the tall, elfish fellow with the longbow had dropped down practically on top of Resnick's team in his attempt to take out their fanged acquisition. The combination of the tree canopy, thick underbrush, and placement of Resnick's team must have fouled up the elf lord's killing shots.

Was it desperation, or just blind hate, which had driven him to expose himself to their team? Resnick didn't have an answer. No one had been able to make tall, blond, and elfish talk.

But Resnick still had a feeling the elf might have been protecting everyone by trying to take out the fanged monstrosity.

"Trees," Resnick said as he glanced over at Ruthven.

"Sir?"

"The damned trees. Robin Hood and our tiny Marion, I'd bet a week's rations they use the trees to travel. Otherwise, we would have found some signs of them long ago."

"Sir," Landry spoke up over the others. "Not sure about trees, but I think I just found another mode of travel. You've got to see this. It's way past interesting, straight into WTF territory."

Resnick took the offered tablet. The feed had been paused and enlarged to take up the screen's entire surface.

His eyes darted over the screen, and he sucked in a deep breath. "We move out now. Back to base, double time. Ruthven, put that thing back in your pack and protect it with your life."

Private Jacobs walked up and tried to glance at the screen as Ruthven stowed the tablet in his pack. "What's on it?"

"I'm not sure, exactly."

Resnick gestured them to move out. "What's on that device is so highly classified they haven't created a designation for it yet. We are going to endure hours and hours of debriefings. That's what's on that damn device."

Resnick kept his voice emotionless and controlled, but inside he was shaking.

He was sure what he'd mentally labeled elf, pixie, and vampire were something science could explain—some kind of mutation, or highly illegal genetic experimentation. Something that had started out human.

What he'd seen on the tablet was not human, not even close. Never had been.

CHAPTER FOURTEEN

*L*illian sat with the rest of the family around the kitchen table. A cooling cup of coffee rested in her hand. She'd been nursing it for twenty minutes but couldn't get it down. The smell wasn't helping the tight knot in her stomach either.

Coffee had been hit and miss with her ever since she'd emerged from her hamadryad healing three weeks ago.

Had it only been weeks? The siren Tethys, the Riven, the human military. It all felt much longer than three short weeks.

Sipping her coffee, she grimaced. The rest of the family was equally as quiet. It had been another long night with only a few hours' worth of sleep. Well, not that she and Gregory had spent the whole time sleeping, either.

She glanced around at her family. Her brother was polishing off a bowl of porridge with more determination than joy by the look of it. Gran sat staring at her oatmeal—

too tired to eat it, by all appearances, which had Lillian worried.

"We need to plan for what comes next. Any ideas?" she asked the table at large.

Gregory cocked an ear in her direction but continued to finish his second bowl of porridge before he answered. "We rest and see what the humans do this day. Tonight, protected by darkness, we stage a rescue. We both scented our allies within that main building just before we fled."

"Yes, but how will we manage it? They were planning to move them to a more secure location yesterday, just before we were discovered. Surely, they have already moved them.

Gregory shook his head. "Darkness says Whitethorn and Goswin are still inside." He sounded a touch displeased. "He took it upon himself to scout the area we did not have time to search. He found them drugged and trapped in clear-walled cages. He couldn't escape with them both, not with them unconscious and during full daylight."

Ah, the real source of his annoyance. Darkness had gone scouting without notifying Gregory first.

Lillian rubbed the bridge of her nose to hide her smile and then turned serious again. "Then we still have a chance to rescue them before they get spirited off to god knows where. I'm glad our debacle didn't spook the military into moving them early."

"If anything, the debacle caused them to dig in and call for more reinforcements," Gran said into her cup. "Our spies are keeping track of things and will inform us if they move our friends."

"Spies?" Lillian asked, feeling like she'd missed something, again.

Gran made a fluttering gesture with her hand. "Like the messenger spells, but these ones watch and report back their news. If the soldiers notice a few more birds, squirrels, and chipmunks than normal?" She smiled. "They will think nothing of it."

Gran's exhaustion now made sense. She'd been doing spell work all night. "We could have helped."

"It was better you slept. There is still lots that needs doing before tonight." Gran gestured at the small television in the corner of the kitchen. "My spies have already overheard many interesting things. We are still persons of interest—though not as much as before now they have something else to hunt. In the meantime, they plan to give the town a clean bill of health and lift the lockdown. They have an ulterior motive, of course. Once they turn the townsfolk loose to gather and gossip, they are going to tail those of interest and see if they can learn something."

"So, every time we turn around, we're going to run into our new best friends," Lillian stated with a snort of amusement. "That's going to make things more complicated."

"We're not going to do anything of interest," Gran said. "In fact, we're going to bore them to death. Lillian, you and Gregory are going to go grocery shopping and run errands. Make sure you hit the coffee shop and the diner for lunch. Jason will go to the hardware store and get the wood for the new gazebo. I'll go meet with the card ladies. Just boring business as usual."

"You're going to turn me loose on the town?" Gregory looked excited at the thought, so Lillian introduced the other part of the equation.

"Yep, lots of places to go in the car."

Gregory's expression fell.

CHAPTER FIFTEEN

*S*hadowlight thought Gran would never leave, but she finally did. Taking the noisy and smelly conveyance she called a truck, she drove off down the lane.

Perched on Gregory's pedestal in the center of Lillian's maze, Shadowlight couldn't actually see Gran driving away, but he could hear it. He waited until the sound of her truck drifted away before he moved.

Jason had gone to something called a hardware store to get wood, which mystified him. Why would they go somewhere to get wood when they were surrounded by forests? Oh well, Lillian's adopted family might be strange, but he liked them anyway.

Lillian and Gregory were out shopping—whatever that was. Gran had just left to play cards. It was all a ruse to trick the humans. He'd been eavesdropping on their conversation at breakfast and thought it sounded like a perfect opportunity to visit with his pet human.

He was supposed to stay on the pedestal and pretend to

be Gregory, which he totally could do, but he was also skilled enough to leave an illusion behind that looked and felt like a stone statue.

After stretching, he jumped down from his perch and created the illusion. He felt a touch guilty. His father had given him the assignment, and it really wasn't honorable to just leave.

Yet, he needed to check on his human.

Somehow, he didn't think his parents would be understanding.

Good thing they were out patrolling the perimeter of the human military camp.

He'd originally wanted to join them, but they'd refused. Something about it being too dangerous.

He made his way out of the maze, searching for any other fae that might be lurking around, especially Greenborrow. The leshii had taken the blame for allowing the medical technician to escape.

Why he didn't know. Greenborrow could merely have said he'd left the human in Shadowlight's care.

The leshii had glanced at Shadowlight while he'd told the lie and taken the blame.

Shaking off the mild guilt the memory inspired, Shadowlight began to run, using his natural magic for camouflage. It wasn't foolproof in the bright light of day, and he felt more exposed than he liked as he ran through the gardens.

He didn't relax until he was once more under the dense forest canopy.

Taking a long winding path to his destination added an extra few minutes to the trip, but it made him feel more secure about his human's safety.

When he arrived, she was already up and walking the edges of the protective dome of energy. Every few strides, she reached out and touched the solid surface and then pulled her fingers away with a little shake.

There was a method to her actions, he realized. She was using a search pattern to cover the entire dome within her reach, looking for a door or weakness she could use to escape.

He stalked forward, maintaining his shadow magic. In a mix of curiosity and playfulness, he paced her, mirroring her move for move to see how much his blood had changed her.

After three steps and no outward change in her expression or body language, a sense of disappointment swept over him. He had hoped his blood would have had more of an effect on her—for her own safety. She needed to be more gargoyle and less human if she had any hope of being accepted by the other fae.

Oh well, no one had discovered his secret. He only had to maintain it long enough to get a little more of his blood in her.

Once she was more of the Magic Realm than the Mortal one, he was confident his family and the other fae wouldn't kill her outright.

Admittedly, he hadn't thought it out thoroughly when he'd saved her, but he was certain the others would see she possessed a noble spirit.

While he'd been thinking of future possibilities, Anna had stopped her search of the dome and was staring at him with a perplexed look on her face. The little wrinkle between her brows deepened.

"You're there, aren't you? I can sense you." Her brow

smoothed as her eyes widened in surprise. Then in a hoarse whisper, she added, "It damn well better be you."

"It is," he assured her as he released his hold on his cloaking magic.

His sudden appearance had startled her, but after a moment she returned to the dome's edge and studied him through it. "Handy trick. How many others can you do?"

At first, he'd been a bit in awe of her outwardly calm exterior—he doubted many humans would possess such an adaptable personality, but then he'd come to realize it was a coping mechanism. To keep her panic at bay, she asked questions and cataloged his answers, telling herself she would take everything she learned and turn it over to her people once she'd escaped. Her thoughts were all there before him, clear as a glacial waterfall.

He hadn't lied when he said he couldn't read her mind—not exactly. At least he wasn't willfully doing it. Her mind was just so focused and disciplined, it was like she was talking aloud, and her thoughts just came to him clear and uncluttered.

"I thought you said you wouldn't be coming back until nightfall. What happened? Do we have a problem?"

He had to admit she was good—using 'we' and making it sound like they were a team, when in fact she was still searching every angle to escape him.

Knowing her thoughts became a boon at that moment.

"There is no problem." Oh, but how to go about telling her she could never return to her people.

"Thanks for saving me. Now it's time to let me go."

"I can't. Not yet." He raised a talon and tapped on the protective dome once, and then stepped through. She leaped back, putting space between herself and the dome before she dropped into a defensive crouch.

She held a knife in her hand. It was the one from the pack. A simple camp knife his father used for little tasks when talons were not sufficient.

It wasn't much of a weapon. Its blade was no longer than his hand.

"I know you think of escape, of taking what you've learned and sharing it with the humans," he said as he held his ground, allowing her to process his words. "But you are no longer only human, you are in part, small though it is, gargoyle." He tilted his head in new understanding of what he'd done to her. "You are neither human nor gargoyle. My blood saved your life, but at a heavy cost. One I'm just beginning to understand myself. How do I go about explaining it to you?"

"One sentence at a time." Her voice came out in a soft rush, the tension behind it obvious.

"My father says humans are not tolerant of anything they see as different. However, he hasn't interacted much with humans. Perhaps his assessment of them is not accurate?"

"Lack of tolerance—sounds about right for a good portion of the population," she said grudgingly.

"And you are now different than you were."

The truth of his words flashed across her face.

"Will your fellow humans accept you back now that you are partly gargoyle?"

A muscle in her jaw ticked. "Oh, they'll be glad to have me back," her throat bobbed as she swallowed hard. "I'll be lucky not to end up on some examination slab, somewhere."

Shadowlight didn't have a reference for the words she used, but her tone said enough.

She narrowed her eyes at him. "You're saying my only hope of safe haven is with your kind?"

"That is not entirely accurate."

The line between her brows deepened. "Feel free to start filling in details at any point."

"You're still too human in your thinking, your loyalties, and your motives. I think it best none learn of your existence for now."

"You're awfully astute for a kid." Her lips compressed in thought and her brows descended slightly. She inhaled a sharp breath. "You plan to keep me as a pet, don't you? For how long? Until you get bored with me?"

Shadowlight felt the first traces of annoyance and anger filter through his being.

He'd saved her, a selfless act.

Shouldn't she be grateful?

Apparently, he wasn't handling the situation well. It didn't matter if she was grateful or not, all his gargoyle instincts and his father's memories said he was still responsible for her. He'd saved her. Now she was his responsibility.

To start, he'd have to protect her from both the fae and the humans. She seemed like a reasonable person. He was sure he could gain her trust...eventually.

"What happens when you get tired of your shiny new toy?"

An ear flicked forward and then back. Even his tail twitched slowly as he worked through the meaning of her question.

Oh, she was the toy.

His ears swung forward, snapping to attention. "You think I would harm you?"

She held her rigid pose. "What am I supposed to think? You just explained I belong nowhere, and you hadn't fully thought out your actions."

In a moment of clarity, Shadowlight dropped to all fours and bounded over to her, butting his muzzle and head under her hand for a scratch. "Foolish human."

As he had hoped, his action so caught her off guard, she didn't use the knife she held.

"I saved you because I liked your spirit. I'm not about to kill you just because you think I now find you an inconvenience." Shadowlight wiggled closer as he felt the first tentative scratch behind his ears. "That goes against every instinct a gargoyle has. We protect. We guard against evil and eradicate it where we find it. We don't harm those we consider our responsibility."

"Because you saved me, you now consider me your responsibility?" Her tone was thoughtful, not flippant, he noted.

"No, not because I saved you. Because my blood changed you. I did not fully think through what I'd be forcing you to accept." Oh, there was more, and he debated telling her now or later. He wanted her trust. Lies and omissions would only bring harm later down the road. "And there is the possibility you may require more of my magic-laced blood at certain intervals to keep you strong."

Her fingers froze in his mane. "Say that again."

Hmmm. Maybe he should have waited a day or two for that detail.

While he was still flailing for something to say, she

squatted down in front of him and stared him in the eye. "How often?"

He flinched at her tone but answered truthfully. "I'm not sure. My mother is a healer. She would have a better idea. Unfortunately, her memories weren't that detailed."

"Is this a 'for life' condition?"

"I think so, yes."

"I need a time out."

With those brisk words, she took herself over to the fallen tree shelter and sat down with her head on her drawn up knees.

She stayed like that for a long time.

With a dejected sigh, he sat on his haunches to give her the time she needed to cope with that new knowledge.

Then he napped, one ear cocked in her direction, so he'd know if she stirred.

But it wasn't the sound of the human soldier stirring which dragged him from his sleep—no this was a tremendous droning tone that swiftly grew until it reverberated within his very bones.

The noise grew closer, and the human jumped to her feet and tilted her head back to study the sky.

Shadowlight flared his wings out, tensed his powerful haunches, and called his magic as he prepared to launch himself into the sky to face whatever enemy was bearing down on them.

"You may want to keep your feet firmly on the ground unless you enjoy a world of pain." She shrugged. "Your choice, my friend, but those big boys are going to be armed to the teeth. Although, I don't think they are after us. Moving too fast. They'll overshoot us in...."

As if she'd synchronized the timing of her words to their flyover, seven mean-looking machines buzzed over their heads and were gone moments later.

"What were those?"

She looked him in the eyes. "Well, the two escorts were ours. The other five were United States Army. Things just got a whole lot more complex for you, my young friend."

He gave her a questioning look.

She clarified. "They have more resources to hunt you down."

"Are they from a neighboring kingdom?" he asked, growing concerned for his family's well-being. His mother and father could hide easily enough. But Lillian and Gregory were known and couldn't just vanish without drawing suspicion.

She arched an eyebrow at him. "You have so much to learn."

He gave a little shrug, entirely unapologetic.

"I was just born three days ago."

Her jaw dropped as she stared on, mute. Shadowlight left while she was still too shocked to waylay him with more questions. He had to find his family and make sure everyone was safe.

CHAPTER SIXTEEN

"Are you done yet?"

It was the fourth time Lillian had heard that question in the last two hours. The first time had been in the first drugstore she'd hit, the second in the long lineup at the coffee shop. The third complaint had been in the grocery store when two miniature tyrants—Gregory's title for them—had rammed him in the hip with the cart. She'd sweetly promised him a special treat of his choosing if he didn't decapitate the two boys.

They'd left the grocery store without further issue. Their silent tails, two dour looking military types, pretended to pick up a couple of things at the store as well.

When Lillian had driven away, she'd spotted their new friends following behind in an armored vehicle. Was that their attempt at undercover? Or maybe they just didn't care if they were spotted.

She made a few more stops, and her tails followed faithfully. She was almost tempted to set Gregory upon them. She was sure he'd have enjoyed tormenting the humans.

It would distract Gregory, too. Which would be handy, she admitted as she pulled into the second drugstore's parking lot.

She needed to pick up a couple more items for her peace of mind. The threat of pregnancy still hung over her head. Gregory hadn't remembered anything from the night of the masquerade, but that wouldn't help her if she was pregnant and began showing signs. Which brought her to her next issue. Being a gargoyle-dryad hybrid, she didn't even know what the symptoms of pregnancy would be.

She didn't have a monthly cycle like a human. Hers came once every three months. She'd always wondered about that, but Gran had said it was a normal genetic blip on her side of the family. Being young and naïve, she'd trusted Gran. Then again, who would have equated a longer cycle than usual with being a dryad-gargoyle hybrid?

"More stops?" Gregory asked, sounding grumpy.

Lillian got out of the car and came around to his side while he was still trying to extract himself from the vehicle. She leaned down and gave him a quick kiss on the lips while running her fingers along his tattoo. "I would say you could wait in the car, but…"

Gregory snorted without humor. "As if I'd leave you undefended."

Yes, picking up a few pregnancy tests from the drugstore without Gregory knowing was going to be problematic.

Feeling ornery and flippant, she waved to her two tails as they pulled into the parking lot. Gregory gave them a toothy grin, and a wave as well.

Lillian marched into the drugstore and snatched up a basket as she ran through her mental list of things to pick up.

She figured if she grabbed lots of stuff, Gregory wouldn't notice a few pregnancy tests among everything else. Not that he would know what they were anyway, but he could read, which gave her an idea as she walked past the magazine racks. She grabbed a local newspaper and gave it to Gregory. "Read it and let me know if there is anything interesting in there we may need to know."

Gregory frowned but nodded and began to skim through the paper. Lillian continued her task with military efficiency and came to the aisle she needed. She didn't pause to read or study the packages, instead grabbing three of each variety on the shelf.

The number would make the girl at the checkout do a triple take, but Lilian wasn't sure when she'd have a chance to get more.

She knew gargoyles were warm-blooded and dryads had breasts, so they were mammals in theory. Also, dryads looked enough like humans that they probably had some shared ancestry somewhere far enough back on the evolutionary tree. She didn't know if they were enough like humans for the test kits to be useful.

Personally, she doubted they'd be accurate, dryads and humans probably didn't have the same hormones. In fact, it had only been two days since the incident so the tests wouldn't show anything yet, anyway. She planned to use one tonight as a sort of baseline test, and then space the others out on a weekly basis to check for any changes. At least she hoped it would work, and she really hoped not to see any changes.

By her estimate, she was maybe two-thirds of the way through her fertility cycle, which once again, told her nothing.

Damn, she really needed an Idiot's Guide to dryads with a bonus chapter on gargoyles.

Basket at her side, Gregory a few steps behind with his nose still buried in the newspaper, Lillian rounded the corner of the next aisle and nearly ran head-on into one of her friendly tails.

It was the taller of the two clones. Up close, she noted this one had brown eyes where the other guy possessed a lighter shade—hazel maybe?

She compressed her lips and then replaced the encroaching frown with a smile instead. "Nice day," she said. "Enjoying the town?" Because really, what did one say to their tails?

"Ma'am," Brown Eyes acknowledged and then glanced down in her basket.

His one eyebrow rose slightly. Yep, he was so adding the basket of pregnancy tests to his report. Damn. As long as he didn't say anything in front of Gregory, she didn't care.

"Well, I'm sure we'll be seeing each other again soon." She sidestepped around Brown Eyes and nodded to military clone number two.

They didn't stop her, so she continued toward the checkout. She was halfway there when the tattoo around her neck tingled and she realized Gregory hadn't followed.

A glance over her shoulder showed him having a staring contest with the taller soldier. She sighed and briefly wondered if there was a sudden bout of testosterone poisoning sweeping through the town.

She ignored the tattoo's second warning twinge and continued to the checkout. Eventually, Gregory returned to her side while she was bagging her purchases, but his attention was still for the two soldiers.

With a sigh, Lillian plucked the forgotten newspaper from his fingers and gave it to the cashier to add to the other items.

Without a word in exchange, and apparently Gregory being none the wiser about what she'd purchased, they returned to her car under the watchful gazes of her two tails.

She'd just slammed the trunk when she heard a loud rumble approaching. The sound increased in volume alarmingly quickly as seven heavy-bodied helicopters, which were armed to the teeth, tore through the skies overhead.

The townsfolk came out to gawk at the helicopters until they vanished behind the tree line.

She couldn't be sure of their destination, but she'd bet the lower branches of her hamadryad, those helicopters were there to transport the prisoners to a more secure location.

She turned to Gregory and whispered, "We need to get home, now."

"Yes," he agreed but didn't take his eyes off the place they'd last seen the helicopters before they'd vanished.

CHAPTER SEVENTEEN

By the time they made it back to the spa, Lillian had discovered everyone else was already home. Gregory stomped into the house loaded down with eight bags of groceries while she scooped up her own bags and ran them upstairs where she hid the pregnancy tests in her bathroom vanity. She was just headed back down the stairs when the second warning tingle crawled along her tattoo.

Gregory emerged from the kitchen, rubbing his own throat and watched her with a questioning look as she crossed the living room floor and returned to his side.

"Sorry," she mumbled as she joined him. "I figured I could run the stuff upstairs and be back before the collars reacted."

Gregory merely nodded and then added, "Darkness is in the kitchen. He has news."

He didn't say or do anything else to outwardly show his excitement, but she could sense it all the same.

The trip to town was almost too much for her poor

gargoyle, and now he was clearly itching to do something dangerous.

She felt her own blood surge at the thought of danger, and she began to wonder if their DNA was coded to hunt out dangerous situations.

Rather like they equated danger with fun. Now she had to lump herself in with them.

She pushed open the kitchen door and was only halfway through when she was scooped up in another strong embrace.

"Father says I get to help with this mission." Shadowlight vibrated with happiness. He spun Lillian around once and then put her down.

Her little brother made an aborted motion toward Gregory, who was still in human form, but her other half lifted an eyebrow in warning and bestowed a grim look upon the youngest gargoyle which promised pain to anyone foolish enough to attempt to pick him up.

Shadowlight dropped to all fours and butted Gregory in the stomach instead.

With a sigh, and a smile he couldn't hide, he gave the youngster a few affectionate scratches before turning to the other gargoyle in the room.

Darkness stood in the corner of the kitchen with the most shadows. He wasn't actively trying to hide. Perhaps it was just an unconscious instinct on his part.

Her mother stood off to the side, speaking with Gran and Jason. Gregory went straight to Darkness. Lillian joined them.

"Those loud flying machines landed at the humans' camp," Darkness was saying. "I overheard one pilot," he hesitated over the foreign word before continuing, "Say to another member of his team he had orders to be back in the air within the hour."

"Not long," Gregory chimed in. "They must be planning to move our people."

"There was a flurry of activity at the base. I agree. They will move your allies soon."

Lillian glanced out the window, eyeing the sun as it started its descent toward the horizon. She knew Gregory and Darkness were able to hide even while the sun was still high. Shadowlight she wasn't so sure about. Though, he was a proper gargoyle and had inherited their father's memories and skills to a much greater degree than she had. He, too, might be able to hide while the sun was still high.

Lillian knew she wasn't ready to infiltrate the base again so soon but didn't see another option. "We have to get them out. Now. In the daylight."

Gregory nodded. "The base is too well guarded. We'll take them on the wing."

Darkness nodded agreement, and they both went over to Gran.

Lillian was left standing with Shadowlight, who leaned against her, happy to be included in the hunt. She finally found her voice and chased after Gregory so quickly, she heard Shadowlight lose his balance and stumble into the cupboard door next to where she'd been standing a moment ago. He made a disgruntled sound but bounded after her.

"You can't be planning to attack those helicopters. It's suicide to even think to try."

Gregory huffed. "They won't expect an attack on the wing. Nor will they be able to see or hear us coming. This way we won't have to deal with the entire armed camp. Just what those machines can carry."

Lillian's stomach fluttered nervously. "Those things house weapons Gregory, ones like the guns the soldiers carry, but the ones strapped to the helicopters will be bigger and meaner."

"We know of these things now and can use shielding magic against them."

"And how do you propose we go about catching them once they're in the air? Kind of hard to rescue our friends if we can't even catch them."

Darkness tilted his head in her direction, and she had the distinct impression he was translating her words in his mind into something he understood. "Oh, but gargoyles can match speed with those things, and if we dive from a much higher vantage point—"

"You'll get sliced to ribbons," Lillian cut in.

Her father's look of disdain didn't earn him any sympathy from her, but he continued anyway. "I saw how those things keep themselves up. It will be no great challenge to bring them down. If getting close proves too dangerous we can do it from afar. Gargoyle magic is adaptable. Those machines are not."

"We can't bring them down. Whitethorn and Goswin wouldn't survive, and the humans are just doing their jobs."

Gregory placed a hand on Lillian's shoulder and gave it a squeeze. "We don't need to harm the humans, but you need to trust me. I am not underestimating the humans, and you should know by now I would not embark upon this quest if I thought you would be placed in unnecessary danger." He gestured to Darkness. "That's why I've asked your father to do a partial memory transfer, so you'll have the skills and knowledge you'll need for this mission."

Oh, he made it sound so reasonable, but she couldn't help thinking about all the ways this attempt could end in painful disaster.

She glanced at her father where he waited patiently for her to see their way of thinking. Even with the memory transfer Gregory talked of, she didn't think this plan had a hope of success.

But if they didn't act now, Whitethorn and Goswin might slip forever beyond their reach.

"Fine, let's do this."

Gregory and Darkness gave almost identical somber nods, whereas Shadowlight jumped to attention, wings vibrating with excitement.

If it were within her power, she would forbid Shadowlight from coming. He was far too young to go on such a dangerous mission. However, she'd been overruled, and they *did* need every set of wings available to rescue Whitethorn and Goswin.

Besides, Shadowlight would likely just follow them, and if he was going into danger, she wanted him near enough to keep an eye on.

Major Resnick decided he was having the mother of all bad weeks. They made their way back to base as fast as humanly possible on foot, the land too rugged for any kind of motorized vehicles to extract them. Not that their radios were working. Something was jamming them again.

He was just exiting the forest and coming out onto the road when he heard the roar of helos approaching. His team was less than five kilometers from the base, but they might as well have been a hundred for all the good it did him.

Thirty seconds later, five US Army helos flew overhead, heading south. His gut told him that was the prisoner transport, and it was in danger. Was the communications blackout the work of his people or something else?

If how this week was going was any indication, the blackout would be the work of something else.

"We need to warn them. Move it." He broke into a run.

The slight breeze tugged at Lillian's tightly folded wings as she sat perched on the highest branch of the tree capable of holding her weight.

The stout oak grew at the edge of a craggy ravine, where it had taken root along a small rocky outcropping in some long-ago century. Now it overlooked a narrow river and provided Lillian a convenient perch from which to launch herself into flight.

Gregory, Darkness, and Shadowlight all waited in the surrounding trees, listening for the approach of their intended targets.

"They come," Shadowlight informed the others. "It's as the Coven reported. I only detect five this time. The other two escorts stayed behind."

Lillian frowned and strained her ears forth and back, seeking what her little brother had heard.

Another minute passed before she heard what Shadowlight had noted. Her little brother had sharp senses. Better even than Gregory? She'd ask about that later. There was no time now.

Together, the four gargoyles launched from their perches and climbed high into the sky.

She beat her powerful wings, but it wasn't solely their strength which catapulted her higher, magic filled her wing membranes and snapped in the air around her.

Shadowlight beat his wings harder and pulled ahead. With a wide grin, she answered his unvoiced challenge and flew faster, darting past first him and then Darkness and Gregory.

Her sleeker body allowed for greater acceleration, and she had a hunch she might be much more agile, too. Although, she hadn't tested her theory yet.

With a joyous roar, she arched higher into the sky.

"We're at a good height," Gregory called across their four-way link. *"Prepare to dive."*

His words tarnished her child-like joy, but she'd rekindle it another time when she could take wing with Gregory for the sheer pleasure of flying. But that would have to wait.

Five dark military helicopters thundered closer to their positions. She thought they were called Black Hawks, but she was no expert.

Within seconds, they'd be directly below, over the pristine waters of the lake.

Lillian angled a wing and dipped a few feet lower to take up position behind the tip of Gregory's tail as he continued to circle above their target area. The lake's blue, calm expanse looked more like a puddle from this high up.

"Ready," he called, using their mental link.

With slight shifts of her body, she mimicked Gregory's

every move, but she couldn't manage his cool battle readiness, not even her father's memories could calm her nerves although she was thankful for them. Otherwise, she never would have mastered either flying or her fear of heights.

Gran and the rest of the ground crew, as Lillian had taken to calling the Clan and Coven members aiding in this endeavor, had reported that two hooded decoy prisoners had been escorted into each of the five choppers. The real Whitethorn and Goswin had been loaded into the second helicopter to take off.

Many fae had taken to the trees, watching the track of the helicopters. Not once had the aerial formation changed during flight. Their targets were still in the chopper flying left of the leader in the wedge formation.

Lillian kept her gaze locked on that target. Her part of the mission was easy.

"Now!"

Gregory and Darkness dived in unison, like arrows shot from a giant bow. Lillian darted after them, Shadowlight nearly wing tip to wing tip with her.

Below, the two gargoyles parted company. Gregory angled toward their helicopter while Darkness headed for the one in the lead.

Shadowlight dipped a wing and dived under Lillian, in pursuit of their father. She banked left to join Gregory.

Darkness flared out his wings, and Shadowlight matched speed. Together their trajectory and momentum slammed them into the helicopter with such force it rocked sideways wildly as it started to spin out of control. They latched onto it. Darkness under the tail, Shadowlight clinging upside down from the landing struts.

Lillian had only a moment to worry about the safety of everyone concerned before her own momentum carried her to her target.

She twisted her body in the air, and as she sailed under the belly of the helicopter, she raked her claws out, grasping at anything to hold her securely to the bottom.

The helicopter shook violently with a second impact. Gregory had just arrived. There were shouts from inside, followed by several seconds of chaos as the pilot tried to level out the wildly careening machine.

Below her, she could see where Darkness and Shadowlight had managed to bring down their helicopter—or maybe the pilot performed some kind of emergency landing. Lillian wasn't sure what had occurred, but the aircraft was down in the shallow, reed-filled waters at the lake's edge.

Her father and brother were heading toward the second helicopter that had swung back around to aid the two in trouble.

From her vantage point hanging upside down while she waited for Gregory to do his part, she watched as Darkness and Shadowlight attacked their second target with undisguised glee.

They were fulfilling their part of the plan admirably. The two helicopters not already engaged had broken formation and arced back around, but they had no targets to shoot at. At that moment, Lillian rather liked being a gargoyle. There was something to be said about being at the top of the magical food chain.

The sound of wrenching metal drew her back to her part of the plan. A second later, a large-ish piece of the helicopter dropped down into the lake below.

Lillian tensed, waiting for what would come next. Then from within came much crashing and thumping as a moment later one unfortunate soldier came flying out.

Shadowlight and Darkness broke away from their helicopter and her little brother scooped up the free-falling soldier before he could hit the water at breakneck speed.

Another soldier was tossed from the opening. This one Darkness caught, slowing his descent enough the human would survive the fall to the water below.

"Lillian, now," Gregory called.

She released her hold on the helicopter the same moment Gregory burst out with two bundles tucked under his arms.

Lillian took the smaller form of Goswin and then they were both beating their wings to gain altitude and put distance between themselves and the carnage they'd left behind.

The bundle in Lillian's arms was limp but alive. Sedated. She scrunched her nose at the scent of chemicals oozing out of the little fae's pores. She hoped the small, delicate Fae was more robust than she seemed.

But until they could get them safely on the ground, it was impossible to judge the severity of their injuries.

Darkness and Shadowlight would join them later, once they had dealt with the human soldiers. By mutual agreement, they had all agreed it was best to strip the humans of their memories before leaving them for their fellows to find. Once that was done, the other two gargoyles would rejoin them back in Coven lands.

With a nervous glance back at the mess of twisted metal, Lillian winced. At least none of the soldiers were mortally wounded. Still, she feared they'd just kicked the hornets' nest.

CHAPTER EIGHTEEN

"Oh, for the love of God!" Major Resnick snarled. "Get Lieutenant-Colonel Harmon on the line. He'll clear us."

"Sorry, sir, these are his orders," the private at the main gate explained. "Any teams coming back in must now be searched and debriefed before allowing them on base."

In other words, they were looking to avoid another incident. Which was all well and good, but today Resnick didn't have time for this kind of bullshit.

"Fine, I need you to get this to Colonel Tremblay or Doctors Fleming and Rodgers. This contains intel about our enemy, and I believe the prisoner transport is about to get hit. We need to warn them."

"Sorry, sir. I can't leave my post, but I'll have the tablet sent ahead."

Resnick didn't want to risk the tablet in someone else's hands but knew it was no use ranting about it. He'd been the one to suggest the new protocol.

He just hadn't thought his own idea would turn and bite him in the ass. Of all the clusterfucks that could have befallen him, did they all have to fall within the same week?

Shadowlight hoisted the unconscious soldier higher on his shoulder as he continued to run through the forest. Running on two legs, he decided, was far less fun than four. The human flopping against his shoulder didn't help either.

At least the destination he had in mind wasn't far, which was good since he still had two more humans to transport.

Each memory-erasing spell was delicate, time-consuming work. Darkness, being much more experienced with such spells, performed each procedure, which left Shadowlight with the task of moving the humans.

There were still two of those noisy flying machines in operation. One had turned back the way they'd come. His father had said it was probably going for reinforcements since the Coven had taken out their other modes of communication.

Whatever that meant.

Which left the last one circling over the area, searching for the other humans he and his father had rescued from the flying machines before they'd crashed.

They'd managed to save all the humans though most had bumps and bruises; one had sustained a broken arm. Shadowlight was feeling a little battered himself. Going inside the machines as they'd spiraled out of control hadn't been as much fun as he'd thought. His one wing still ached fiercely, and the ribs on the same side had suffered some abuse. In the chaos, he didn't remember it happening. It wasn't until he was on the ground again, running to do his father's bidding, that his injuries made themselves known.

On this trip, his third such one, he'd gone a little farther out of his way because he wanted to check on his pet human. His shielding dome should both hide and protect her, but with that helicopter thing circling, he didn't want to take a chance she might be located.

Wiping all these humans' memories wouldn't do one speck of good if the searchers found Anna Mackenzie.

He slowed as he made his final approach. The area seemed undisturbed. He remained cloaked as he came up to the dome. Inside, Anna was sitting by the fire, waiting for her tea to steep by the scent of it.

She scanned the shadows and then homed in on his location, telling him his gargoyle blood was still working its changes upon her body.

"Shadowlight?" she called softly and then glanced in his direction. "If that's not you, I'm so screwed."

He dropped his shadow magic and his human burden at the same time.

Her expression shifted from annoyance to shock, and then her eyes narrowed.

"What? You planning on starting a zoo?" she jerked her chin in the newcomer's direction.

Shadowlight's ears flicked forward in question, not knowing what she was referring to again. What was a zoo? He would search the language memories his sister had shared with him later. At the moment, he didn't have time.

"Never mind," she continued and then added, "That one's U.S. Army. You went and did something stupid, didn't you?"

He stepped over the unconscious human and continued toward Corporal Mackenzie. When he was still several feet from her position, he wrinkled his muzzle.

"Yeah, I stink," she barked with a good deal of grumpiness in her voice. "See how good you smell covered in three-day-old battle." Her arms folded across her chest, her expression turning belligerent. "You're going to get me clean clothes and something to wash with, but first," she pointed at the lump of soldier behind him, "explain."

He shrugged, seeing no point in not telling her. "We rescued two of our fellows. A sidhe and a sprite were being transported elsewhere by these humans."

"I suppose this has something to do with those helos from earlier?"

He puzzled over her words but then picked the meaning from her thoughts. "Yes."

"And then that lone one hightailing it back?"

"Yes, my father said it was going back for reinforcements."

"I don't doubt it."

Shadowlight felt his ears swinging forward again wondering where she was going with this.

She shook her head at him. "Do you know what your little stunt just accomplished?"

He had an idea, but since she had that look that said 'I'm going to tell you anyway' he decided to hold his silence.

"It means you and your family just declared war."

Shadowlight's ears drooped of their own accord, and his tail gave a half-hearted flick. Lillian and Gran had warned against that, told him of the dangers. "Gran isn't going to like this."

"I can only assume she's a smart lady."

"Gregory entrusted his other half, my sister, into her care. Gran is almost as fearsome as a gargoyle for all she descends from mostly human bloodlines." His wings clamped tight to his back with worry. Gran tended to withhold treats when she was annoyed with someone. "We didn't kill anyone," he said, hope kindling in his heart, or maybe that was his stomach. He'd worked up an appetite.

"Well, that's a plus." But her expression didn't improve much. "And you brought down how many helicopters?"

"Three of the machines," Shadowlight said with renewed pride. Less than a week old and he'd already been victorious in battle twice.

"Oh, just a few million dollars' worth of damage. They'll just hunt you down, no thermonuclear device required."

She said it with such a straight face, he wasn't sure if it was mentioned in jest or not.

But he didn't have time to figure out human thought processes now.

After stretching to loosen stiff muscles, he turned back to where he'd dropped his earlier burden. "I will come back later with more food and clothing once I've returned this one to his fellows."

"Where exactly are you taking him?"

"Back to the human military camp."

"Shit, kid. You like living dangerously."

Turning back to her, he gave her a huge toothy grin. "I'm a gargoyle."

She shook her head again, a smile twisting her lips and flashing the point of one fang. "Adrenaline junkie. You're going to get your ass shot off." She sobered after a bit. "Be careful, kid."

He smiled. "You do like me."

"Nah, just don't like the idea of starving to death here under the dome once you get yourself killed or captured."

Her words would have hurt if there hadn't been a twinkle in her eye.

"I'll be careful not to get captured or shot. I don't like the idea of being haunted by your disquieted spirit."

With the sound of her laughter still following him, he ventured back into the forest with his sleeping burden bumping against his back.

CHAPTER NINETEEN

apping an index finger against his thigh, Major Resnick frowned as the last member of his team was waved through the checkpoint. None of them were allowed to move on until the entire team was finished.

He was sure his blood pressure was crawling slowly higher toward stroke level range.

When they approached the last checkpoint, there was another team waiting to meet them.

"Major Resnick, I'm Corporal Jordan," a fresh-faced soldier said and motioned them forward. "We're here to escort you to command."

Resnick swallowed back his frustration and acknowledged the other officer. "Did my intel reach them yet?"

"Yes, they are sending other helos after the convoy. If you will come with me." He started away, and Resnick followed on his heels.

With Jordan's team clearing a path, they made good time and were soon at the community center.

They didn't make for the elevators. Instead they headed to the stairs which led down to the arena floor which was now converted into a field lab.

The room lacked the usual bustle. They'd cleared out most of the non-essential personnel. Colonel Tremblay, his senior officers, and the lead scientists heading the project were all clustered around a central terminal.

Doctor Rodgers was gesturing at the screen enthusiastically.

"This isn't us," she was saying.

Resnick and Jordan's teams saluted the general and the other senior officers and then took up positions.

Doctor Rogers and Fleming weren't into niceties. "Where did you find this? Were there other signs? Prints, hair or skin samples caught in the underbrush, maybe? The terrain they were running through has dense undergrowth—there should have been some physical evidence."

Outwardly, only a slight shift in his position gave away his displeasure. The science types always rubbed him the wrong way. The less he had to interact with them, the better.

What had he expected? He'd brought this newest intel in from the field—of course they were going to have questions.

This was going to be a lengthy debriefing. He turned his gaze toward the screen with all its impossibilities.

A winged beast for God's sake. Two actually. He cleared his throat. "We didn't take the time to study the area. When we saw the two creatures on the recording and took note of the wings, I ordered my team to return at once, fearing something like this might, theoretically, pose a threat to our prisoner transport." Though admittedly he didn't know how something like these creatures could keep up with, let alone attack, a helicopter already in flight. Yet he'd seen too many strange things in recent days. Besides, in his gut, he knew these two were trouble.

"A pity," Doctor Fleming said, "but understandable why you came back at once."

Colonel Tremblay took over the conversation at that point. "We haven't been able to raise the helicopters, I've sent out other units to search, but with the interruptions to communications, we don't know anything yet. So, tell me your thoughts on those." He pointed to the screen. "Any chance it's a fake?"

One of his advisors gave a little shrug. "We have our experts working on it. Nothing yet."

"But it would explain one of the intruders we had last night, and how he escaped. We were right on his tail when he suddenly vanished. The grass showed a clear trail for a thousand meters, and then it just ended in the middle of the field like he had up and vanished. Or flew away."

Doctor Fleming reached out and touched the screen. "I'm not sure if they could fly, the body mass to wingspan ratio... I'd love to get a closer look at their locomotion." He tapped a button, and the recording advanced a few frames at a greatly reduced speed. "Quadrupeds but look at the length of the strides."

Resnick noted that too and did a quick estimate of stride and determined the beast could probably outrun a horse or most anything else. One thing for sure, it was a hundred percent predator. No herbivore had claws and teeth like that.

Once again, the Colonel shut down the scientists before they could descend into a debate. "But what is it? Some kind of genetically engineered and weaponized new species?"

"I don't know. Maybe," Doctor Rodgers said as she zoomed in on one of the creatures—the darker colored one. "But it's not one of ours, if it is. It's not one of us."

Resnick frowned. A one-year-old could have taken a look and known it wasn't human. What was she getting at?

She tapped the screen with more force as she gestured at them all. "The other ones we've captured, we know they are not human, but they are genetically our next closest relative —closer than chimpanzees. They are part of our evolutionary tree, on the same branch even," she paused and then pointed out the wing joints of the newly found creature. "This isn't us. This isn't part of our evolutionary tree. Six limbs. They both have six limbs. This isn't of our Earth."

"Non-earth evolution?" The general asked, but it wasn't a question, not exactly. He'd already come to the same conclusion as the doctors. "We need to verify this recording and scavenge the area for evidence.

"I need blood and tissue samples," Rogers said as she looked from one person to the next. "We need to capture one of them."

Oh, he knew where this was going. With a touch of trepidation, he glanced back at the frozen still, studying the creature's natural weapons. Damn it all to hell. The creature looked like it could take down a velociraptor without breaking a sweat. This assignment was proving too interesting for his liking.

Major Resnick had known the recording was going to be bad for his peace of mind.

"We're going to need bigger guns," he muttered.

CHAPTER TWENTY

*L*illian trudged up the stairs to her bedroom with all the zeal of a dog going to visit the vet. She hurt everywhere. She hurt in places she didn't even know existed, but they were letting her know of their existence now.

Gregory looked equally worn. He doggedly took the steps one at a time, without his usual spring powering him up the stairs like he didn't know what gravity was.

They'd flown Whitethorn and Goswin to safety, and at the time she'd been so full of adrenaline an armored vehicle could have broadsided her and she would not have noticed. Now, a half hour after their flight, she was witnessing just what prolonged flight did to the body. The thought of a hot bath was the only thing keeping her going.

It certainly wasn't the scent of food Gregory had taken from the kitchen as they made their way through. Actually, the smell of food was tying her stomach in knots.

She wondered if she was coming down with something—

though that was unlikely. She'd never been sick a day in her life. Probably protected from common germs by her kick-ass gargoyle immune system. She'd never thought to ask Gregory if gargoyles could catch diseases.

It was on the tip of her tongue to ask when she stopped dead in her tracks.

No. Not possible.

Her stomach plummeted, and her heart lurched like she'd been kicked in the chest.

It couldn't be. No.

Oh God, with her spectacular luck, it was entirely possible.

Wasn't that why she'd gotten all the damned pregnancy tests?

It was too soon. It had been, what, three days?

Yes, entirely too soon to be having morning sickness. She was probably just feeling sick from extreme exhaustion.

Placing one foot ahead of the other, she continued to follow Gregory up the stairs. A long hot bath would help soothe her aching muscles, and then she'd pee on a stick to help soothe her racing mind.

If it had been possible, she would have preferred to confide in someone who might know more, someone like her mother perhaps. Unfortunately, she couldn't do that without it getting back to Gregory. Besides, somewhere deep inside she was still uncomfortable with the idea of talking to her mother.

Oh hell, what a messed-up week it had been.

Lillian arrived in her bedroom and made for the bathroom and then slapped her hand up to forestall Gregory from entering. "Nothing in the bathroom is going to eat me. I don't need accompaniment while I pee." She patted him on the chest to soften the blow. She had slapped with a touch more force than intended. "I'm going to draw a hot bath, and then you can have the shower." She smiled. "Or you can share the bath."

She stood on her tiptoes and stretched as far as she could to place a kiss on his cheek. "I'll let you decide."

She closed the door on his face. When it became apparent he was going to give her a few minutes, she flew over to the vanity where she'd hidden the test kits. She grabbed the first box her questing hand found and read the instructions.

She ran the bath while she waited for the results, refusing to look at it, even avoiding looking in that direction. What she couldn't do was stop herself from glancing at her watch and pacing.

Gregory was going to get suspicious if he heard her pacing. She forced herself to stop. Then she hurried over to the vanity, grabbed the pregnancy test and shoved it behind some of the candles she had spaced around the big bathtub. She turned the jets on and added a touch of her favorite bubble bath.

No point in making him suspicious.

At her soft call, he joined her before the tub. One wing folded down around her a moment before his arm pulled her against his side.

He rested his forehead against hers and murmured, "I did not like taking you into danger."

"We pulled it off. No one was injured," she said and then

wrinkled her nose. "Is that helicopter fuel? Don't go near the candles! Get your butt in the shower before we have a gargoyle firebomb."

She shooed Gregory toward the shower, and he went willingly enough. While he was adjusting the shower, she stripped and stepped into the tub.

Ah, wonderful heat.

When she was certain Gregory was busy with his own shower, she glanced at her watch where she'd left it near the candles. It was time.

After another glance in Gregory's direction, she dragged the test stick out of hiding. Taking a deep breath, she looked down at it.

Purple. The entire test area was one big purple blob. She looked closer. No little lines like the instructions showed. Just one big purple patch.

Purple. What the fuck did purple mean?

CHAPTER TWENTY-ONE

*A*nna gave the fire another poke, not because she was cold but because she was bored out of her mind. So bored in fact, she'd gone straight to frustrated, which was probably why she couldn't sleep.

Being annoyed out of one's mind didn't allow for a person to reach the level of calmness which might morph into sleep. Physical exhaustion, her other go-to cure for insomnia was out of the question as well. Being trapped inside a clear energy dome, or magic fairy ring, or whatever the fuck else you wanted to call it, didn't allow for a lot in the way of physical diversions either. Unless one counted pacing as exercise.

She'd give almost anything to go run a tour right about now.

A rustle in the forest south-east of her position snapped her out of her pout, and she tensed. Her ears strained to hear, but even that newly sharpened sense couldn't pick out anything over the breeze whirling among the trees. Unfortunately, her eyes were still blinded from staring into the fire.

Of all the dumbass things to do, she knew better than to half-blind herself by looking directly at the fire.

She bit back the knee-jerk reaction to call out, even though Shadowlight had promised to return later. Well, it was way past later, and now he was just plain late. Middle-of-the-bloody- night late.

She frowned as she scanned the surrounding forest. Nothing moved. All was silent.

It was high time for a change of scenery.

Too many more nights in a forest feeling exposed to invisible eyes and she'd need to see the shrink. Damn it, she was better trained than this. No more losing her shit over something no more dangerous than an opossum.

She was just turning back toward the campfire when its light caught and reflected off something dark and shiny at the tips of her fingers. Staring down, unable to look away, she slowly returned to the fire where the light revealed with clarity what her brain hadn't wanted to acknowledge.

"Oh, you've got to be fucking kidding me!"

Yes, those were inch-long, black talons on the end of each finger.

"Magical mental link my ass!"

The kid had some serious explaining to do.

A soft scuff and a crackle of dried leaves had Anna bolting upright, nearly stumbling into the fire in her haste to stand.

"Easy, it is only me," said a familiar voice.

She scanned the shadows looking for the young gargoyle but couldn't spot him. She could, however, sense him.

"Ah ha! There you are. Next time speak up before you scare three years off my life."

"How is it my fault if you fell asleep?"

"It just is. I'm always right. It's one of the fundamental laws of existence. Get used to it."

"Ah. If you say so," he said as he became visible a second after he'd crossed the protective dome barrier. "I brought the supplies you requested. Soap. Clean clothes. A few other items I found in my sister's bathroom. I don't know what they all are for, but you're both females."

He left it at that like he'd just explained one of the mysteries of the universe.

At the moment, he could have called her a female ape for all she cared. She pounced on the bag of supplies and rummaged through it as she backed toward her favorite 'chair,' one of the larger branches of the fallen tree that made up her shelter.

"I'll go hunt us up something to eat," he said with a note of amusement in his voice.

Great. A kid was laughing at her eagerness. Oh well. Upending the sac, she found what she'd most hoped to find. Toothpaste. There were even two unopened toothbrushes.

Who actually had a stockpile of toothbrushes just lying around?

"They are from the spa," Shadowlight explained. "When I couldn't find doubles in my sister's possessions, I borrowed from the building complex they call a spa. Though I don't know why they would need so many of such things."

"You really were just born three days ago, weren't you?"

"Yes," he said and turned away, more interested in finding food than talking, apparently.

"Rabbits," she shouted at his retreating form. "Not squirrels again. Then we are going to talk! About these!"

He half turned to look back over his left wing and shoulder. She raised her hand and flashed her shiny new talons. The kid looked sheepish for a moment and then fled into the forest.

When she was sure he was gone, she gathered her new things and walked to the area where a small stream flowed under the energy dome. She'd already investigated the area which allowed the water to flow under or through it—she wasn't really sure which, as she'd gotten a good zap for her troubles and decided it didn't matter. There was no way she could wiggle under it. The stream was too shallow, only a few inches of water flowing over a rocky stream bed.

Three feet in from the edge, the stream flowed into a little dip in the terrain. It wasn't deep enough to bathe in, but she used it for washing. It was cold, but now that she had soap and clean clothing, the temperature seemed like a minor inconvenience.

Shadowlight padded through the forest on two legs instead of the preferred four. This way he figured it would take longer to get back. Besides, he'd forgotten to take the sack with him, and the three rabbits he'd caught were easier to hold in his hands than his mouth.

Ducking under a particularly low evergreen bough, he cleared it and spotted the shimmer of the dome ahead. He strained his ears but didn't hear any sounds of splashing water, so deemed it safe to return.

The human sat next to the fire as she worked on her damp hair. It was longer than he'd thought, about midway down her back. She was the first human he'd seen with a proper mane.

Earlier, she'd had it fashioned into tiny braids that marched down her scalp, with the entire mass gathered at the back of her head where the braids were fixed to themselves in an intricate pattern which mystified him. She'd somehow managed to fit all that under her helmet.

He was surprised she hadn't just cut it all off like most other soldiers he'd seen.

"Ha! Picked that one up!" she crowed. "The thought leaking thing is a two-way street, my friend. No way am I cutting all my hair off. It's the one damn vanity I'm still allowed."

Slightly taken aback by the fact she was able to pick up on his thoughts, he froze halfway to her side. His blood was still making changes to her.

"Nice rabbits," she said in her usual droll tone. "Bring them here, and we can get them cooking. I'm not going to get any less hungry while I wait."

He hesitated a moment longer and then brought his kills over for her to spit. She seemed to know how to manage a cooking fire, so he left her to it.

She glanced his way. "You any good at foraging? You know, fruits and berries that won't make either of us sick?"

"Maybe I can help," came a voice from somewhere behind Shadowlight's left shoulder.

He felt his stomach physically lurch with fear as he spun around to face Greenborrow. The leshii stood watching them from his position outside the dome. The dark frown, which had replaced his usual jovial expression, promised trouble for Shadowlight's newest friend.

How had the leshii found him? He'd taken extra precautions always to hide his trail when he came to visit his human friend.

Actually, it didn't matter how the other had found him, he'd just have to fix this new development.

"I can explain," he said by way of introduction.

Greenborrow snorted and leveled him with an intense look. "I highly doubt you have enough words in your vocabulary to explain this... situation... to my satisfaction. However, it will surely be entertaining to let you try, so go ahead."

Anna eyed the newcomer, knowing her continued existence was about to come into question again. While the newcomer, with his baggy clothes, bare feet, and wild hair didn't look formidable, one of her freaky new senses picked up on something and warned her.

Yeah. This one fell into the category of 'scary dangerous,' and it had nothing to do with his appearance.

Well, as she saw it, she'd won over the gargoyle, now she'd just have to gain this one's trust. She didn't fool herself. If she failed, she was dead.

No pressure.

She stood and strolled over to the stranger and held out her hand. "Name's Corporal Anna Mackenzie. Shadowlight filled me in on the basics. By his response, you're either Clan or Coven and likely here to finish what the Riven started. If I'm allowed input in the outcome, I'd prefer a clean death."

Shadowlight made an alarmed whimper, but she continued to stare at the wild man with her hand outstretched.

He held his stony expression for a moment more and then burst out with a robust belly laugh, which sent more than one bird winging for safer locales.

He clapped both his hands around her outstretched one, giving it a hardy pump before releasing it.

"And mine's Greenborrow," he managed between bouts of laughter. "If your death is required, I promise I'll try to make it quick. In the meantime, let us see if we can find another resolution first, shall we? The boy is looking a wee bit upset."

Anna glanced over her shoulder and saw the young gargoyle on all fours as if he was prepared to launch an attack. His ears were pinned back, and he shifted his weight from side to side, seeming undecided whether to snatch and grab her, or stay and fight Greenborrow.

It was kind of cute, like a half-grown puppy snarling and snapping to protect its toy from a bigger dog. Somewhat cute, or not, she didn't need the kid getting involved and making matters worse.

"If my death isn't required at this exact moment, mind if I check dinner? One of the rabbits is a bit close to the fire."

Greenborrow gestured, waving her forward. "By all means. Plans are best discussed over food."

Anna turned her back on the two and attended to the rabbits. With her back to them, she was sure they couldn't see her hands shaking. She'd called the other fae's bluff, and if she kept a level head for the next few hours, she might live to see her next birthday. Twenty-five seemed like a good goal.

When she had fussed with the fire as long as was possible,

she turned back to the older fae and asked, "So, which one of you would have won the fight? Just genuine curiosity."

Greenborrow laughed again. "A gargoyle usually wins most fights, but Shadowlight is very young, and I've learned a fair number of dirty tricks over my lifetime."

So, like she'd thought. The older fae would have creamed the kid.

Her gargoyle friend looked displeased by the other's words but didn't contradict them, which was telling all on its own.

Greenborrow took a seat on the other side of the fire from her, perching on the fallen tree trunk like he did it all the time. Then he turned his head in Shadowlight's direction and looked expectant.

When that didn't elicit a response, Greenborrow sighed. "Well boy, are you going to go get those blueberries half a kilometer back or not? You do realize humans are omnivores; they need more than just meat."

Shadowlight's indecision was almost humorous if they hadn't been thinking the exact same thing. It would be easy enough to do what needed doing while the young gargoyle was away for a few moments.

"Oh, please," Greenborrow's great shaggy eyebrows rose. "You both have my word no harm will come to the human while you go get the berries. Take the sack and pick only the darkest ones with the dusty coating—they'll be the ripest."

Greenborrow tossed a canvas bag in the general direction of the gargoyle. Shadowlight hesitated a few moments more.

"I promise not to tell her anything until you return." Greenborrow proceeded to pull a knife and a chunk of wood from somewhere. Had he just pulled them out of the air? It sure looked like that.

After turning the raw chunk over several times and studying it from many angles, he began to whittle an image only he could see. He ignored all else around him as he worked and even started whistling an unfamiliar tune.

Shadowlight hesitated a moment more, and then with a twitch of his ears—one she was coming to equate with a shrug—he turned and vanished into the forest.

Well, wasn't he trusting?

Anna wasn't feeling half so trusting herself, but there wasn't anything she could do about it. So instead, she tended the fire and the rabbits while she waited for Shadowlight to return.

It was one of the longest half-hours of her career.

CHAPTER TWENTY-TWO

The smell of dripping fat and wood smoke had her stomach growling for the third time. The rabbits weren't ready yet, but she was eyeing them anyway. If the damned gargoyle didn't get back here with something else to eat, she was going to start picking off the most done bits.

As if her silent thought summoned the kid, the gargoyle appeared out of the woods. He walked through the energy barrier like it wasn't there and dropped down next to her. With the help of the fire's light, she could see the wet blueberry stains on his claws. Glancing at his muzzle, she grinned.

His pearly whites were more purple than pearly.

He held out the bag to her and waited like a dog on point.

"Thanks, kid." She took the bag and tentatively patted his shoulder, holding back the 'good boy' his happy wiggling inspired.

If it weren't for the wings and horns, she would have sworn gargoyles and canines had a common ancestor somewhere not too far back in the family tree.

"Ah, good, you're back," Greenborrow said, setting aside his carving and coming over to investigate the cooking fire. "Though if I know anything about gargoyles, you probably ate as many as you picked."

He fell silent again, and both Anna and Shadowlight tracked his every move as he re-arranged the coals and turned the rabbits on the spit.

As Anna waited, she mentally coached herself not to lose her cool. Showing anger or annoyance to this fae could be very, very bad.

But oh, how she wanted to shout 'out with it, old man' but she didn't.

Shadowlight flicked first one ear and then the other in Greenborrow's direction. Finally, the older fae finished what he was doing and returned to his seat.

"Oh, yes, what were we going to talk about again?" he paused, looking thoughtful, and then a smile spread across his face. "Right, Shadowlight was going to test his vocabulary and explain to me why he put all our lives at risk to save one human when he'd been instructed to report any and all battle sites to me. Honestly, I suppose this mess is equally mine. His mother and father were needed elsewhere, and they had entrusted his safety to me. I should have gone to him, not have had him come to me. That way Shadowlight never would have come upon such a scene without an adult at his side." Greenborrow made a little shrug. "That makes any trouble the kid gets into while on my watch my responsibility. However, we have a deal. So, Shadowlight, start talking."

Anna found herself leaning forward. It was more than just because her ass was on the line—though that was part of it, certainly. She admired the kid's spunk, his bravery, and self-lessness in saving her. She didn't want to see him get hurt.

Shadowlight looked down at his hands as he thought over what Greenborrow had said. "She had killed three Riven by the time I found her. Well two and a half. The last one was impaled on a trap she'd set. She was brave even when she first saw me." He paused. "She didn't want to become a Riven. She asked me to kill her."

Anna reached out and touched Shadowlight on the fore-arm. "I would never have asked had I known you were only a child."

He flashed her a toothy grin. "I know. You have a pure heart—a noble spirit. It fought to remain free of the Riven's taint, but there were too many bites, and you were losing that battle." Shadowlight looked over at the leshii. "I would have done my duty had she not asked to die by my hand. I'm a gargoyle, born knowing my duty—age does not factor into this. She asked to die, so she wasn't yet a Riven. She didn't want to harm others. She wasn't afraid for herself. Even at the end, she worried about what would happen to others when she rose a Riven."

Shadowlight stood and paced around the campfire. "But she also wanted revenge against those who had murdered members of her team, her military family. Her heart and spirit burned as brightly as any gargoyle's. I couldn't kill her." He dropped his head, his shoulders drooping in defeat. "I know I failed my duty to the other fae, but I would have betrayed a part of my gargoyle nature if I hadn't tried to help her. She serves the Light as surely as I do."

Greenborrow nodded. "That's all I wanted to hear. Well, all I wanted her to hear and you to admit. You did nothing wrong, my fine young gargoyle. Don't let anyone tell you otherwise."

Shadowlight's entire being perked back up, and he darted forward to give Greenborrow a sloppy looking kiss. The leshii batted at the gargoyle and made half-hearted exclamations of annoyance.

"Thank you for understanding," Shadowlight said with one final wet-looking kiss before he dropped to all fours and settled back by the fire.

Greenborrow dragged his forearm across his face a couple times before continuing. "However, everyone is still going to make an attempt on your pet human's life. I had planned the same thing until I was close enough to see you two interact."

Again, Shadowlight was on the defensive. "I didn't have a choice. The Riven taint was too strong to be removed by normal magical means, but my father's memories pointed to another solution."

"You gave her your blood," Greenborrow stated. His guess was damned accurate Anna noted.

"Yes," the gargoyle admitted, sounding entirely too guilty about it.

Now that couldn't be a good thing.

"Did you give her a choice?"

Anna was sick of the other two talking over her head. "Yes, he gave me a choice. He even read the list of risks involved, and how I probably wouldn't survive."

"Did he tell you the blood exchange would form a magical link between the two of you if you did survive?"

"Yes. We can already pick up a few of each other's thoughts." She glanced down at her fingernails and flexed them so the leshii could see. "But I'm guessing there are a few more things still to be discussed."

Shadowlight cringed. "Those and the other changes came as a surprise. I was going to tell you about that," he said, sounding very young and uncertain. "But I didn't have a chance, and then Greenborrow found us."

"The boy didn't fully think through his actions," Greenborrow said with an assessing look directed at her. "Now it will be up to us to protect him from harm."

A thrill of alarm hummed through her being at his words. "Are you saying his people will try to harm him because he acted to save me?"

"Yes, and no." Greenborrow rubbed at his whiskers. "The boy could certainly come to harm while trying to protect you from the other fae, and he could be equally harmed by your death."

"What do you mean?"

"Our young friend has done something never done before when he saved you, a mere mortal. Gargoyles rarely share blood. Their blood is tied to their magic. Gargoyles are immortal, as in they don't age, and they are hard to kill. Occasionally, they will take a dryad mate to increase their numbers." Greenborrow held up a hand to silence her when she was going to ask a question. "But there are no female gargoyles, well, there is one, but that's a discussion for another day."

"His sister, Lillian. Shadowlight told me about her, and the Avatars."

"Well then, hasn't Shadowlight been an informative fellow."

Shadowlight whined and thumped his tail on the ground.

"He was very forthcoming. He told me about his parents, the Avatars, and an evil demigod bitch who wants to rule all the known universe. Oh, he also told me the basic history of the Magic and Mortal Realms. That about sum it up? Or did he miss anything?"

"The Spirit Realm?" Greenborrow suggested.

"Oh, right. Shadowlight mentioned that, too."

"We were both in the Spirit Realm not long ago." Shadowlight inched closer until his head was resting in her lap. "We may even have been friends there. Maybe that's why our paths crossed in this Realm." His eyes drifted closed. "Compared to us, Greenborrow has been away from the Spirit Realm for a long, long time."

That confirmed Anna's earlier assumptions about Greenborrow's age.

"Anyone would seem old compared to you, young pup," Greenborrow said. "Yes, I'm old and have seen many things. I was born long ago in the Magic Realm. Though it was long after the Twins had started their war. Back then, the Mortal Realm looked like a safe haven."

"What started the war? Shadowlight never said." Anna wanted to know as much about those twins as possible because they sounded like bad news.

"Love."

Anna arched an eyebrow, and Shadowlight perked his ears as if that answer had surprised him.

"Yes, love. The Lady of Battles once had a consort, the Shieldbearer, but he became corrupted by greed and envy. He wanted the Lord of the Underworld's power for himself. The Lady of Battles did not see or turned a blind eye to that ambition."

Greenborrow took another drink from his flask. "Unfortunately, the Shieldbearer may not have been the wisest creature to ever walk the universe. He challenged Lord Death. As you might imagine, he didn't live long to regret his foolish mistake. The Lady of Battles took exception to her twin's actions, and the war grew up out of the bitterness between them."

As much as the story was interesting, she wanted to know how something that happened forever ago applied to her current situation but didn't dare interrupt. Greenborrow seemed the type who liked to do things in his own time. He'd eventually get to how all this related to planet Earth.

"The Twins' dispute drew the attention of the Divine Ones—and as punishment, the twins were cast out of the Spirit Realm, forbidden to return until they saw reason. Lord Death did not know how to gain his twin's forgiveness, so he has kept her focused on him for all these millennia so the Magic and Mortal Realm need not suffer the Battle Goddess's rage more than needed."

"Are you saying we have Death to thank for our continued existence? That's so fucked up."

"Not your existence, no, but for keeping his twin in check. They share a duality curse. While one is trapped within their temple in the Magic Realm, so too is the other."

Shadowlight blinked open his eyes sleepily. "The Lord of the Underworld hasn't left his temple in over thirty thousand years, so the Battle Goddess is forced to remain in hers."

"But her servants are not," Greenborrow said. "And she still has many loyal servants and soldiers—an entire army's worth."

"Well, doesn't she just sound like the charismatic, demigoddess, dictator type?"

"It gets worse—some of her worst nearly killed you."

"The Riven."

"Yes, they were one of her captain's experiments that didn't work out as planned. They were too cunning and vicious and turned on their masters."

"They are also the reason why we now know there are other beings on this planet as intelligent as us," Anna muttered. "For the record, I would have happily continued on in ignorance."

"Wouldn't we all love to live in peace and ignorance," Greenborrow laughed. "Alas, that's not what fate has in mind for us."

"So, I take it the Lady of Battles is bad for Earth even if she isn't taking a direct interest in us mortals."

"There is a war coming, and it will likely spill over into this realm." Greenborrow's expression was somber. "We all are very much in danger. For a long time, many of the fae have simply hidden away, but that tactic is no longer viable."

Anna held up her hand to stop the fae's words. She would have stood and paced, but Shadowlight had fallen asleep with his head resting on her lap.

Poor kid had had a rough time of it.

Divine Ones, demigods, Avatars.

Well, fate certainly had been rolling out the worst case scenarios lately, so by that way of reasoning, the old goat was probably telling the truth.

She was going to have nightmares for a year.

"So, you're saying there is a whole host of less than benevolent beings out there capable of swatting this planet like a fly?"

"Hmmm, it would take considerable power, and this is only one planet of many, and said being would have to have an excellent reason to want to annihilate you, but yes, in theory, there are a few beings out in the wilds of the universe capable of such power."

"They don't cover this kind of shit in basic training."

"Well, you'll be happy to know the Divine Ones love all creation and have some safeguards to protect it." The leshii gave the fire's embers a stir and then checked on the rabbits. "The Avatars are one such safeguard."

Greenborrow removed one of the rabbits, transferring it to another stick before handing it to her so she wouldn't burn her hands. Suddenly, she was far from hungry.

"Unfortunately, the Lady of Battles found a way to force the Sorceress—the female half of the Avatars to be born within her domain. There she remained until the male half of the pair became aware of the danger to his other half."

Anna nibbled on a thigh. The meat was a little stringy, but her stomach reminded her it was starving. "Thank you for the scary history lesson," she added around a mouthful of meat, "but that still doesn't tell me about my present problem." She waved her black nails at Greenborrow.

"Just setting the stage."

She looked down at Shadowlight. He was bound to be hungry. As she reached out to shake him awake, Greenborrow shook his head. "Let the boy sleep. It is better he does not hear what I have to say next."

Anna froze with her teeth still sunk into her dinner. She rolled her eyes to meet the leshii's gaze.

"I've told you a bit about the Battle Goddess but very little about the Lord of the Underworld. He, too, has an army, every bit as fierce as his twin's." The leshii gestured at the young gargoyle. "All gargoyles call Lord Death their liege. That the male half of the Avatars always chooses to be born a gargoyle should tell you something of their valor and loyalty. No one ever thought a gargoyle could be swayed from the Light."

"But one was, or we wouldn't be having this conversation, I assume."

"Yes, though it has yet to be determined how great the taint has spread." Greenborrow looked thoughtful for a moment before he decided on what to say next. "For the Battle Goddess to capture the Sorceress, she first needed a dryad and a gargoyle to conceive her. The dryad was easy enough apparently, for the Battle Goddess's oldest confidant and loyal servant was one of that race. Capturing a gargoyle was another challenge, but one she managed."

Anna flexed her new talons as a reminder.

"Oh, it will become clear in a moment," said Greenborrow with a nod. "The Lady of Battles imprisoned the gargoyle with her loyal dryad. The gargoyle didn't learn until much later that the dryad wasn't a fellow prisoner like he'd thought. I'd have loved to have been a fly on the wall for that conversation." The leshii sighed dejectedly.

"However, there was nothing the gargoyle could do. He'd already fallen in love with the dryad and given her a child. I imagine he hadn't intended that to happen, for no creature of the Light would willingly beget young in the Battle Goddess's domain." Another shrug. "Darkness hasn't yet told me all the gritty little details."

Anna nearly choked on a bit of rabbit. She knew Shadowlight called his father Darkness. She looked down upon the gargoyle child, and everything snapped into place. The cryptic comment earlier about his parents wanting to help Lillian but unwilling to leave Shadowlight behind enemy lines.

Well, fuck.

Shadowlight and his sister were created in part due to this Battle Goddess's manipulations.

Greenborrow took a flask from an unseen pocket. "You see why it's better the boy not be reminded of where he came from?"

"Hell yeah."

"I do not believe the boy is evil, but I certainly don't trust his mother. She only betrayed the Lady of Battles because her love for her children was slightly stronger than her fanatical loyalty to her overlord."

"How do you tell a kid his mother happily serves the Antichrist and is also a willing member of a terrorist organization?"

Greenborrow nodded. "He was likely created to be the equivalent of a weapon of mass destruction. Because I can guarantee you, the Battle Goddess planned for Shadowlight's birth as surely as his sister's."

Anger kindled in her stomach. She was familiar with human monsters, had seen enough of their work, but what kind of monster breeds for children specifically so she can use them to achieve her own twisted plans? A demigoddess, apparently.

Greenborrow took another sip from his flask and then handed it to her.

She took a big gulp, and the alcohol burned all the way down.

"Moonshine?" she wheezed.

Greenborrow laughed. "Only the best."

He sobered and studied Shadowlight for a few minutes.

"I see no darkness upon him. Even the unicorn and the pooka detected no traps or taint within him. After what happened to Lillian, they know what to look for." He looked up at her. "But Lillian's demon seed remained dormant for twelve years before it roused. Darkness swears there is no evil within his son, and I believe him."

"Believe or believed?" Anna stressed the past-tense.

"Shadowlight possesses the purest spirit I've ever seen, and the unicorn concurs."

Anna breathed out the lungful of air she'd been holding.

"But there is something clearly odd with his blood."

"How so?" she asked guardedly and found her one arm coming up to circle protectively over Shadowlight's head while he slept.

Greenborrow waved at her. "You, dear. You're the proof. You're living, breathing proof something is not as it should be. His blood should have killed you or healed you, not changed you."

"Maybe you're overreacting. It's only my nails after all." She flexed her fingers to study the oddity in question.

"It's not just your nails. Your eyes are solid black like a gargoyle's, and your ears are pointed."

"Okay, so I can't see my eyes, but I'd know if my ears were suddenly pointed." Her seeking fingertips circled the lower lobe. It felt normal, and then she moved on up to where the top curve should be yet wasn't. A defined point met her seeking fingers. "Fuck. Fuck it! Fuck it all to hell!"

"I think you may need to expand your vocabulary a little more. You seem overly fond of a certain word."

Glowering, she demonstrated the depth of her vocabulary in a creative string that went on for over a minute.

Greenborrow arched an eyebrow. "Or continue as you were. We can finish this later if you prefer."

"Sorry." She bit out and swallowed a few other choice words she'd had all lined up. "Go on."

"Shadowlight may not even know your changes aren't normal, or there might be some instinct or implanted memory from his mother's bloodline that's guiding him. Either way, I doubt he's aware your changes signal a darker purpose."

Greenborrow reached out and took her hand, pressing at the base of each nail bed and watched as the talon flexed out until it was fully extended. "These differences are why you and our young friend are in danger. While the other fae may not know if Shadowlight serves the Battle Goddess, the possibility alone will be enough for some of them to act and eradicate that risk."

"Then why am I alive? Why tell me all this? Surely you could have just killed us before we were even aware." She was on the verge of shaking Shadowlight awake. Maybe together they could overpower the leshii.

"Just because the Battle Goddess has plans for our young gargoyle here, and you now by association, doesn't make either of you instantly evil. As I recall, the Battle Goddess had plans for Lillian and Gregory as well. So far, they are doing a fine job of foiling her plans. I hope you and Shadowlight will continue the tradition." He shrugged. "Or you and he may bring about the destruction of all, but either way, it's bound to be an interesting few years."

Anna gaped at the old reprobate, speechless for the first time.

"Wake Shadowlight or his meal is going to get overdone."

Still too flummoxed to think, she gave Shadowlight's shoulder a shake. It took two more tries before the kid stirred.

"It's dinner time."

CHAPTER TWENTY-THREE

Shadowlight startled awake but was quick to accept the hot meat Anna handed him. He'd eaten his kills raw before but found he liked them cooked better. He devoured his portion and looked around for more. A spurt of guilt assaulted him when both Anna and Greenborrow offered him half of theirs.

Anna gave her offering a little shake. "Take it. You're three times the size of us and still growing. You need it."

He took what they offered.

After his belly was full, his brain kicked in, and he realized he'd drifted off to sleep while their dinner had cooked. A wave of hot embarrassment swamped his body. So much for staying alert and keeping watch.

Wanting to at least sound more like an adult than a fat pup who had overslept, he asked, "What plan of action have we devised?"

Anna laughed, and he realized she'd picked up on his thoughts again.

"The kid wants to know what he missed while he napped." She ruffled his mane affectionately. He didn't like that she'd embarrassed him in front of Greenborrow, but he did rather like the scratch behind his ears. He leaned into her fingers and forgave her earlier laugh at his expense.

"We talked some boring old history and then some adult conversation you'll get to hear about in a few years," Greenborrow said with an accompanying wink.

Shadowlight's curiosity spiraled up another three notches.

He rolled his eyes up at Anna.

"He told me about my new eyes and ears. Also, a bit about gargoyle history, the other fae, and why they won't view a human—even one with gargoyle blood—as a friend. That's about as far as we got."

Oh, good. He hadn't missed much then.

"I'll help you hide her," Greenborrow said as he picked up his knife and started carving his piece of wood. "You can't keep her out in the open like she's part of a zoo exhibit."

Shadowlight felt his ears wilt. "It was the best I was able to find given the time I had."

"I'm not criticizing you. Just saying it's time to find a better lair. I just happen to know a good one."

Shadowlight stared doubtfully at the large, three-story home Gran called the Cottage. He'd been inside it before, had, in fact, slept an afternoon away inside one of the second-floor bedrooms the day after the battle with the Riven. His parents had shared the room with him, likely to be certain he didn't wander off and get caught by the human soldiers who had been sniffing around.

"I don't think this is a good plan," Anna whispered close to his ear.

He was inclined to agree. Turning his questioning look to Greenborrow, Shadowlight used his tail to tap the leshii's shoulder.

"Oh, ye of little faith." Greenborrow gestured at the home. "It's a great place to hide. The entire top floor is an attic, but there is a hidden room in the northeast corner with fully functional facilities. I've stayed there a time or two before. It's a fae safe house, designed to be soundproof as well."

"Safehouse? Really?" Anna questioned.

"During the Wild Hunt the occasional young hothead gets hurt, and we need a safe place to stash them so they can mend where no human will find them. We have other such places throughout our territories. Though this one is the closest." He shrugged. "It's empty now, and since Shadowlight's parents will likely wish to stay close to Lillian and Gregory, our young gargoyle will have the run of the place without drawing suspicion. It certainly shouldn't be too difficult to sneak food. Besides, gargoyles all eat like horses. No one will be surprised if a young, growing gargoyle takes some back to his room for later."

"It might work," Shadowlight admitted.

"Of course it will work. Let's see if we can get our human friend up there without anyone knowing."

"Don't gargoyles have a super sense of smell? At least Shadowlight does. Aren't I in danger of getting tracked down by scent?"

"We'll have to use a spell to cloak your scent as we travel through the house, but once you're situated in your new quarters, you should be fine. None of the gargoyles go up into the attic. If it was the middle of winter with all the windows closed, we might have had to try somewhere else. However, this is the best we can do for the short term."

Greenborrow glanced toward the east. "We need to do this now. It will be dawn in another hour and a half. Then others will start to stir, and I don't know about you, but I don't want to be the one who has to explain to Gregory why we're sneaking a human into his territory without his knowledge."

Anna made a small, unhappy sound. "He's one of those Avatars, right? Let's not run into a demigod."

"I'll make introductions if we are so unfortunate," Greenborrow added cheerfully.

Shadowlight whined.

Anna hardly dared to breathe as she made her way up the stairs. Greenborrow led the way while she and Shadowlight hung back. The young gargoyle was using his shadow magic to hide their presence, but it wouldn't shield them from another gargoyle.

In other words, if they met anyone getting up for a piss, she really hoped it wasn't a gargoyle.

The trip up to the second floor was uneventful. Greenborrow led them down a long corridor, flanked by what she assumed were bedrooms on either side. When they reached the end, he turned right onto another short hall. This one ended at a brown wooden door. He produced a key, unlocked the door, and opened it to reveal another set of stairs. These ones obviously leading up to the attic and what was to be her new prison.

They made their slow way up the stairs, Greenborrow pointing out the seventh and tenth treads were 'blighted noisemakers'. Anna committed them both to memory. It was bound to come in handy later when she planned her escape.

Unlike when she'd been trapped under the energy dome, she now had a hope of escape.

Even if they erected other protections to keep her here, she figured they couldn't summon another dome. At least not without putting up a sign the equivalent of a drive-in movie screen saying, 'come look what we've hidden in the attic.' She liked her new odds much better.

"What is a drive-in movie screen?" Shadowlight asked.

Oh. Shit.

"Something I should know?" Greenborrow asked.

Shadowlight explained, and the leshii's broad shoulders shook with silent laughter. At least he didn't make enough sound to give away their location.

She just reached the top of the stairs when a bright silvery light seared her eyeballs, and she raised her hand to cover her watering eyes. When she was able to see through the floating spots obscuring her vision, she located Greenborrow holding a small glowing ball of light.

Anna blinked while she took in the strange sight. The leshii and the gargoyle had used magic before, but it was still all so new to her; she just had to stand and stare. Her mind kept looking for logical reasons to explain the impossibilities that kept cropping up.

But she still hadn't found any. She compressed her lips and frowned. How the heck would she explain all this to her superiors?

"You'll have your physical changes to act as proof for some of your story," Shadowlight added helpfully.

"I thought you said you couldn't read my thoughts? That I had to project them?"

Shadowlight patted her shoulder. "With my magic cloaking both of us, it's the same as if I was touching you. Physical touch strengthens our magical link."

"Why on Earth did you just give me that information? I could use it against you later. Kid, learn some basic survival skills."

"I have. I now know how a human thinks."

"We're not all the same you know."

"No? I'll learn what I can from you anyway. Would you actually try to run away if you could? We're linked through my magic. I could track you before you got far."

She sensed hurt accompanying the young gargoyle's words. He took it as a personal failure that she wanted to escape instead of staying and being his friend. He didn't word it as such, but it was there in her mind. Poor kid was starved for attention.

An unhappy twist of emotions churned within her. The kid was so damn sincere about everything, and she'd hurt his feelings. Damn it. She shouldn't care if she hurt his feelings. He was her captor. Guilt still kicked her in the gut.

"Do you know what duty is?" she asked at last, after a lengthy internal debate.

Shadowlight nodded his head. "All gargoyles are born

knowing it is our duty to serve the Light, to protect those weaker than ourselves."

"The same duty rules me, too. I serve and protect my people. It's my duty to share what I've learned so they can better protect themselves. It's not that I wish to abandon you, kid. It's that I have a duty to my people first and foremost."

Shadowlight butted her in the shoulder. "I'm your 'people' now too. I'll help you keep the other humans safe."

His response touched her in a way she wasn't ready to admit, so she fell back on snark. "You're such an innocent."

And she realized no matter what happened to her, she couldn't let the other humans ever get their hands on Shadowlight.

"See. Told you." He sounded far too pleased with himself, but she could only smile at his boldness. He was correct, he was one of her 'people' now too, and she would protect him. Something within her demanded it.

"Now children," Greenborrow whispered. "We don't have time for group hugs. We need to get Anna settled into her quarters.

Anna nodded sharply and walked into the room. Inside it was not precisely cramped, but not spacious either. She'd slept in worse. The room was sparse. Its only furnishings a narrow bed, nightstand, lamp, and dresser. That was about it. The walls were unfinished plywood, but the floor was carpeted. It would help muffle noise, and Greenborrow had said the room was sound proofed by magic.

Off to her left was a small bathroom.

"Is there anything else I can get you?" Greenborrow

asked. "Shadowlight doesn't know a lot about humans, so he may not have stocked your bag with useful items."

"Razors and tampons would be nice since you're asking." That reminded her of something, and she went over to her pack and rooted through it until she found the pregnancy test. "I certainly don't need this, but since Shadowlight said he took one of everything he found in his sister's vanity, someone might want to return this before she misses it and starts asking questions you don't want to answer."

Greenborrow stared at the box she held out for all the world like he was gobsmacked.

Shadowlight leaned in closer for a look. "I didn't know what that was, but she had several stuffed behind other items. I didn't think she'd miss it."

Greenborrow jerked his gaze to Shadowlight. "She has more than one?"

"Yes, several. Why, is that bad?"

"It doesn't concern you but thank you for letting me know. I will see this gets to where it needs to go." Greenborrow gave Anna an old-world bow. "Now I must be off, and our young gargoyle needs to go find his bed before his parents find it empty. Dawn isn't far off."

Anna watched as they left, closing and locking the door behind them. She was a prisoner for now, but she would get free and then run to the nearest military personnel she could find. At least now she knew where she was, and which direction led to the rest of civilization.

All in all, it had been a harrowing few days, but she'd survived and had gathered more intel since meeting the young gargoyle than the whole science team had in three months leading up to this. She just had to find a way to get it to her superiors without endangering Shadowlight. She didn't want to see the leshii come to harm either, but he was old and wise. She bet he could take care of himself just fine.

CHAPTER TWENTY-FOUR

"That was an epic waste of time and money," Lillian mumbled as she stood in front of the vanity and looked down at the pregnancy test in her hand. Like the other two varieties she'd used, this one just showed a purple blob instead of the marks it was supposed to.

Well, what had she expected? She wasn't human. She shoved the useless test in the garbage, tossed some crumpled facial tissue on top and made a mental note to find a better way to dispose of the used tests. As she washed her hands, she remembered the one military tail had seen in her basket at the drugstore and had raised an eyebrow at her purchases.

Yep, she'd best burn them all in a bonfire later tonight. That way there was no chance of them falling into the hands of some scientist.

Lillian exited the bathroom, her eyes going to the bed where Gregory was still asleep. Her fingers reached to touch the brand around her neck. At least the bed and bathroom were close enough together the tattoos didn't flare painful warnings.

However, she was hungry.

But if Gregory was still asleep, then he needed his rest. Sighing, she went to her side of the bed and carefully sat down so as not to wake him. She brushed his thick mane from his face, his gargoyle features somehow less harsh, softened by sleep. Or maybe she was just so used to seeing him in gargoyle form now, she saw the beauty in him?

With him asleep, she could fulfill his need for intimacy without jeopardizing her secret. She curled up next to him, and he shifted in his sleep, making room for her. A moment later his strong arms encircled her, and she rested with an ear pressed against his chest. The steady thump of his heart reassured her, but still, silent tears flowed down her cheeks.

He stirred then, and she felt warm breath in her hair a moment before his deep voice rumbled in her ear.

"What is wrong, beloved?"

Lillian swallowed hard, snuggling closer to his warmth, and told him the truth. "I am afraid for our future."

"Ah," he rumbled softly, and she felt him press a kiss to the top of her head, and then he shifted again. Fingers came to rest under her chin as he gently guided her head up so he could look her in the eyes. "I do not know the future, that has never been one of our gifts, but know whatever comes, I will stand with you always."

He enfolded her in his wings and held her close, but she didn't sleep. Instead, she looked over the curve of his shoulder to watch the east-facing window. As the sky lightened to a pale grey with a flush of pink, Gregory drifted back to sleep.

Lillian continued to watch the sunrise.

A pounding on her bedroom door jerked Lillian from sleep. She swung her legs out of bed and pulled on a robe while Gregory was still shifting a wing so he could look over his shoulder and scowl at the door.

"What now? Are we under attack?" Lillian asked as she tied the robe's knot.

Gregory huffed. "No."

The pounding came again, sharper this time.

"One moment," he shouted at the door, and then more quietly to her, "I promised your mother she could start your training this morning." Gregory rolled out of bed, dropped to all fours, where he stretched every muscle twice and then made his way over to the door.

"Why wasn't I told about this?"

His tail twitched. "She only asked last night. You were in the bathroom. As I recall, we became distracted after your bath. The last thing on my mind was your mother."

Lillian felt her cheeks flame red. "Okay, fine. You're forgiven." Turning her back on him, she went over to her closet and grabbed some workout clothes. "How many of these mother-daughter workout sessions did you agree to?"

"We didn't discuss an exact number. However, the training sessions will be every morning before breakfast."

"My God, that early? In case you didn't notice, she and I don't exactly know how to relate to each other on a good day. That's asking a lot before my first cup of coffee. Maybe even too much before a second or third cup."

Gregory made another of his huffing sounds of displeasure, and then she felt him touch his thoughts to hers. *"I wish to study your mother."*

She looked up sharply. *"So, I'm not the only one who doesn't trust her?"*

"No. Although, there might be hope for her yet. It won't be easy and may take years, but I think she might be redeemable."

Lillian wasn't so sure.

Lillian inched closer to the wall as she eyed the dimensions of the newly discovered training room adjacent to the wine cellar. It wasn't as large as the massive weapons storage room where Gregory and the fae metalsmiths had been storing all the newly forged weapons, but it was large enough to serve as a practice area for normal opponents.

She hadn't known the massive forty by sixty-foot storage room existed until just recently, so she supposed this new room shouldn't have come as much of a surprise.

But it did.

Gregory apparently knew about it.

She'd lived here for twelve years.

She bloody well should have known what was under her feet.

"Are you sure this space is big enough?" Lillian asked her mother. Two fully grown gargoyles didn't qualify as normal opponents, and the room seemed a little small.

"It is fine," River said without taking her eyes off the weapons rack situated along the north wall of the room. Lillian inched back farther until her shoulders bumped the wall, and she still didn't feel far enough away from where the two gargoyles circled each other with swords drawn.

At least the branded tattoos were happy with the close quarters.

Darkness gave his two swords an experimental flick. Testing the balance?

Gregory did the same and continued for another half circle. By some mutually agreed upon signal, both gargoyles attacked in the same heartbeat.

This was no half-hearted test strike to measure each other's skill. They were just blurs of darkness and bright silver flashes where light reflected along deadly blade edges.

"Someone is going to lose a wing, or maybe a head," Lillian muttered.

The two combatants continued their lethal dance while Lillian held her breath.

"Don't be silly," River said in a long-suffering tone. "Gregory is the Lord Protector. He has had lifetimes to perfect the sword. And Darkness was a skilled warrior long before he was captured by the Lady of Battles. Once he was under her power, I took over his training, and I took him from admirable skill to a higher form of mastery."

Lillian's gaze left the gargoyles to land squarely on her mother. Of course. What her mother said made sense. She was the confidant, and perhaps protégé, of the Battle Goddess. River had demonstrated her skills with the blade when she first arrived and went about the business of eradicating Riven with lethal ease.

"And I will expect to see that same level of skill in my daughter one day." She lifted a medium-sized sword from the rack. Giving it a flick, she spun it in her hand before holding it out hilt first to Lillian.

After taking up the offered sword, Lillian gave it a couple of test slashes. It felt well balanced in her hand. She didn't know the name of the sword for it was of sidhe design, but it looked similar to a Japanese katana, but one with a broader blade and more ornate hilt.

Gran had only put human swords out on display in the house. It wasn't until recently Lillian had learned Gran's collection was much larger.

"Vivian told me she trained you in some basic sword skills —something by the name of fencing? Yes?" River tilted her head and eyed Lillian up and down.

Lillian relaxed her stance and spread her feet a little wider. "The opponents wear protective equipment, so no one gets run through." She paused and gave her sword another test slash. "Gran said it was time I graduated up to a saber, but even so, fencing is more about knowledge, skill, and daring. This sword is for slashing, gutting, and killing."

"That is a sword's true purpose." River made a gesture at the sword. "This one greatly increases the odds your opponent will not get back up to continue the fight even if you don't deliver a killing blow."

"It's heavier than I'm used to."

River made a delicate sniff of disdain. "You will build core strength and muscle memory for your new weapon of choice. You will master both it and yourself."

Lillian had a feeling there wasn't going to be much choice. "It will take time to learn a new weapon."

"Most certainly, but that little metal stick Vivian showed

me and called a sword would be mostly useless in battle. I own deadlier hair ornaments."

"I think a few historians might disagree."

"They would swiftly change their minds once one of our swords shattered their inferior mortal blades into useless shards."

"Prejudiced much?"

River's expression took on a hint of doubt or perhaps that was confusion over Lillian's meaning, but it cleared a moment later as her expression smoothed out. "How can it be prejudice when I have spoken only truth?"

Lillian winced. "Okay. We can agree to disagree."

"Very well."

She knew dealing with her mother's quirks was going to be painful and slow going, but Gregory may be correct. There still might be hope for River. It would be a long journey, full of much frustration but when it was over, her mother might morph into a potent force for the Light.

"Come, let's see what other bad habits that mortal woman has managed to teach you."

Or not.

Either way, the coming hours were bound to be painful.

CHAPTER TWENTY-FIVE

Shuffling into the kitchen, Lillian followed Gregory's larger form and blinked against the bright light. Even after getting showered, she still only felt half alive. Missing most of a night's sleep and then having an evil dryad mother demand to begin sadistic sword fighting lessons at the butt crack of dawn will do that. She sighed and made her way to the coffee pot.

Only Gran and Greenborrow were in the kitchen, and they were deep in conversation, discussing what they should do next.

Secretly, Lillian was glad. She wouldn't have to talk or think for a few minutes yet.

She waved at them as she crossed the kitchen, coffee pot firmly in her crosshairs. She was almost at her target when she saw a narrow, surprisingly familiar box sitting in front of the coffee maker.

A pregnancy test.

Sitting on the kitchen counter.

Her stomach plummeted, and her heart lurched like she'd been kicked in the chest. It quivered and fluttered and then broke into a full panicked gallop.

Unable to move, Lillian stood frozen, staring at the relatively tiny box.

There was writing on it.

Her eyes narrowed.

Someone had taken a sharpie and written something on the side of the box. She took a step closer and then picked it up to study the cryptic message for a moment and still couldn't figure out what 'P=P' stood for.

What the hell did that mean?

Obviously, someone knew more than she wanted them to. Who, and more importantly—did Gregory know? Had they told him? Were they going to tell him?

A glance over her shoulder showed Gregory going through the fridge. He was pulling out milk, yogurt, and cream.

He hadn't seen what sat in front of the coffee maker. If he were aware, he wouldn't be half so mellow. She closed her eyes, refusing to think about how Gregory would take the news of what he'd done.

Turning the box over in her hand, she spotted another handwritten note on the other side of the box. This was done in a different hand.

She read it once. Her mind refused to understand. She read it a second time.

Purple equals pregnant.

Her breath froze, her mind slowed. Her heart might even have stopped for a beat or two. The buzz of white noise filled her head, and her vision greyed at the edges.

"Oh my, someone catch her!" Gran shouted as she came to her feet.

Gregory's strong arms closed around Lillian, holding her up when her knees wanted to buckle. She didn't know if she would have passed out or not. Lungs demanding oxygen, she took several deep breaths and her vision cleared. Her heart, however, was still pounding in sympathy with her mental panic.

"Lillian, what is wrong?" Gregory asked. With them touching, she could feel his thoughts brush hers, his worry and confusion coming clear across their mental link. She forced her eyes away from the box in her hand and tried to focus her mind on other things. Finally, she got herself under control and said, "Sorry. It must be stress and lack of sleep. I'm fine, really."

"Do not lie to me."

Something in his tone scared her. He didn't sound angry or hurt, only intense—a predator on the hunt for the truth.

"I," she started, "I'm sorry. This doesn't concern you. This is my fault."

"Lillian," Gregory reached down and gently pried the package from her. He turned it this way and that as he took in what it was, and the notes penned upon the outside.

"And was it purple?" he asked, voice devoid of emotions.

But he couldn't fool her, she sensed the barely controlled riot of emotions swirling beyond his surface thoughts. He was nowhere near as calm as he pretended to be.

He deserved an answer, but it kept sticking in her throat. She couldn't look him in the eyes either.

"Beloved," he prompted a second time gently.

"Yes. Three of them turned purple. I know they can't

possibly be accurate. They're designed to react to a human hormone. I'm not human. I was just using them as a baseline test out of desperation. Nothing would show that fast even if they actually worked. And it was only the one time!"

Lillian was babbling, but now that she was talking, she couldn't seem to stop.

"On a genetic level," Gran explained, "sidhe, dryads and a few of the other fae are more closely related to humans than you might expect. We speculate the same evolutionary branch. Though the pregnancy tests are just a fluke dryads discovered a few years ago." Gran cleared her throat, "but I digress."

She took one of Lillian's hands in her own. "A dryad's body knows within hours if a mating was successful. Fertilization is different than in a human woman. A dryad's cycle is seasonal, and her egg seed lays dormant in the womb until fertilization occurs and then it takes root within minutes." Gran smiled reassuringly. "I was only told to keep you ignorant of your heritage, not that I needed to be ignorant too. The other dryads shared a great deal of information with me when they learned a gargoyle had entrusted me to raise one of the sisterhood. In those early days, I had a dryad at my side almost constantly. At the time, I didn't think I would need such information, but now I'm glad I had it."

Lillian snapped her teeth closed as a large hand settled over her stomach. She chanced a glance at Gregory. He'd been silent, and now that she could see his wild-eyed expression, she knew why. So there was something capable of confounding her gargoyle.

After another long minute, he gave himself a shake. "I can't believe I was unaware."

He turned her in his arms and dropped to his knees before her. A soft exhalation of breath against her belly was the only warning before he jerked up her shirt and his sensitive nose was running along her abdomen. He inhaled a few more times and then pressed his ear against her stomach.

Lillian held her breath and waited for Gregory to confirm or deny what the test had claimed.

After several agonizing long moments, Gregory straightened and placed a finger under her chin. His dark eyes reflected some emotion she couldn't label.

Slowly his arms encircled her again, and his chin came to rest on her head.

"I smell the barest hint of new life upon your skin." His voice rumbled over her head. "It's so slight, I wouldn't have noticed it for another day or two had I not been looking for it. There is no heartbeat, not yet..." his voice choked off, thick with emotion.

Lillian drew in a shaky breath. "I've doomed us all. We're not supposed to.... this is all my fault."

Gran barked out a short humorous laugh. "No baby is ever 'all' the woman's fault. Fifty percent can be firmly placed on the man's shoulders. Gregory has big, broad shoulders. I'm sure he can handle the added responsibility."

As if in response to Gran's words, Gregory tightened his hold. "Lillian, beloved, I will be a good mate. We will get through this together."

"But I broke one of the most forbidden taboos. What if I birth a monster? This is exactly what the Battle Goddess wanted."

Gregory chuckled—there was a strong hint of relief in his tone. "No. Actually, the Lady of Battles will be quite put out,

I imagine. She wanted a child born of the Sorceress and the Gargoyle Protector. This child is not that. As your hamadryad is presently the Sorceress, we were saved from that fate."

"But I am still linked to my tree. How can we know for sure until after the child is born? And won't I still have to give the baby to the tree to gestate? What happens then?"

Gregory continued to caress her belly, as if in awe, but his voice echoed in her ears again. "We are still here. Had we come together as the Avatars without divine will driving us, we would have been hunted down by Lord Death within moments."

"But I thought he was imprisoned."

"He would not need to leave his temple. But for such a violation of the divine law, he would be forced to act. He would dispatch every gargoyle, djinn, and celestial warrior within the three realms to hunt us down and bring us to him. Then we would be sent back to the Spirit Realm for judgment." He leaned down and nuzzled her neck. "That you are alive to worry about the baby and trying to hide it from me, tells me the Divine Ones are not...concerned enough to have us returned to them immediately."

Lillian shuddered. Returned, he meant killed. "So just like that—we are free and clear. No consequences."

"Consequences?" His voice took on a darker tone. "There will be those aplenty. We may still have to face the Lord of the Underworld. He may demand our child into his service. All gargoyles are his to command—even me to some extent since I always choose to be born as a gargoyle. Also, one day we will rejoin in the Spirit Realm, and there will be a lengthy confession before our creators."

"I'll take the blame. It was my decision that got us into this mess."

Gregory nipped her playfully on the shoulder. "We will be one. There will be no you or I at that point."

Lillian turned in his arms and rested her head against his chest. "You're taking this well."

"Hmmm, this life is a test, I'm sure of it," he acknowledged. "One thing I've learned is fighting that which cannot be undone only leads to more bruises."

A tremor of unease slid through Lillian. "Would you undo this if it was within your power?"

He sighed deeply and then placed a talon under her chin and guided her gaze back to his. "Never." A smile touched his expression. "Long have we wanted a way to express our love that didn't destroy ourselves or our vows to the Divine Ones. This is not the first time either of us has been a parent, but it is the first time we begot the young together. I have no words to explain the emotions inside me. The thought of watching our child growing inside you, a child I put there, pleases me more than it should. All children are a blessing, regardless of who sires them. But I cannot be unhappy with a child created solely between us."

"I'm glad." For the first time, Lillian felt hope bloom in her chest. She was with child, Gregory's child, but their world wasn't about to end. It was going to grow bigger.

"There is one thing I must know." A thread of worry had crept into his voice. "Why don't I remember it happening? You made me forget for some reason. To protect me?" He sighed. "I need to know the truth. We can have no more secrets between us."

Lillian's heart sank to her toes. Why did he have to ask that? Why couldn't he just leave well enough alone?

"I know it must have happened the night Tethys enchanted me with her song," he prompted.

Lillian remained silent.

How could she tell him without making him hate himself or her?

"If you will not tell me then show me." His fingers caressed her arms, and he nuzzled the side of her neck again.

Still, she remained silent and refused to think anything that would give it away as she stared at the kitchen tiles.

"You're blocking me," he said, sounding surprised and unhappy. "All of you, out."

Lillian turned to see their audience had grown beyond Gran and Greenborrow. Her little brother had appeared at some point, and her parents were just entering the kitchen. Darkness was still on the threshold. He took one look at Gregory's expression, bowed deeply, grabbed River around the waist and dragged the startled dryad backward out of the room.

Gran patted Lillian and then jerked her chin at Greenborrow and Shadowlight as she left.

Greenborrow cleared his throat. "Come on, Shadowlight. Grab as much food as you can carry and let's get out of here. I'll explain what an uncle is on our way outside."

Shadowlight looked confused but took the items Greenborrow handed him and allowed himself to be hurried outside.

"Lillian," Gregory's clipped tone sounded more exasperated than angry. With a sigh, she stepped back into him. As one of his wings tucked her close, her jaws finally unlocked and allowed her to speak.

"Promise me you won't run off and do something stupid."

He touched the brand on her neck. "I won't, but not because of these. Nothing you say or do will ever drive me away. We are one being. I will keep telling you that as often as you need to hear it." He rubbed his cheek against hers. "As for doing something stupid, that I cannot promise. We both seem to excel at that in this lifetime. Maybe this realm just disagrees with us."

Lillian didn't know how he could find humor at this time, but it gave her the courage to lower her defenses and allow Gregory into her mind. He preceded slowly and gently. She knew he could simply seek out what he wanted in seconds, but he allowed her to set the pace of the memory sharing.

Outwardly, he was as still as if he'd turned to stone, but she still heard his heartbeat change as she soaked in his warmth and scent.

He rumbled something once in the gargoyle language. She wasn't sure of the meaning, but it sounded like a profanity. He was silent after that. Shifting away enough so he could press their foreheads together, he closed his eyes and just breathed in her scent.

"Forgive me, beloved, for the pain and fear I caused you. That was not well done on my part."

She reached up and stroked his mane. "You were not yourself. What happened wasn't your fault."

"I allowed the Siren to ensnare me."

"Yes, but you said she couldn't have held you for long. Had I just not..."

"Shh," he pressed a finger to her lips. "We've been over

this before. You did what you could to protect the humans and us from her wrath. It was I who harmed you, not the Siren. I will do all in my power to earn your forgiveness for that shameful act."

"Gregory, it was consensual. You realize that, right? You weren't in control. You weren't yourself, but I was willing. It wasn't rape...not on your part."

He huffed softly. "Perhaps not, but neither was it the gentle, loving act it should have been." He sighed at length. "I rutted on you like an animal."

"It wasn't like that."

"Yes, it was."

Lillian ran her fingers along the side of his muzzle. "It was nice to be able to give you something you needed. I know it was wrong, but I'd do it again."

"You did not fear me, even a little?"

"No." Lillian pressed little kisses along his muzzle and one side of his face before wrapping her arms around as much of him as she was able. "Not even a little."

"Then when you are ready. I will endeavor to replace the memory of that act with much more pleasant ones."

"The thought of losing you, or you blaming yourself for what happened—that is why I lied to you. I can't lose you, not your respect or your love."

He shook out his wings and wrapped her in them. "It will never happen. I am yours always."

To say he was shocked down to his core would have been an understatement. Being kicked by the Divine Father wouldn't have caused him much more surprise. Lillian was pregnant. With his child. They were mates in every way. Yet their vows to the Divine Ones weren't shredded beyond repair.

They'd managed the impossible.

Giddiness swamped him—elation, nervousness, excitement. Adrenaline pumped through his blood, urging him to run and hunt, to build her a lair, shelter her from all danger. He wanted to provide for his mate.

Of course, not even one of those ideas were possible at the moment—there were too many humans out in the forest. Rescuing Goswin and Whitethorn was bound to have stirred the humans into action.

Still, he wanted out of the house and to feel grass under his feet, to walk on all fours. Maybe cloaked in shadow magic with Lillian clinging to his back?

"Nope. Running around in gargoyle form is a terrible idea." Lillian's voice introduced reason back into Gregory's thoughts. "And there are other things that need our attention."

"No doubt." Disappointment flashed through him. Lillian was correct. There was much he needed to do. Defensive spells were on the forefront of his mind. While they'd rescued two of their allies, it had likely put everyone else at risk. He'd feel better if he could start work on the protective spells sooner rather than later.

And he also needed to return to work on the spell weapons and continue with the preparations for an invasion. The Battle Goddess was just as much a threat as she'd always been.

"But first, why don't we go have breakfast under my hamadryad?" Lillian asked, interrupting his thoughts.

He glanced down at her, gazing at her still flat stomach in mild wonder. Her requirements would increase in the coming days, and he planned to fulfill her every need.

"I will hunt us up something to eat."

"I was thinking of something now," Lillian admitted. "We could have a picnic under my hamadryad."

Gregory merely nodded and began to gather up the items she suggested. Besides, it was a good idea. There was still much they needed to talk about. Lillian would know nothing about dryad pregnancy, and she must be curious now that she could ask questions freely without betraying why she wanted to know.

CHAPTER TWENTY-SIX

Shadowlight remained cloaked in shadows even though he was certain no one was in the upper parts of the house. Lillian and Gregory were off in the maze. Gran, Jason, and Greenborrow were all down in the dungeon discussing adult things, and he hadn't been included. Shadowlight was actually glad. It gave him a chance to visit with Anna and bring her a stockpile of food.

Only his parents still worried him, but he was certain Darkness was busy keeping River from accosting Lillian about the baby. At least, that's what his father claimed.

He didn't know exactly how he should feel about his sister's pregnancy. Not that he would admit it to anyone, but secretly he felt a little left out. Now, he doubted he'd have his mother or sister's full attention. As for his father, he didn't doubt Darkness's love, but his attention was focused on outside dangers, and he had little time to lavish on Shadowlight.

Greenborrow still made time for him and was likely

helping to distract the others so Shadowlight could bring food to his pet human. With his sack of food tucked under one arm, he stalked up the three flights of stairs to the attic. Maybe Anna would be pleased to see him.

He eased the attic door open and stopped short. Her door was ajar.

A soft scraping sound came from the northwest corner of the attic. Old furniture and boxes of assorted other items blocked his line of sight. He eased slowly in that direction, picking his way around piles.

Anna stood in front of a window barely large enough for her to fit through. She already had the window glass out of its casement. It sat propped next to her feet. On her other side was a long coil of rope she'd already tied knots into for ease of climbing. Where had she gotten the rope? Then he noticed most of the boxes were open, items scattered everywhere.

As he watched, she eased her head and shoulders through the window. Studying the terrain? Or orientating herself?

He came up behind her and waited until she extracted herself from the opening. While she was still straightening, he slapped a hand over her mouth.

A second later, her elbow slammed into his abdomen, and he realized his mistake. The back of her skull cracked against his muzzle with a painful thump even as her one foot stomped on his unerringly.

He grunted in surprise more than pain. She grabbed his left wrist and shoved it away and then twisted and kicked out at his knee.

Instinct and memories took over, and he jerked out of her range before she could inflict more damage.

"Shadowlight?" she whispered and then relaxed her battle

stance.

"You were expecting someone else?"

"No," she hissed back. "What the hell was that? Say something next time if you don't want me to rearrange your kneecaps."

"You're trying to escape?" Hurt crept into his voice.

"Hell, yes. What did you expect? I'm being held prisoner. If anyone finds me, the leshii pretty much said I'm dead." She stopped and looked him over. "I'm sorry kid. My chances of survival are better if no one knows where I am."

"That's a half-truth."

"Okay. We've been over this. I'm a soldier. I'm duty bound to report what I've learned."

"They will imprison you, too."

She looked sad. "Only if they can catch me. I didn't say I'd report in person. I'm not suicidal. I know what will happen to me if they catch me. Best case—I'm locked in a cage for life. Worse case? Well, I don't want to end that way. But I still have intel that could save lives."

Ah. He'd almost forgotten. She was a protector as well. The introduction of his gargoyle blood would only heighten those instincts in her. Protecting those weaker than himself was something that made sense to him. His path became clear again, and with a happy wiggle, he leaped at her and planted gargoyle kisses on every bit of exposed skin he found. "I'll help you then."

"Argh!" Her hands slapped at his muzzle, but her blows weren't painful, so he knew she was holding back. "Enough. Stop. You win."

He dropped to all fours and then padded over to the canvas bag he'd dropped before snatching her from the window. Grabbing the handles in his jaws, he walked into the bedroom and hopped onto the bed, pawing and rearranging the covers into a more comfortable nest. That done, he dug through the packages for the peanut butter cookies he could smell.

"Kid! We are not done talking yet."

Shadowlight glanced up from his search. Anna was standing on the threshold, her hands on her hips, looking more than a little annoyed.

"We're not?"

"No." The one word was long, drawn out and made him think of his mother when he did or said something she didn't agree with.

He tore open the package of cookies and watched her thoughtfully while he chewed.

"Oh...give me that," she said and held out her hand for the bag. "Have you eaten breakfast yet?"

"No. I thought we could eat together and talk."

"Sounds like a good plan. Just one problem. Cookies aren't real food." She took the sack and pulled out a number of items. Some she put in a pile off to one side—fruits and other things that weren't as tasty as what she called cookies, landed in another heap.

To his disappointment, the cookies, rocky road bars, and almond bark all vanished back into the bag.

That left a selection of muffins, fruits, and a container of something called cottage cheese.

"Don't suppose you brought cutlery?"

He shook his head. Cutlery—those things humans like to eat with. He'd forgotten about those items.

"Hmmm. Fingers it is." She shoved the cottage cheese off

to the side and took an orange and a banana. She peeled the orange, but her attention was all for him. "It was noble of you to offer your aid, but I can't accept it. You shouldn't be anywhere near my people. It's not your responsibility."

His ears twitched, and his tail flicked gently in confusion. That had to be one of the oddest things she'd said to him.

"Of course it is my responsibility. I saved you and put you in your present circumstances where you are now forced to question your loyalty and morals."

"That is not how it works. I'm not your responsibility. I'm the adult. Doesn't matter the species. Adults protect the young."

"I'm a gargoyle. I exist to destroy evil. My physical age has no impact on my duty to serve the Light."

"Screw that," Anna barked. I want no part in serving your 'Light' if it requires children to be conscripted into its army. Having children fight your wars for you is pure evil. I don't condone child soldiers, and I certainly won't allow you to put yourself in danger because you think I'm somehow your responsibility."

Her words were the truth, he felt it resonate within him. Yet, he was a gargoyle. His nature demanded he be a protector—a destroyer of evil. Those two truths did not rest comfortably within his mind. Children didn't fight in the Divine Ones' armies. Gargoyles did. Unable to hold her gaze, he rubbed his muzzle against his forearm, scratching a fake itch as a distraction.

His inability to hold her gaze didn't stop her words. "Your family shouldn't have included you in the attack on the transport. It was wrong on so many levels."

"They didn't want me there. Nevertheless, they needed

another gargoyle to have any hope for it to be both bloodless and a success. They knew I'd only have followed anyway." He glanced back up hoping she'd show even a little bit of pride in his accomplishments, but her expression wasn't warm or proud. "None of the humans were seriously hurt." He ducked his head and stared down at his talons. "I just wanted to make my parents proud."

"Oh, kid." She came over to him and patted his back somewhat awkwardly, but he didn't care and tucked his muzzle along her side, being careful his horns didn't catch her in the throat. After a moment, her arms came around his shoulders in a comforting hug.

"Kid, you'd make any parent proud. You're smart, brave, noble, and have the biggest heart. You don't need to put yourself in danger to prove anything. You're still a kid. Promise me you will work on just being a kid. No more of this warrior stuff, no more live-fire missions, hand-to-hand combat, or infiltrating behind enemy lines. There will be lots of time for that when you're older."

Shadowlight sighed. She'd basically just told him not to be a gargoyle. However, it was nice to be hugged, he decided as he snuggled closer. He would try to do as she asked.

"I won't seek out trouble." He agreed at last.

"Good." She patted his back and then straightened. "If your mother is half the battleax I sense she is, I'll deal with her if it becomes a problem. No more of this child soldier crap."

He frowned. "What if danger comes hunting me?"

She gave him a grin, flashing her new fangs. "Then I'll kill it."

"And if you can't?" he asked in the most reasonable voice

he could manage.

"If it gets past me, you're free to do what comes naturally. We'll worry about morals later."

Relief flooded his body. At least he'd tied himself to a malleable human. They were such a backward species in some ways, but he had hopes for this one's trainability.

"Ha! Trainability! I'm not a dog. Nor am I the unreasonable one, my friend."

He decided it was time to change the subject. "I'm going to be an uncle." The word still tasted strange on his tongue, but he was excited all the same. Then something occurred to him. "What does an uncle do?"

"Uncle? Wow." The human's expression turned judgmental. "Your sister's younger than me, and she's having a kid? She's, what, all of nineteen or twenty?"

Shadowlight tilted his head, wondering what had caused the new round of questions tinted with displeasure.

"She's twenty."

"Kid's having kids, great."

This time, Shadowlight laughed. "She may only be twenty years old in this lifetime, but the Avatars are much, much older."

She pinched the bridge of her nose and then ran her fingers along her braids. "Thanks for the reminder that I'm now housemates with billion-year-old-demigods. That'll be fun to explain in the report." Sitting heavily in the chair across from the bed, she gave him a bemused look. "So, the demigods are having a baby?"

"Yes. I'm going to be an uncle." Shadowlight wiggled happily. "Do you think it will be a dryad or a gargoyle?"

Anna's laugh sounded a tad bit hysterical.

CHAPTER TWENTY-SEVEN

A current of magic swept past Gregory's feet and on out into the surrounding land as he stood at the entrance of the maze. It had been four days since he'd last been here. He was neglectful in one of his duties.

The Sorceress missed him.

"What is it?" Lillian asked as she rubbed at her arms. She too felt the chill of Spirit magic. "Scratch that. I know what that is. Are we in danger?"

"No," he said truthfully. They were likely safer than they'd been since they'd first come to the Magic Realm over twelve years ago. The Sorceress was awake and watching over them. He hadn't expected that, though perhaps he should have. Normal hamadryads were moderately sentient. Combine that with the soul and magic of the Sorceress, and a humble hamadryad became something more.

"No? Care to elaborate?"

"Your hamadryad is becoming the Sorceress in truth."

"Ah. That totally does not tell me anything more than I already knew."

"It might be best to show you." Gregory gestured her forward into the maze.

They made their way deeper, plodding through the familiar passages until they reached the last bend and stood on the threshold of a small meadowland glade. In the center, the Dawn Redwood stood tall and proud.

He narrowed his eyes.

Make that taller and proud.

"Oh, my God!" Lillian muttered.

"Goddess in this case," he corrected her.

She glanced at him and scrunched her nose up while giving him a slow shake of her head. After that, she focused back on the tree.

"It has grown fifteen or twenty feet in four days. Someone is bound to notice."

"Doubtful, humans rarely look up. I think your tree is safe from discovery."

"But why the sudden growth spurt? And how much bigger is it going to get?"

"She," he corrected her again. "And I think this is likely a response to your pregnancy. The tree is preparing to receive our child in a few weeks. She probably wanted to be stronger to handle the gestation. I think this may mean the child will be a gargoyle, not a dryad."

Lillian gaped at him again, her hand dropping to protectively cover her stomach. "Weeks?"

"Yes." He took her hand and guided her over to the tree. He set the basket of food on the ground and motioned her over to the tree's base. With her hand still captured in his, he pressed her unresisting palm flat against the trunk.

Above and all around them the hamadryad shifted, her branches swaying even though there was no breeze.

Lillian jerked her head up to watch. "That's new."

A branch brushed Gregory's shoulders, the soft needles tickling his skin. He turned his head enough to touch the branch and then gave it an affectionate rub. "I missed you too, my Sorceress."

The tree quivered, every branch shifting and swaying.

"Is my hamadryad about to uproot herself and go for a stroll? Because someone is sure to notice."

"Of course not." Gregory wondered where Lillian got some of her strange ideas.

"Uh, Gregory?" Her tone turned questioning as she slowly backed away from her hamadryad. A mass of questing branches followed her, attempting to pull Lillian back toward the trunk. "I thought you said she wouldn't want the baby for weeks yet. She seems pretty eager to grab me now."

Gregory laughed at Lillian but was forced to keep half his attention on the hamadryad. The over-eager branches had nearly knocked his feet out from under him twice now. "She is just happy to see us. We have been through a lot. This is how she is showing her affection."

Several branches suddenly twined around him, snapped taut, and hoisted him off the ground before he could warn Lillian. The tree shifted him higher up within seconds.

"Gregory!"

"I'm fine," he called down to her. "I'll be but a moment while I extract myself." He attempted to do as he said, but found for each branch he pushed away, three more would take its place.

Since struggle got him nowhere, he relaxed in the tree's grip and let her do as she wished.

Three smaller branches emerged from the tangled mass holding him in place to flutter around his face and head. Realizing what the tree wanted, he tilted his head back so she could reach his neck.

Delicate needles stroked his throat, and he felt the Sorceress's magic flow over his body. The tattoo ringing his neck flared to life and slapped out at the hamadryad's magic. The tree seemed unconcerned. Well, from what he could tell. Never in all his long lives had he seen what a concerned tree looked like, so he had nothing to compare it to.

The hostile power circling his neck flared a second time, unpleasantly burning the surrounding skin.

"Gregory! My tattoo is getting pissed off about something."

"Easy. The Sorceress is examining my tattoo. She will not allow us to come to harm."

"You know that for sure because...?"

Gregory sighed at her flippant tone. The hamadryad's magic flowed over him in another stronger wave, sinking into his muscles and bones. Unable to help himself, he reached out for his own link to the Spirit Realm and was surprised when it answered his call without needing Lillian to first give him an order. Hope burned hotly in his gut.

Gregory's lips pulled back in a toothy grin. Perhaps his Sorceress would free him from the cursed collar earlier than he'd thought possible.

The tree shifted him off to one side and then with another

great shifting of branches he heard Lillian squeal. It was in surprised alarm, not a sound of pain, so he waited, and as he expected, her sounds of disgruntlement grew louder as she joined him up in the tree's canopy.

If it hadn't been for the unpleasant heating around his neck, the hamadryad's chilled Spirit Magic would have been soothing and renewing. Between one heartbeat and the next something changed. He stiffened, gasping as the wellspring of his Spirit Magic flowed into him faster than he could release it into this realm. He only had a moment to realize something had gone terribly wrong, and then even the trickle of magic he'd been bleeding off into the Mortal Realm stopped, but the magic rushing into his body didn't. Too much. It was far too much power for any one body to contain, even his.

His wings quivered, as his body instinctively fought both the hamadryad's hold and the magic continuing to flow into him. "My Sorceress, please stop this."

"Gregory! What's wrong?" Lillian cursed long and loud. "Talk to me!"

"My Sorceress," he continued reasoning with the tree between waves of pain. "I appreciate your aid, but if you force this slave collar into killing me, we all will be returning to the Spirit Realm in defeat. I, for one, would very much like a chance to raise our child."

The hamadryad didn't respond with words or thoughts, but Lillian was suddenly thrust in front of him. When her wild-eyed stare landed on him, her brows scrunched up. "God Gregory. What the hell?" Then her lips parted in understanding. "I order you to stop drawing magic from the Spirit Realm. Stop now!"

Blessedly, the magic flowing into him slowed and then

stopped. Yet, he still felt like his body was going to split apart at any moment.

"Beloved, talk to me. Tell me what the hamadryad did to you."

"I don't know." Which was true, but as his mind began to process what had just occurred, he began to get an idea of what had gone wrong. Gregory was still panting in pain and shock, so said the first thing that came to his mind. "Your tree, did you sense anything unusual about her just now?"

"Besides your pain! No. But I'd say death by homicidal tree counts as unusual."

Her answer confirmed what he believed had just happened.

Lillian fought to free herself. When that failed, she reached out to touch him but stopped, clearly horrified. Then in a softer tone, she whispered, "Beloved, you look like Frankenstein's monster."

Gregory groaned as the tree loosened her hold on him. He didn't know of what monster Lillian spoke, but he felt instant sympathy for it if it suffered half as much as he did at this moment. Blood welled up and flowed across his skin from a thousand tiny stone-ridged fissures. Even as painful and ugly as they were, the surface wounds were minor. It was the internal ones that were of more significant concern. His body was already going about the business of healing them, but it would take days at this rate.

"Gregory, please talk to me. Why did my insane tree just try to kill you?"

He met her gaze and saw the fear in hers, concern for him. Then he glanced down at himself. Yes, between the hamadryad and the slave collar, they'd made a mess of him.

He understood why Lillian might think her hamadryad had tried to harm him. "I will recover. And, no, the Sorceress wasn't trying to kill me. She was trying to free me from the slave collar but triggered some kind of trap."

"You know that for a fact? Because from what I'm seeing, I'd say she has another agenda."

"Order me to heal myself."

"I don't think more magic will solve anything." Lillian had liberated her upper body from the hamadryad's embrace and was now trying to leverage her legs free.

"I have internal injuries," he admitted.

Lillian swore again. "Heal yourself. I'm here now and won't let my hamadryad harm you again."

Warmer magic filled him at her words. He'd never been so happy to call on the warmer, less turbulent power from the Magic Realm. It was a much slower process, but he was more than happy to just sit and wait for it to heal him.

He grunted in another pained gasp as the hamadryad shifted him closer to Lillian's position. His beloved uttered an unladylike profanity and then she was suddenly within touching distance.

Slowly the magic engulfing him withdrew, his pain already fading as his injuries repaired themselves.

"Do you know what happened?" she asked a second time.

"Something changed the slave collars, mine at least. I can no longer summon magic from the Spirit Realm, not without killing myself and possibly anyone near me." For the first time in any of his lifetimes, he found himself afraid of his most potent power. He could only hope the Sorceress had learned something valuable from all his pain.

As the warrior-protector half of their pairing, he was

formidable and skilled in his own right, but in the past, the Sorceress had exerted an iron-like control upon her magic which he'd envied. Lillian once had challenged him to admit the Avatars were equal in power—and yes, he was a great worker of magic, but he secretly thought the Sorceress's strengths were greater.

Now with his primary power out of reach, he needed to rely upon the Sorceress. Dare he trust her?

With another shuddering shake of her branches, the hamadryad began to lower them to the ground.

"Gregory," Lillian's voice drew him from his thoughts, and he heard her deep worry. "Tell me you'll be okay."

"I will be fine." Gregory pressed his forehead against the trunk's shaggy bark and then studied the fine white lacing of scars which now crisscrossed his skin. Lillian helped brace him while he gathered the strength to stand on his own two feet. "We will be fine."

But he only hoped his words were the truth.

CHAPTER TWENTY-EIGHT

Commander Gryton stood at the maze's north exit, his magic held carefully in check. He was nearer to his enemies than was safe, but he'd felt the hamadryad calling the Avatars to her, and he had been coming to investigate when his slave collars blazed a warning, telling him someone was attempting to tamper with them.

For once fate had been kind, and he'd arrived in time to avert a disaster. The hamadryad Sorceress had been examining his slave collars, and by the complex currents of magic he felt shifting through the earth and air, she had been far too close to unraveling his spells.

And that was not part of Gryton's plans. It should have come as no surprise though. Containing something as powerful and elemental as the male half of the Avatars wasn't a static task, but an ongoing, ever-evolving one.

Even without the hamadryad's help, the Gargoyle Protector could override Gryton's spells given enough time. That was the nature of magic from the Spirit Realm. It cleansed that which did not belong, and nothing could withstand its power. Nor could anything, not even Gryton's greatest spell-work, prevent the Gargoyle Protector from calling to that high power and having it answer.

So, the Protector's near escape shouldn't have come as a surprise.

But it did. The hamadryad's interference in this was most unwelcome. Worse, somewhere deep inside, in a tiny flawed part of Gryton's being, he felt betrayed by the hamadryad as if she had welcomed him and offered a mother's protection and then took it all away. It was foolish. He'd known within moments of his birth he could trust no one, not if he wanted to survive.

This little incident just solidified his wavering resolve. He would root out and crush that tiny seed of weakness. It wouldn't happen again. He would deal with his personal weakness just as brutally and swiftly as he'd corrected the flaw in his slave collars. Just a minor change to each collar was enough to prevent the gargoyle from harnessing and controlling his Spirit Magic.

And should a power that vast just happen to lack any kind of outlet? Why, there could only be one fatal outcome.

Gryton's lips stretched into the slightest of smiles. The Lady of Battles might not be happy with him should the Protector be killed by his own power, but somehow, Gryton couldn't be bothered to concern himself with that at the moment, not when the Avatars had been so close to escaping his control. His own survival took precedence. The Battle Goddess would just have to start over once the Gargoyle Protector was reborn.

Gryton's collar should now, if not wholly neutralize the

Gargoyle Protector, at least make him somewhat less lethal—though he didn't know if his fixes would keep the hamadryad from meddling. Likely not.

After all, the Avatars were still powerful enemies, ones he wasn't yet ready to attack openly. He needed to separate Lillian and Gregory from the hamadryad Sorceress without getting himself captured or killed.

The hamadryad had allowed him his freedom so far, but if he threatened her dryad or her beloved Gargoyle Protector further, there was no guarantee she would remain peaceful.

Gryton eased away from the threshold, heading deeper into the maze as he debated his options.

A direct attack was out of the question. Yet, a subtler trap might be discovered by the Gargoyle Protector or be neutralized by the hamadryad long before Gryton could use it to capture the Avatars.

He cautiously exited the maze and was heading for better cover in the forest when his magic stirred with interest. Never one to ignore its guidance, he followed where its tug led and found himself gazing toward the stone cottage where the Avatars sheltered. A small drama was playing out in a window on the topmost level of the abode. A human female was hanging half out of the window when River's son slapped a hand over the human's mouth and dragged her back inside.

The human was of little interest to him but seeing the gargoyle child opened other possibilities.

There just might be another way to return the Avatars to the Lady of Battles. Fate was being abnormally kind to him of late.

While the Avatars might be too much for him to take unaware, the gargoyle child would be easy enough to capture and returned to the Battle Goddess's domain. Once the child was within the Lady's grasp, Gryton would bet his life Darkness and River would come to the youngling's rescue. More importantly, Lillian wouldn't sit idly by if her little brother was in trouble. Presently the Sorceress or not, where Lillian went, Gregory would follow.

All the Battle Goddess's plans might still come to pass. Gryton might just live through this whole debacle. It just hinged on capturing one young gargoyle. Easy prey.

Gryton just needed time to lay the groundwork for a trap. A day or two should suffice even in this magic-starved realm.

CHAPTER TWENTY-NINE

*A*nna counted the nicks on the bathroom doorframe. Taking out the knife she'd filched from Shadowlight's bag, or rather the bag he had filched from his father, she made a third notch below the first two lines.

Three days.

Seventy-two hours.

Four thousand, three hundred and twenty minutes.

Dawn would be hello to day four.

And here she was still trapped in this godforsaken room.

Oh, she didn't fool herself. Her life could be so much worse. Shadowlight brought her food and clean clothing. The kid was entertaining, she'd grant him that, but she was still a prisoner. After Shadowlight had caught her trying to escape a second time, he'd had Greenborrow strengthen his spells since she was able to circumvent any spell of Shadowlight's making.

In the last two days, she'd discovered there was more than just physical changes. She now could 'see' the energy Shadowlight called magic, and she could even unravel the weavings. The unforeseen side effects were more instinct than memory, but she'd still been quick to take advantage of it.

Regrettably, she hadn't been able to bypass the leshii's shielding spells. She'd tried. Repeatedly.

Referring to the barrier as magic spells and wards, while still mildly weird, was starting to seem familiar. Which was more disturbing than the changes in her body.

Some of the alterations were beneficial, like her ability to see in the dark, and her heightened sense of smell and hearing. She'd bet she had greater stamina and strength, too.

Not that this tiny room allowed her the chance to test her theory.

She was going stir crazy. The inability to do anything might just kill her. Wouldn't that save everyone a headache? Too bad she was too stubborn to roll over and die—even if no one had ever, actually, died of boredom.

Even pacing was out of the question in case the room wasn't as soundproof as Greenborrow claimed. The last thing she needed was for more fae to learn of her existence. With only the two, she still had a hope of escape.

Sighing, she sat down on the bed and rummaged around in the nightstand for the books Shadowlight had stolen for her. He'd had an agenda she'd soon found out. The kid loved to be read to, which shouldn't have been such a surprise. All kids liked to be read to, didn't they?

Unfortunately, of the five books he'd brought—one spy novel, one detective, and two rather steamy romances, only the Jane Austen was anywhere near kid-safe reading. So, every night, she'd read Pride and Prejudice to the young gargoyle for a couple of hours before she chased him off to bed.

Rolling onto her stomach, she spread the remaining books out on her pillow to sort through them. She'd already finished the detective novel the first day, so she picked up one of the romances. At least it was a historical. Maybe she'd learn a little history among other things.

With a chuckle, she flipped to chapter one.

Hearing soft footsteps outside her door, she folded the corner of the page down. It wasn't like she had a bookmark. Besides, this one was so dog-eared, one more fold wouldn't be noticeable.

Shadowlight tapped softly. She knew it was the gargoyle because Greenborrow didn't knock, and if she'd been detected, it wasn't like anyone else would knock before storming the room. So, she always knew that soft, three-part rap was the young gargoyle.

At least someone had taught the kid manners. It certainly wasn't the leshii.

"Come," she called. Though she wasn't sure if he could hear through the barrier which doubled as both sound-proofing for the room and cage for her.

Shadowlight stuck his head in at her soft call. Guess that answered her question.

He spotted her and then came in carrying supper. The scent proceeded him.

"Oh, my god," she muttered as she jumped off the bed and snatched the tray from his hand. It was warm. In the past, he'd only been able to snatch cold leftovers. Apparently, gargoyles didn't do microwaves. "This smells delicious."

She set the tray down, looked around, grabbed the only chair, and dragged it closer to the bed. Shadowlight placed his own dinner down next to hers and then jumped up on the bed as he always did. There was no way he could fit in the chair anyway, so she felt zero guilt about having the only seat with a backrest.

She took the lid off the covered tray—who actually had covered trays in their kitchen?

"The trays are from the spa," Shadowlight admitted. "Gran intended me to take the extra food to Lillian and Gregory, but they went off hunting in the forest."

"Mmm...no use wasting food. Keep up the good work." She grinned around a forkful of the divine-tasting stir-fry and watched as Shadowlight tried to navigate the rice to his mouth without wearing it. She was just opening her mouth to tell him to forget manners and just dig in when the door shoved open with a crash.

Anna shot out of her chair. She snatched up the knife she kept in the nightstand. Shadowlight was faster and lunged off the bed, his talons extended, and his lips curled back in a snarl.

The young gargoyle didn't reach his target. A fiery wall of power leaped up between him and the newcomer.

Before that power had utterly obscured the newcomer, her heightened senses tagged what had invaded her room as deadly. Her talons lengthened, every instinct screaming this was a lethal opponent that needed killing swiftly.

How exactly she knew that she had no clue. She'd only had a glimpse of crimson and black armor and sharp edges.

She circled to the side, her small, stolen knife in one hand, the chair gripped in the other, ready to whip it at the newcomer if she saw an opening.

Shadowlight's magic slammed into the fiery barrier. Steam hissed and curled up from the point of impact. She didn't know much about magic, but she did know Shadowlight's power was cold, a chilled mist across her senses. This newcomer's magic must be as hot as it looked.

She wasn't about to let the bastard land a blow just to confirm her theory, though.

Speaking of landing a blow—that looked to be next to impossible. He was covered head-to-toe-in some kind of fantasyland scale armor like he was ready for a movie set. It didn't stop Shadowlight from trying his damnedest to eradicate the newcomer though. Anna inched closer, waiting for an opening.

Tin Man reached out and grabbed Shadowlight's right wing, jerking it hard enough to send the young gargoyle stumbling into the wall. Seeing her chance, she swung the wooden chair with all the force in her arm. It flew true to its target, splintering on contact.

The newcomer didn't go down as she'd hoped, but her move gave Shadowlight a chance to free himself.

The gargoyle dropped to all fours, attacking from a new angle. Anna knew they were in trouble when Tin Man deflected blow after blow without even looking at the gargoyle.

Tin Man's attention was riveted on her instead. She didn't know what he found so fascinating.

"Scrutinize this." She lobbed the small knife straight at his visor's eye slits.

His arm snaked out and he caught her knife by the hilt before it could embed itself in his eye.

Shit. The fucker had reflexes.

"Well," Tin Man said. "I see the boy is already showing his potential. I had not expected him to start building our new gargoyle army until he was mature. The little prodigal has been busy."

Tin Man heaved Shadowlight off him and then slapped out with some kind of physical wall of magic that sent the gargoyle flying backward.

Shadowlight's lower legs hit the end of the bed, and he slid, half rolling all the way to the headboard. He slammed into it with enough force to put a hole in the wall.

"Mortal," Tin Man drawled, "I need a moment for a few words with you."

A force hit her square in the chest, and she was flying backward until she slammed into Shadowlight's still form. She wasn't sure if he was still conscious.

Instinct told her he was still alive. Thank God.

Shadowlight moaned a moment later, assuring her he was, indeed, still alive, and mostly conscious. He rolled to his side, planning she knew not what, but his motion was aborted when he met some kind of barrier suspended just inches above them. The heat rolling off it warned her not to make contact. Then she realized it was descending toward her, and she might not have a choice.

"Now, little human—there is no need to fear. I'm not going to cook you for my next meal. However, I do need to examine you, so you'll be coming with us."

He didn't want to kill Shadowlight, or at least not immediately. What he did want was a mystery.

Tin Man glided to the bed and muttered a few words over the struggling gargoyle. Shadowlight went limp between one second and the next and the fiery barrier vanished.

From somewhere on his person, or maybe he pulled it out of the air, a length of delicate silver chain appeared in Tin Man's hand, followed by a far-from-delicate collar.

With another mumbled word, the collar flared with magic and Tin Man reached down and slipped it around Shadowlight's neck. The chain fused itself to the collar in some fashion she couldn't see.

Screw that. Shadowlight wasn't a dog.

In a move more bravado than brains, she twisted on the bed and kicked out with her right leg. The toe of her sturdy boot caught him in the side of the head. His helmet took much of the impact, but he still rocked sideways and dropped the chain he'd been holding. While he was off balance, she lunged at him, tackling him in his armored chest.

The impact felt like she'd been in a collision with a tank.

Tin Man only staggered under the impact a half step. Nonetheless, she accomplished what she'd set out to do. The hilt of one of his large daggers now rested in her hand.

It would have been nice to have been able to snatch the other one. Alas, she was lucky to have gotten this one.

"Hey, Tin Man, your blade has a really nice balance."

His eyes narrowed, clearly not loving that anyone would challenge him.

A roar echoed through the room, catching them both off guard. Ah, naptime was over.

Shadowlight, a blur of sharp talons and white fangs, launched from the bed a second time, slamming their enemy clear off his feet. Tin Man and the pursuing gargoyle tumbled out of the room and halfway across the attic. Stacks of boxes and pieces of furniture toppling over made enough noise to alert everyone within the house that something was amiss.

Anna darted after them, looking for a place to strike. Shadowlight had Tin Man in a choke hold, dragging him back toward the stairs. At that angle, she doubted Shadowlight could see the glowing ball of fire in Tin Man's other hand.

"Fireball. Right hand," she barked out the warning and lunged at the pair, her knife at the ready. She'd see if he could still do the handy fireball thing without that hand.

Just then Tin Man kicked out with both legs, his booted feet catching her squarely in the chest. Again, she found herself flying backward. This time a wall was kind enough to stop her.

She grunted and wheezed and cursed as she crumpled to the ground. The bastard was half horse to judge by that kick. She lay a moment more, her body unresponsive to her brain's demands to get up. White and grey snow blurred her vision.

Turning her head to search for signs of Shadowlight and their enemy, all she spotted was a broken off two by four and a few pieces of shattered balusters, which had once been part of the stairwell's guard railing.

Grunting, she heaved herself to her feet and ran after the two combatants.

They were at the bottom of the stairs, the narrow hallway hindering them both, but Tin Man had managed to get the upper hand on the young gargoyle. He had the length of chain in one hand, trying to attach it to his own wrist, where a small circle of metal glowed evilly.

Her stolen knife gripped firmly in her hand, she descended the stairs three at a time. She didn't know what the leash and collar were capable of, but Shadowlight's desperation as he fought to free himself told her enough. She landed in a crouch at the bottom of the stairs.

Tin Man cursed and lobbed a fireball at her. She dropped to one knee and lurched sideways, her newly sharpened reflexes saving her from a nasty burn or worse.

Shadowlight roared, the sound echoing down the hall and farther out into the house.

Someone was bound to hear and come to investigate. It just might not be soon enough.

Tin Man had Shadowlight on his back and had looped the chain around the young gargoyle's throat. With a mighty heave, he dragged the gargoyle backward, while sending fire back in her direction.

She dodged. Mostly. The smell of burnt hair and a new throb covering most of her left shoulder and neck said she hadn't dodged the last one fast enough.

Behind her, the fire was starting to lick at the carpet and walls. As it spread, its heat radiated against her skin, fed by new fuel. She couldn't spare the fire any more attention, or she'd be just more fuel.

Shadowlight still fought, his tail whipping around, the lethal blade-tipped end seeking a weakness in Tin Man's armor.

Which gave her an idea. She darted forward in the same moment Shadowlight twisted and heaved himself back to his feet. He headbutted Tin Man in his armor-plated chest, which didn't do much damage, but it succeeded in keeping Anna from getting charbroiled.

The kid had heart.

Now if she could just land a blow. While Tin Man and

Shadowlight grappled for the chain, she sprang at them. She slammed into Shadowlight's back, and their combined weight felled Tin Man like he was a tree in a hurricane.

She drew her arm back and then stabbed down toward the slit in his helmet's visor.

Something slowed her strike, a force she could feel in her arm, wrist, and fingers. Whatever it was stopped the blade from sliding all the way home. The muscles in her arm flexed, trying to force it deeper. She might as well have been trying to penetrate concrete.

Shadowlight's claws curled around her hand in a crushing grip, and their combined strength forced the blade a few inches lower, its tip sliding past the visor's opening.

Tin Man screamed. Fire raced up the blade's length to engulf both her and Shadowlight's arms before her brain ordered her to jerk back. The same invisible force which had messed up her strike now lashed out at them with punishing force. A second wave tossed them both clear of Tin Man who continued to howl in pain.

His howling turned to something more akin to cursing, but it was in a language she didn't know. He slapped a hand over his visor in an instinctive action—it wasn't like it would do anything for the pain and blood—and struggled to his feet.

But she spotted another opportunity to inflict some damage.

She rolled to her knees then picked up the knife with her left hand. She tried not to look at her right hand, but still glimpsed a charred, blackened mess. After the initial flash of pain, there was only a kind of numb deadness about it.

That probably wasn't a good thing.

Her vision was starting to blur strangely. No wait, that

wasn't her vision. Tin Man was muttering and moving his right hand in an intricate pattern. Something was forming along the north wall.

It shimmered as magic danced and sparkled. Whatever it was took the form of a large window, or maybe a door.

He'd said he was taking Shadowlight home.

Oh. God. They were out of time, and Shadowlight was hurt, unmoving beside her. The need to protect forefront in her mind, she studied her target one last time and prayed her aim was true. Her dad had taught her how to throw a knife, had always drilled her to keep practicing with both hands until she was as accurate with her left as she was with her right. Too bad she'd never gotten that good.

If she lived, she promised to practice until her arms were ready to fall off.

With the last of her strength and a desperate prayer, she sent the knife flying toward its target. A wet, meaty sound registered on her ears. There was another loud hiss, and then with a pained grunt, Tin Man yanked the knife from where it had embedded up under his arm joint where his armor didn't protect.

A lick of fire curled up from where the knife had embedded itself, but it was gone so quick Anna wondered if her eyes were playing tricks on her.

He made no other sound or showing of pain as he turned his attention from the magic door, which now showed a view of a deeply forested area. She couldn't see his expression behind the helmet's visor, but the intensity of his banked rage weighed heavily upon her. Or maybe that was just gravity and physical weakness turning her muscles to water.

Then Tin Man took a step in her direction as flames burst

to life along both arms, hovering just above his armor. With a disdainful flick, he tossed the dagger back toward her where it clattered on the floor before bumping to a stop against the toe of her boot.

"You both will learn your place even if I must burn the reminder into your flesh."

Now that sounded like a world of pain.

A glance down at Shadowlight confirmed he was still out cold. No chance he could escape Tin Man's wrath.

Anna threw herself down upon the kid and already knew her attempt to shield him would fail. He was just too big.

Another roar shook the house. It sounded a lot like Shadowlight's, but this one was deeper and definitely meaner. It came again, and she could feel the floor tremor slightly.

Tin Man whipped around and drew a sword from a scabbard at his hip. While he was distracted, Anna palmed his discarded dagger. If he was stupid enough to arm her, she was more than happy to sheath it in some other part of his body.

Something partially obscured by shifting shadows burst from around the corner and up the final few stairs.

Tin Man didn't wait for the fight to come to him and loosed more of his fireballs on the newcomer. The gargoyle, she could see him now, ran straight into the wall of fire coming toward him. She sucked in a concerned breath, but the fire didn't slow the gargoyle as he lunged at Tin Man.

The armor-clad enemy sidestepped the gargoyle at the last moment, but the gargoyle snapped at Tin Man's thigh as he surged past, tearing away a chunk of armor with a small spray of blood and fire.

In a blur she was barely able to follow, the gargoyle attacked again. Tin Man struck with both magic and steel.

The sword sliced through part of the gargoyle's wing membrane, causing a nasty three-foot tear. By the angle of the strike, Tin Man had been aiming to take the gargoyle's head.

The two opponents circled, sizing each other up. Tin Man chanced a glance in her direction, and she could practically see the frustration seeping from him. Yeah, he very much wanted to take Shadowlight with him.

"Tough luck, fucker," she said and gave him the finger.

The two opponents resumed the fight. She would have said the two were evenly matched, but that wasn't really the case. Tin Man had already defeated her and Shadowlight—though she'd managed to score a couple of hits on him—and from what she saw now, she knew he had been taking it easy on them. He hadn't wanted to kill either of them.

But he certainly wasn't terribly concerned about that stipulation now. Tin Man slashed at the gargoyle again and then slammed his armored fist against the gargoyle's head.

While the gargoyle was stunned, Tin Man kicked out, catching the gargoyle in the side and slamming him into a wall.

Tin Man came within inches of losing his own head as another opponent arrived on the scene. Anna only had a moment to register Greenborrow's presence before he swung a massive club at Tin Man's head.

In a move to make any martial artist proud, Tin Man darted to the side, deflected the blow and then stepped in behind the leshii.

Anna fully expected to see the point of a sword burst through the front of the startled leshii's chest but heard the ring of sword on sword instead.

She glanced past the leshii to where Tin Man was sparring

with yet another opponent. When Greenborrow turned to aid the newest arrival, Anna discovered it was a diminutive woman who looked barely strong enough to lift one sword, let alone the two she wielded with grace.

But damn, she was good as she danced around Tin Man in the narrow confines of the hall. The woman darted in and slashed with one sword while she parried with the other. Tin Man spoke in a foreign language. While it was an elegant-sounding language, Anna imagined what he said to the woman was anything but nice.

The smaller woman brought her two swords up in a clear attempt to remove his head from his armored shoulders.

At some point, the gargoyle had rejoined the fight. He landed a blow with his long tail that Tin Man hadn't seen coming.

It unbalanced him, sending him stumbling toward the leshii who swung his club with such force and speed it made her think of a professional baseball player.

The armor along Tin Man's right shoulder crumpled under the impact, and he roared in rage—pain too probably, but she was sure that was mostly fury.

From that point on, the fight took on the feel of a brawl, no—make that a melee.

Anna slumped to the side, taking her weight on her least injured shoulder just as her senses hummed a new warning. The air around her vibrated. She could feel it in her breastbone and even her lungs.

She dropped flat a second time as an intense wave of fire blew outward from where Tin Man stood.

The bright fiery blast, as intense as a grenade, blew apart a portion of the ceiling and walls nearest it and sent the other opponents flying backward. Anna felt the fire race over her and on down the hall.

She hurt, so she was alive. It took longer to figure out what had happened. At first, she'd thought he'd blown himself up like a suicide bomber.

As she picked herself up off the floor and blinked spots from her vision, she saw him bolt past and dive out a second story window at the end of the hall.

The strange gargoyle and Greenborrow rolled to their feet, looking a little worse for wear, but they followed him out the window just as more people came charging up the stairs.

Through an increasingly fuzzy, grey field of vision, Anna tried to study the newcomers.

She struggled back to her feet and protectively stood over Shadowlight, Tin Man's dagger clasped in her good hand, ready to protect the kid with her dying breath if it came to that.

Friend or foe she wondered?

The smaller woman with the swords spoke to the newcomers.

Friends, then, Anna guessed.

An older woman with a long, gray braid falling over one shoulder and hefting a substantial-looking staff in one hand tilted her head at Anna, giving her a once over.

After a moment, Anna recognized the woman. It was the nice grandmother everyone in town just called Gran.

"Who the hell are you and why are you in my house?" Gran asked.

Anna drew herself up straighter and nearly fell flat on her face when her one knee gave out. She settled for just staying on her feet, borrowing some of the wall's strength to do it.

"Corporal Anna Mackenzie. I'll gut anyone who tries to hurt the kid."

Anna's vision darkened more, and she knew that last bit was pure bullshit. She weaved like a drunk, her feet or the floor rolling out from under her and suddenly gravity was winning.

She didn't even feel the floor when she hit.

CHAPTER THIRTY

By the time she and Gregory ran back to the house, Lillian had found they'd already missed the primary battle, but she'd been in time to see the human standing over Shadowlight faint dead away. Deciding to voice what everyone else was thinking, she asked, "What's going on?"

Jason approached the fallen woman and felt around for a pulse. "The hell if I know, but this is Corporal Anna Mackenzie apparently. She's alive. Guess that makes her our problem now."

"Wait. I do know her," Lillian said. "She's the soldier who helped round up our 'horses'."

Gran stormed forward and pushed Jason out of the way. "Go get as many others as you can and follow Greenborrow and Darkness. I'm pretty sure that was Commander Gryton. We cannot let him get away."

Gregory huffed out an affirmative, his tail still flicked with agitation. He looked like he wanted to go hunt down Gryton then and there, but he hovered near Lillian, and she thought it was more than just the collars that kept him there.

Jason nodded sharply and then hurried to do Gran's bidding. River used the opening Jason created to reach Shadowlight's side. Lillian made to follow, but Gregory blocked her.

"Gregory, does the human actually look like she's capable of hurting anyone at the moment?"

"She's not human, not fully." But he grudgingly stepped toward Shadowlight and allowed Lillian to go to her little brother's side. With Gregory's help, they were able to move the human and gently roll Shadowlight on to his back and take inventory of his injuries.

He looked no better than the human.

"What do you mean she's not fully human?" she asked with a cursory glance at the woman.

She detected no hint of Riven upon the soldier. Other than her grievous wounds, which should have killed a human by now, there was nothing overtly strange about her. Then again, she couldn't scent anything over the stench of blood and burned flesh.

"What do you know that I don't?"

"Open your senses wide. What do they tell you?"

Aiming a questioning look at Gregory, she did as he asked even though she wanted to help her brother more than solve some mystery about a human she neither knew nor really cared about.

"Shadowlight will recover. He'll be sore for a few days." Gregory gestured at the human again.

Lillian was still more concerned about her little brother but turned her attention fully upon the human. "Why is there a soldier here? Would Gryton conscript humans to do his bidding?"

"I don't know why Gryton is here, but this human was protecting your little brother, not trying to capture him. I think we may have this human to thank for Shadowlight's present freedom."

Now that put a different spin on things.

"She was protecting Shadowlight of her own free will?" Lillian muttered in astonishment.

"Hmmm, I imagine they were trying to protect each other."

"I can explain," Greenborrow shouted as he came stomping back up the stairs. "Darkness and the other fae are out hunting for our dear commander. I thought I should return and explain about the human before anyone does anything...regrettable."

He stomped his feet and rotated his shoulders like he was aligning his joints back in place.

"Tell us what you know." Gregory didn't look up at Greenborrow, much more interested in Gran's healing.

"Anna is Shadowlight's pet human," Greenborrow chuckled. "Though, I think he knows not to call her that in her hearing."

"A pet human? Never in all my..." Gregory just shook his head and studied the two in question. "And under our noses, too."

"Yes, it serves us right for leaving a week-old gargoyle to his own devices for long periods."

"How long have you known?" Gran glanced up and glared at Greenborrow. "Children make mistakes in judgment. A ten-thousand-year-old leshii should not."

He waved his hands in surrender. "Only a few days."

"Days," Gran snorted. "Old fools and children will be the death of me yet."

"Go on," Gregory prodded, not willing for this to descend into a bickering contest.

"The boy found the human just after the Riven battle. She'd killed two of the beasts and had done a fine job on a third. As you can imagine, she was infected by the time our young gargoyle found her. Shadowlight was impressed by her bravery. She'd asked him to put her out of her misery, but he couldn't bring himself to end such a brave, determined spirit without trying to fight for her first."

Greenborrow waved at the unconscious gargoyle. "He didn't really understand what he was doing when he gave her his blood in order to save her. If you look past all that blood and burns, you'll see some of the changes. I don't think that will be the last of them either."

"But she's human," Lillian whispered, "I thought it only worked on dryads. Even then, it doesn't change the dryad."

"Interesting, isn't it?" Greenborrow stated.

Gran stood. "We will discuss this later. First, we need to treat these two."

After some muttering, shifting of bodies, and barking of orders, Gran won. Shadowlight and the human were moved into a medical area situated in the far back of the basement.

"How many more secret rooms are there that I don't know about?" Lillian asked.

"A few," Gran said and rolled her eyes. "It has never come up in conversation."

∼

After being shuffled to one side of the room, Lillian paced back and forth while River and Gran worked on Shadowlight and the human.

Gregory tilted his head and then cleared his throat. "Darkness reports he lost Gryton's trail. He believes the commander used a pre-set magic weaving to transport himself to another location."

It had been too much to hope they would have tracked him down.

"Your father doesn't know where it took Gryton, only that the spell wasn't great enough to take him back to the Magic Realm."

"Well, that's a blessing."

"Wounded as Gryton is, Darkness doesn't think our enemy will be able to return to the Battle Goddess under his own power any time in the next three days, not with the wounds they dealt him before he escaped."

"Don't suppose he'll do everyone a favor and crawl off into some hedgerow somewhere to die."

"No," Gran barked. "He will likely be seeking another way home before we have a chance to track and kill him."

"You said he's not powerful enough to get back to the Magic Realm at the moment."

"Not under his own power, no. However, we know of one being capable of meeting his needs." Gran didn't look up from her work.

"You're talking about my hamadryad. Why would she aid him? She is the Sorceress now, and as Gregory and I can attest to, she does possess higher thoughts. She's waking to her power and memories. Surely the tree will recognize what

Gryton is and prevent him from traveling between the realms."

"Yes," Gran said, a frown easily heard in her voice, "the Sorceress must have known Gryton was here. He had to have come here using her power. Otherwise, we would have felt a surge of a foreign power at the time of his arrival, and we would have investigated the cause. Which can only mean the Sorceress wants him here for some reason."

Lillian touched the tattoo branded around her throat. "Gryton made these."

"Exactly," Gran said.

Gregory looked upon them both like he was seeing them for the first time and was horrified by what he saw. "The Sorceress would not side with evil."

"Perhaps not," Lillian said, "but what if she wants something from Commander Gryton, and she brought him here for that reason? Gran has to be right. Otherwise, Gryton couldn't have hidden his arrival. We would have felt it." Lillian tapped the matching brand encircling Gregory's throat. "But what if Gryton being here is part of my hamadryad's plan to free us from these slave collars? Gryton created them, after all, he must know how to get them off."

"The Sorceress does not need his help," Gregory countered.

"But what if that is the Sorceress's plan?"

"Doesn't matter at this exact moment," Gran cut in. "We need to heal Shadowlight and the human. I don't like that Shadowlight hasn't regained consciousness."

River pressed her palm against Shadowlight's forehead. Lillian felt the flare of magic, like a slight vibration against her skin. Her mother continued to pour magic into Lillian's little brother for a few moments more.

Removing her hand, she frowned. "I do not like what I feel either."

Gran waved her hands in Lillian and Gregory's direction. "Go join the other fae and relieve Darkness. He'll want to be here with his son." She bestowed a stern look upon Gregory. "If you make it an order, Darkness won't feel like he's forsaking his duty just to be with his son."

Gregory agreed, ushering Lillian from the room.

"Oh," Gran called over her shoulder. "Take Gryton's dagger and the piece of armor to the other fae and see if you can come up with a way to track him."

Gregory huffed a second agreement.

They left the room in silence. Lillian didn't have to touch their mental link to know Gregory's thoughts and emotions.

His earlier rage had been replaced by a limp tail and drooping wings. He wouldn't meet her gaze.

She waited until they were far enough away that Gran and River wouldn't overhear their words.

"This isn't your fault, Gregory." She reached out and touched his arm. "You couldn't have known Gryton was here."

He pulled away from her touch. "Of course it is. I am the Protector, Lord of the Gargoyles. One such as Commander Gryton should never have been able to venture into this Realm without my knowing! I failed in my duty."

"How so?" she countered but didn't give him the chance to answer. "I think it's likely my hamadryad is behind this, at least in part. I told you she was hiding something from me."

"You don't know what you're saying. The Sorceress would never side with evil."

"You're a hard-headed male. I'm not convinced the old rule book still applies in this lifetime. We've bent those old rules so badly I think we're dealing with a whole new set."

Gregory grunted and hunched his shoulders as if that would change the course of their discussion. "They have not changed merely because I am foresworn."

Lillian stopped. Well then. So that was the broader issue. She should have known.

"Hmmm, if either of us is guilty of not upholding our duties and our vows, that would be me. Each knuckle-headed, moronic decision which has nearly led to disaster has always originated with one of my ideas or actions. That we are still here is due entirely to benevolent gods."

"You may say it is so, but that does not make it true. I have allowed myself to be distracted far too many times. I will endeavor to do better." He turned to her suddenly and wrapped his arms around her. "I will not fail you again, and I will never fail our child."

Lillian's need to finish the conversation faded, but the knowledge that this present mess was not Gregory's fault did not diminish.

She would find out what her hamadryad was planning, but first, they had to stop Commander Gryton from returning to the Magic Realm.

She squeezed Gregory fiercely and then released him. "Come on. We've got a sample of Gryton's blood on the daggers. Let's see if we can use that to track the bastard. Then we'll make him pay for attacking Shadowlight."

CHAPTER THIRTY-ONE

"Argh!" Anna cursed as she jerked awake. Three things became immediately apparent.

She was alive.

She'd been injured.

And she sure as hell wasn't on base.

Oh, right. Gargoyles, magic, and other strange shit.

"Hello," said a voice from a chair to her left. She turned toward the sound and found her body didn't want to move. Her one arm was wrapped in several inches of bandaging, which was why she had trouble moving it. She eventually turned far enough to meet the gaze of an older woman with a long braid.

"Name's Vivian, but everyone calls me Gran."

"I remember. And Shadowlight has told me more about your family since I met him."

The woman shifted a seven-foot quarterstaff from her lap and rested it against the chair. She wiped her hands on a rag.

At which point Anna realized the other woman had been cleaning and oiling the staff's dark wood.

She eyed the length of wood a second time. She hadn't seen one in years, but her father had an obsession with antique weapons. That length of wood lying across the old woman's lap was no walking stick.

Something told her this was not a 'Gran' to pick a fight with.

"The human is awake?" This voice came from the other side of the room, behind a curtained off section. A moment later, the curtain parted, and another woman came into view. This was the same delicate-looking woman from the sword fight earlier, though, her two swords were now absent. That had to be a good sign.

She looked human. Both women did. However, the newcomer addressed Anna as 'the human,' so she was likely the only homo sapiens in the room.

"Where is Shadowlight?"

But her heightened senses already told her he was behind that screen. Or at least another gargoyle was. She'd never been close enough to any of the others to compare scents.

But there were other instincts telling her Shadowlight was behind that curtain.

She tossed back her blankets to find she was wearing a long nightgown.

"Easy," Vivian cautioned and came to her feet.

Anna ignored the warning and stood up. Then gritting her teeth, she stormed toward Shadowlight. Okay, it was more of a stumble than a storm.

The delicate female made to block her.

"River, I would suggest you allow her to see Shadowlight. I felt the shadows reverberate to her anxiety."

"The human mongrel is no match for me."

Mongrel?

Seriously?

"Who the fuck are you?"

"I am Shadowlight's mother."

Anna managed to hide her surprise. Shadowlight had said his mother was a dryad. He'd explained the whole born-of-a-tree thing. "You should be fired. You suck at motherhood. I'm Shadowlight's new babysitter, or legal guardian, big sister or something—so get out of my way. Who in their right mind lets a child do the things he's done?"

If livid was a color, mommy just turned it. But just then the shadows shifted, and the curtains flowed apart like an unfelt breeze pushed them. Another gargoyle appeared beside Shadowlight's mother.

Anna didn't step back, foolish as it might be to provoke this eight-and-a-half-foot tall wall of solid muscle.

She did, however, suck in a breath at her first look at an adult specimen. He bowed his muzzle down to sniff at her. She wasn't intimidated by his size.

Nah, not intimidated at all.

She swallowed hard. "You're dad?"

His eyes narrowed, and then he nodded.

"You suck too."

The big gargoyle laughed. "I cannot fault you for your reasoning. Neither River nor I have given our son the time he needs. We will do better."

River, yes, that was the mother's name, she'd forgotten.

The dryad began scolding in a foreign language. The gargoyle only rumbled back at her.

While those two were arguing, Anna squeezed past and found herself standing next to a massive bed with Shadowlight taking up a good amount of it.

His wounds and burns were bandaged so she couldn't see how bad they were, but the number was concerning.

Shadowlight shifted in his sleep, and his ears twitched as he came awake with a pained grunt. His eyes slowly blinked open and focused on her.

"Hey, kid. How are you feeling?" Okay, it was a dumb-ass question to ask, but she had to say something to distract him from his parents' bickering.

"I hurt," came his honest reply. His attention continued past her shoulder and riveted on something behind her. She had a good idea what.

The parents were still arguing in another language. Whatever they said must have made sense to the kid because his ears drooped, and an expression of pain and fear crossed his features. Anna was damned sure it was emotional pain, not a physical one that made Shadowlight look like he was going to weep.

She was sorely tempted to go over to the world's worst mom and box her ears. Instead, she stroked Shadowlight's mane, tucking a few wild locks behind his large, deer-like ears.

"You'll heal, and I'm not going anywhere until you're back on your feet." She sat down on the side of the bed. "It's going to be okay, kid."

"No, it's not. Mother wants you killed." Shadowlight hauled himself up onto his forearms and then launched himself at her, his arms locking around her like a vice as he buried his muzzle against her side.

He did cry then, his whole body shaking with silent sobs.

Anna glanced over at his parents, prepared to give them the evilest look she could muster only to see Gran rapping them both on the shoulder with her quarterstaff. She then pointed at Shadowlight with the staff in case the dryad was too dense to figure out what the smack was for.

Darkness, apparently possessing a thimble-full of common sense, glided over to his son's side and whispered in that dark, beautiful language again.

He bounded up onto the bed and nuzzled his son gently.

Shadowlight didn't seem overjoyed and clamped onto Anna harder, digging in like a tick.

"My son, forgive us, we will not harm the human, I promise." Darkness had said the words directly into Shadowlight's thoughts.

Anna figured she was hearing the private conversation because Shadowlight was linked to her at the moment.

"Mother will. She promised to kill the human. I overheard her."

"She will see reason. We were just surprised to learn you healed a human in this way. That is all. Your mother loves you."

Anna barked out a loud laugh. She couldn't help it. Mommy had a weird way of showing her love. Aloud she said, "Don't worry kid. We adults will smooth things over. Besides, I'm still alive. Your mom had lots of time to do me some harm while I was out cold. She didn't, which proves this is all just bluff and bluster."

Secretly, Anna did wonder why she'd awakened at all. They'd had lots of time to 'take care of the human problem' while Shadowlight had still been unconscious. They could have blamed it on the injuries Tin Man had given her.

But they hadn't. Which made Anna wonder what they wanted from her.

Shadowlight finally allowed himself to be consoled and went into his father's embrace. River joined them both, and Shadowlight returned his mother's hug and leaned into her.

Anna just held her place. She couldn't go anywhere anyway, not with the kid's tail wrapped around her waist like a boa constrictor.

After ten or fifteen minutes, his tail relaxed its grip, and his father laid the now sleeping youngster back on the bed. River tucked him in, and three sets of eyes firmly swung upon Anna.

The one called Gran came over and looked down upon the young gargoyle and checked his bandages a final time. When that was done to her satisfaction, she turned her gaze back to Anna.

"We need to talk."

"Yeah, I gather."

The talk didn't happen right away. Gran said she had to summon everyone, alert the acting council, and make a few preparations.

A few preparations must have been code for 'go have a nap, we'll be back in a few hours.' Those few hours ranked up there as crappiest moments of all time.

Darkness stood guard at the door while Anna sat on her bed and kept herself busy putting the ruins of her hair back in braids. Though it would take someone with far more skill than her to address the scorched and burned off parts.

Messing with her hair also allowed her to pretend to ignore River, where the dryad stood tending to her son while periodically shooting death glares at Anna.

At long last footsteps sounded in the corridor outside. Darkness exchanged a quiet word with the newcomer.

It was the leshii, Greenborrow, followed by Gran, another big male gargoyle, and a woman she recognized as Vivian's granddaughter.

Gran zoned in on Anna. "We will take you before the council shortly to discuss your future, but first a few key players want to talk to you."

Lillian stepped out around Gran, covered the distance to Anna in two strides, and then held out her hand in the first normal, friendly gesture she'd seen in a while.

"I'm not sure if you remember me, but I'm Lillian. Welcome to the Twilight Zone. Just when you think things can't get any stranger, they will."

Anna took Lillian's hand and gave it a good pump. "I remember you. I'd say it's nice to see you again, but well, the events leading up to this meeting have been anything but."

"I don't doubt it," Lillian said. "But I do understand what you're going through."

Anna highly doubted that.

"I thought I was human until four months ago. Didn't have a clue about magic or fae or gargoyles. Went from thinking I was just your average twenty-year-old, to finding out I'm not human."

"There never was anything average about you," Gran said.

Anna raised an eyebrow, realizing something she hadn't

until then. "You're Shadowlight's sister. Somehow, I pictured you with horns."

"I suppose Gran is correct," Lillian laughed. "Did I mention that I actually shift into a gargoyle upon occasion?"

"Shapeshifting? Shadowlight might have mentioned something about that. Is there anything gargoyles can't do?"

"Subtle." Gran and Lillian said in unison.

"Yeah," Anna said with a sharp nod, "I've never seen the kid do subtle either. Did you really take on five helos?" She pointed her question at Shadowlight's dad and got a grunt in response.

So, lethal, yes. Subtle, no.

Small talk didn't seem to run in the genetics either. Guess that made Shadowlight the odd one out of his family. That kid loved to talk.

"You seem to genuinely care for my baby brother. We all saw the injuries you took trying to protect him from Gryton. The others didn't expect that."

Anna frowned, feeling a little like her loyalties were being called out or tested, or something. "He's a kid. What was I supposed to do? And he doesn't want to harm anyone. I saw that right away. Well, maybe not right away. I wouldn't have asked a kid to put me out of my misery after the Riven attack." Anna swung back around on the parents. "However, I wouldn't have expected to find an eight-year-old anywhere near that shit storm firefight with those vampire-Riven things."

Antagonizing the parents was probably foolish, but by dad's admission of guilt, she had hope he might be able to reform. Mom was probably a lost cause.

Besides, Anna wasn't going to forget the mongrel comment any time soon.

Darkness bowed his head slightly and then glanced over at his sleeping son. "We arrived in this Realm just before the Riven attacked the Coven lands. There were many Riven already here. I did not have a safe place to stash my son, so I kept him at my side." Darkness fell silent, and she thought he was done, but his glance tracked back to her. "My decision almost cost him his life. Then Commander Gryton nearly stole him away from me. If you had not intervened, he might very well have succeeded. Thank you for protecting my son where I have failed."

Anna was just about to mumble an awkward 'you're welcome' when a delicate snort of disdain drew her attention back toward River.

"The human wasn't acting out of her great noble intentions. She did exactly as she was supposed to do when she saw Shadowlight was in danger."

What the hell did that mean?

By the looks River was getting from the others in the room, Anna wasn't the only one baffled by her remarks.

Darkness's expression turned thunderous while Lillian's showed bafflement. Gregory, the other demigod in the room, just looked thoughtful as he studied Anna.

Gran and Greenborrow both dragged chairs from the corner of the room and then sat down like they were about to watch an evening's entertainment.

"You know something about why our son's blood is changing this human," Darkness accused River. "What has that meddling Battle Goddess done to our son?"

"She made him perfect," River said, her voice softening as

she explained. "My lady changed Shadowlight while he was still in my hamadryad."

My lady?

Holy shit.

Another piece of the puzzle fell into place. River was still loyal to her goddess in some twisted fashion. Sure, she'd defected to save her children—maybe—but that didn't mean she was friendly. Certainly not toward humans, and Anna wasn't sure how much River cared about the other fae either.

Why, oh why, was this fanatic still free?

River continued like the others in the room weren't thinking of bars, locks, and sturdy walls. "When Shadowlight is mature, he will be able to convert other species into full-blooded gargoyles. He will be their master."

"Sacrilege!" Darkness roared, making River stiffen.

Shadowlight jerked awake and jumped out of bed. Still half asleep, he took up a defensive stance next to Anna.

She patted him on the head, ruffling his mane affectionately. "Easy, kid. Your dad's just having a conversation with your mother. She said something that surprised everyone."

Shadowlight took her at her word and slowly stood up, sheathing his talons. He still wasn't steady on his feet. She wasn't the only one to notice.

Lillian and Gregory came over to help steady the youngster. Then, in a very un-demigod like fashion, Gregory licked at Shadowlight. The tender action reminded Anna of a mother dog grooming her pups. The young gargoyle seemed to crave the reassurance and leaned against the older one.

"Why is everyone upset?" Shadowlight asked at last.

Gregory huffed something, but it was Lillian who answered. "We just learned the Battle Goddess changed you, sweetheart. You're different than other gargoyles. Apparently, when you're mature, your blood will be able to convert others into full-blooded gargoyles. It alarmed our father, but it doesn't change how we feel. I'm different too because of the Battle Goddess's manipulations."

"Oh," Shadowlight mused. "That's why my father's memories didn't explain about the changes I saw in Anna. Why would the Lady of Battles want to grow her brother's army larger? She hates him."

Lillian planted a kiss on the top of Shadowlight's head. "The converted gargoyles would look to you for leadership. I assume the Battle Goddess had planned to raise you as her own to ensure your loyalty."

Shadowlight whimpered. "I don't want to lead an army, not for her."

"You won't have too," Gregory said. "We will not let her have you."

Anna suddenly decided she liked the demigods. Who knew?

When Shadowlight had first told her about the Avatars, she had mentally added them to her list of Big, Bad, and Scary. Now she decided she needed to move them to a new list. Big, Scary, but mostly benevolent.

"So," Anna mused while studying River, "if Shadowlight's blood is supposed to create full-blooded gargoyles enslaved to his will, why am I not either full gargoyle or a puppet to his will?"

"He isn't yet mature," River answered in a short, clipped tone, and then eyed Anna with a calculating stare, "though as he matures, you, too, might improve."

Anna was beginning to think there wasn't anything in the

world which might improve River's attitude. However, airing that thought wouldn't do much to improve the situation.

"What will happen to Anna, now that everyone knows what I've done?" Shadowlight asked.

It was the one question Anna had been too chicken to voice.

Gran stood up and crossed the room, giving the gargoyle an affectionate scratch. "That's one of the things we need to discuss at the council meeting."

"But what if the other council members deem Anna too much of a risk?"

Gregory, who had been reclining on the floor until now, stretched and came to all fours and padded over to Anna.

She held her ground while a demigod sniffed her over.

With a huff, he reared up to stand on two legs and then walked away. When he was halfway to the door, he reached out, hooked an arm through Lillian's and then addressed the room in general. "Anna is now family. I protect my clan. No one will be permitted to harm our youngest gargoyle or his pet human."

Shadowlight loosed a happy whine, bounced up so fast he nearly knocked his father over, and then launched himself straight at Anna.

"What? Wait...!" She didn't even get her arms up in a defensive position before the young gargoyle was upon her, his weight tumbling her right over the narrow bed and to the floor on the other side.

She had the wind knocked out of her but otherwise was unharmed. Unfortunately, she had no protection from the dozen sloppy gargoyle kisses he was applying to her face, arms, and even her bandaged hands.

"Ah! Uck! Get off."

The kid was hoisted off her a moment later. She climbed to her feet in time to see Darkness holding Shadowlight a couple of inches off the ground.

The young gargoyle seemed unperturbed by the change in locations and just transferred his sloppy kisses to whatever part of his father he could reach.

Anna scrubbed her face dry on a bedsheet and then looked up in time to see a softer expression on River's face as she looked at her mate and their son.

Huh. Maybe River was not the full embodiment of the cast iron bitch after all.

When Shadowlight finally got himself under control enough that Darkness could release him, everyone else in the room began to file out, heading to the so-called council meeting.

Darkness gestured her forward. "You must come too."

"Yeah, sure."

"What we discuss will affect you as well as the other humans of this world."

That was certainly one reason to go. The meeting might also be her last chance to escape long enough to get intel to her CO.

She didn't delude herself into thinking she could avoid recapture for long. Shadowlight would probably track her down through their mental link within minutes.

She'd just have to plan carefully and act quickly.

CHAPTER THIRTY-TWO

Gregory led the way back up through the house, Lillian close to his side with the others spread out farther back. He missed the military efficiency of the gargoyle army. Not that he was even sure if they would still accept him as their commander with this cursed tattoo around his throat.

Only the Lord of the Underworld could tell him that.

And he wasn't ready to face Lord Death just yet.

He glanced over his shoulder at the disorganized procession behind him and sighed. Yes, he missed his gargoyles.

Very much.

But they were firmly on one side of the Veil between the Realms, and he on the other.

Ah, well, he should be thankful for the allies he had. His senses stretched back toward where the human-gargoyle hybrid marched between Shadowlight and Darkness, plotting her escape.

That one hadn't quite gotten the hang of shielding her thoughts, though she was exceptional at projecting her intent to the other gargoyles. Even Lillian was glancing back, a wicked grin on her lips.

"Was I ever that bad?"

"At shielding or sheer stubbornness?"

Lillian punched him in the arm. "Shielding!"

"Yes."

She chuckled. "Fine. Is someone going to train the poor woman?"

"Eventually. Once things settle down, Darkness and I will take turns training you, Anna, and Shadowlight on the finer points of being a gargoyle."

"You're taking this really, really well," she said, suspicion tinting her voice.

His one ear flicked at her in question. "What did you expect me to do?"

"Well," she coughed into her hand to cover a smile. "You've never been the humans' biggest fan."

"Ah. I am coming to respect them a touch more. Besides," he half turned and gestured behind them. "What do you see when you look at the human?"

Lillian sighed. "This game again?"

"Humor me."

She did and studied the human in silence. "I see one big security risk that's pretty determined to get back and warn the other humans what's coming. Yet she seems to care for Shadowlight, and I don't think she wants to put him at risk. I imagine she's torn. She's a good person at her core. I can see that easily."

"Exactly," Gregory grinned. "She is a pure spirit, not one the Battle Goddess would have chosen for Shadowlight's second in command. I see the Divine Ones' hand in this, and the unraveling of another of the Battle Goddess's carefully laid plans. She will be irate when she eventually learns of this development. That gladdens my heart."

"Hmmm," Lillian looked thoughtful. "I hadn't thought of it like that. I see your reasoning."

Gregory reached the back door and led the procession out into the gardens, heading toward the maze where the other counsellors waited at the center.

"It's high noon. Are you sure no one can see or track us?"

He gave her his best put upon look.

"Sorry I asked." She raised her hands in surrender and then marched to the maze's center in silence.

Within the small central glade, he saw the entire council was present, even those members he'd not seen since before the Siren came.

The banshee stood between the pooka and the unicorn. Greenborrow was making his way over to that group. Even Whitethorn and Goswin were present, though their ordeal at the humans' hands was still easy enough to see in their hunched shoulders and pale complexions.

Hyrand hovered near her daughter as if mother and daughter were both expecting human soldiers to recapture Goswin at any moment. Jason joined the sidhe and the two sprites.

Lastly, three large wolves in the company of the dryad Russet emerged from the base of Lillian's hamadryad.

Russet bowed to them both and then straightened. "Allow

me to introduce the new high alphas of the dire wolf clans. This is Kendrick and Natasha, and their daughter Brigid."

The three large dire wolves lunged up and shapeshifted into their human forms, their transformations smooth and possessing an elegance only achieved through long hours of practice.

"Lord Gargoyle, Lady Sorceress," the alpha female said, "I am sorry the dire wolf nation could not have been at your side sooner. We are here now and ready to serve."

"Oh. My. God. Werewolves."

Gregory sighed at the uncouth comment and turned his attention to Anna long enough for her to figure out she'd drawn attention to herself she really didn't want.

Shadowlight whispered something in her ear, and she looked chagrinned.

"Mmm, sorry," Anna called from across the meadow.

Natasha raised one eyebrow in question. "Why is there a human here?"

Lillian pounced on that before it could twist from neutral to accusation. "She's one of the family."

"Indeed?" the male asked, stepping closer to Lillian so he could peer past her for a better view of the human. "I have never seen her before."

Gregory studied Lillian as she turned a few different shades of pink as she tried not to notice the alpha male's lack of clothing. The dire wolves were far too sensible to worry over something as silly as physical modesty.

If their creators really wanted their creations to swath themselves in yards of fabric and buttons and zippers, they'd have been certain to gift it to them at birth.

Though it *was* a touch amusing to watch as Lillian addressed the foreheads of the two alphas, clearly too flustered to meet their eyes or look anywhere else she might see too much.

After watching Lillian squirm at the mercy of her embarrassment, Gregory stepped up to the alphas one at a time and rested his hands on their shoulders then thrust his muzzle under their jaws and along their necks in the dire wolf way of greeting.

They returned the gesture, sniffing along his neck. Once he'd deemed they'd sniffed their fill, he dropped his hands from their shoulders and stepped back.

Dominance established and social needs met, both sides relaxed, and the atmosphere took on a much more mellow quality.

"Gran has informed us of the dangers this Commander Gryton poses to our world should he make it back to the Magic Realm and warn the Battle Goddess," Kendrick said with a frown "Gran also presented a piece of his armor for our people to scent. All the packs have his essence now, and we are prepared to hunt at your word."

Gregory nodded in thanks. "Your aid is much appreciated."

Jason came over, his arms heavily loaded with clothing. "Gran sent these—said there was no point encouraging the mosquitoes and other opportunists." He sighed dramatically and then slumped his shoulders.

Brigid barked out a sound more canine than human and took the offered clothing.

Turning to Gregory, Jason added, "Gran says she and the others are ready to start."

"Good." He followed Jason back to the center of the glade.

Several picnic tables had been dragged together, end to end, in a way reminiscent of the last time he'd stood before this council.

Unlike the first time, he considered these beings friends and allies, not potentially hostile strangers.

This time, he was going to ask them to trust again, taking a chance on an even greater risk than last time.

Lillian followed Gregory as close as his shadow. He hadn't confided in her about his plan. She sensed it was something big, and she wanted to be able to support him.

But, damn, that would be easier to do if she knew what he planned.

Something to do with their newest family member, the human soldier, but what?

Gran called the group to attention, and they got down to the business at hand.

It was more of a war council than a council meeting. There was no bickering, just effective planning.

Members of both Clan and Coven had worked all through the night to complete hundreds of tracking spells like the messenger spells Gran had been using for communication. The tracking spells were keyed to Commander Gryton's blood and would make tracking him possible even if he used transportation spells to move from place to place.

They merely needed to be placed in a vast grid pattern for kilometers around the hamadryad's location.

Lillian listened while Gran explained at length that they were banking on Gryton moving on the tree. He had no choice. When he did, the tracking spell would relay his present position.

"It's like you can just roll out a full surveillance package, no tech required. Whenever, wherever you want," the human soldier said, real awe in her voice. "No wonder we had no idea we shared the planet with other intelligent beings. You were always three steps ahead of us."

The banshee came to her feet in one graceful motion, which was no small feat Lillian mused since everyone was seated around picnic tables. "Who is this human? Clearly, she isn't Coven. If you want us to fight for you, you owe us an explanation."

The table broke out in a chorus of shouted agreements. Gran stood next, rapping her quarterstaff against the top of the table hard enough to echo.

"The Avatars do not owe us an explanation. They do not even have to ask for our aid. It should be freely given."

Gregory chuckled. "Though an explanation is always nice, all the same."

He proceeded to explain at length who and what the human was. He ended with the simple fact that as a human-gargoyle hybrid, she was now firmly one of the Clan. As such, she was as much fae as any other sitting on the war council.

Lillian knew the opposition was not truly silenced, but everyone was also sensible enough to know Gryton was the greatest danger at the moment, and all conversation soon turned back to him.

Then she realized Gregory's plan—the obvious solution

that linked both Corporal Anna Mackenzie and Commander Gryton.

The others at the table still hadn't seen the truth hovering in front of them.

"How can we possibly get the tracking spells spread this far in the next few hours? The area is far too vast," the pooka said, his yellow eyes dimming somewhat. "Even I cannot run so fast. We don't have enough bodies to cover this much ground."

"Even if we do manage to cover even half this distance," Whitethorn took up where the pooka left off and tapped the outer edge of the mapped area, "we will be too spread out to fight Commander Gryton. If he can best gargoyles in a fight, the rest of us won't be enough to stop him alone—many would not even survive their first encounter with him. We need greater numbers to drive him into an ambush."

There were several nods of agreement to Whitethorn's statement, but still, no one thought to use the human. Lillian narrowed her eyes and then summoned a touch of gargoyle magic, reaching toward the Corporal with it.

Ah, the human had come to the same conclusion as Lillian herself had. She waited, and still, Anna did not speak up. Neither did Gregory. What were they waiting for?

"I can think of a species capable of gathering the numbers needed to track, herd, and lay an ambush for Gryton," Gregory finally said in the drollest tone Lillian had ever heard him use. "We enlist the aid of the humans."

The table fell silent as one by one all the occupants turned to look at him aghast.

"Gargoyles truly don't do subtle." Gran sat back in her chair with a loud booming laugh, "Well, if you turn Anna loose, I'm sure she knows enough to stir the military up really good, but will it be enough to get the humans hunting Gryton? Or is it just more likely to confuse the hunt? We'll end up avoiding the military as much or more than hunting the commander. I don't see how that'll be much of an improvement."

"I'm not proposing we 'stir up the hornet's nest' as you might say, I'm proposing we form an alliance with the humans of this world," Gregory explained at last. "My other half once told me the humans have as much right to defend their lives and lands as the rest of us. I did not agree with her at the time, seeing only the humans' many weaknesses and the damages they had done to this planet. Now I see they are trying to make it better, fix what they've caused to go asunder. This is their home as well. The Lady of Battles, should she gain enough power to defeat her brother, will be looking for new territory to conquer."

Anna cleared her throat. "If I quote you on that last part, I can probably get them combing the forest for this Commander Gryton. However, they will be hunting the bunch of you as much as Gryton. There will be no alliance—no lovefest, no singing Kumbaya, not after how a certain group of gargoyles decided attacking five helos was a good idea."

"Actually," Gregory said as he tilted his head down to meet the human's gaze with such intensity Lillian felt sorry for the woman. "That is exactly what you are going to tell them. Remind them what two adult gargoyles and two fledglings were capable of. Then have them imagine what an entire dark army will do to their planet and lastly, tell them that together we can track and kill Gryton before he has a chance to inform his goddess.”

Anna stood and began to pace. “I’m all for warning my people so they can defend themselves, but they aren’t going to just agree to this alliance, not for days and days. If at all. Even then, they are going to want assurances. Not to mentions samples and specimens to study.”

Gregory tilted his head thoughtfully. “Then we will give them that.”

The banshee stood suddenly, preparing to leave, but paused long enough to bark out her thoughts. “Why would we agree to such? You’ve all seen what the humans did to Whitethorn and Goswin. If they learn more of us, that will be all our fates.”

Anna gave a hoarse cough. “That cat is already out of the bag. We humans already know other non-humans are roaming the forest. There isn’t going to be something called common sense or reason, or peaceful co-existence. Even if you’re willing to show goodwill on your part—which I do not see a lot of here at the table—peaceful coexistence will be a long way off.”

Lillian found herself agreeing with many of the human’s points.

Gran came over and leaned a hip against the table, looking down at Anna. “That’s where a bit of old-fashioned Coven persuasive magic will come in handy.”

“You’re crazy,” Anna challenged but leaned back and gave her head a shake. “Nuts, but I’ll try to convince my superiors Gryton is so scary, we need an emergency response team hunting him down ASAP. Anything else that happens after is out of my hands.”

Gran grinned. "Don't worry dear. Coven magic will help smooth the rough edges. At least enough they won't shoot or dissect you on sight."

"That's very reassuring, thanks."

Again, Lillian found herself sympathizing with the human, and thinking this plan sounded about as well thought out as one of her own.

CHAPTER THIRTY-THREE

"This is a stupid plan," Anna mumbled as she walked at the edge of the forest, cloaked in shadow magic. "I'm going to get locked in a cage for the rest of my life—make that the rest of my *short* life."

"I won't let that happen," Shadowlight said in a cheerful tone.

"You'll be in the cage next to me, drugged out of your mind. Just how are you going to rescue me then? I'm curious."

"No cage will hold me," he countered, far too excited at the thought of infiltrating HQ to see reason.

"Having you here is even stupider than the plan cooked up by Gran and the demigod." She frowned. "Don't come crying to me when you get a tranquilizer dart in the ass."

He huffed and stalked away a few paces, still close enough to hide her approach from the patrols walking the perimeter, but far enough away for her to gather he was upset at her.

"I'm sorry, but I still think this is a bad idea, we shouldn't involve kids in this mission." She directed the last at Vivian.

"And you're how old again?" Gran arched an eyebrow at her.

"Three times his age."

"Hmmm, a sage old twenty-four, yes?"

"At least I'm an adult and a military brat. Third generation." Anna continued her march, annoyance fueling her strides. "I've got older brothers in the forces. Been training long before I enlisted. Shadowlight's a kid. He shouldn't be here."

Gran huffed, rather like a gargoyle's sound of annoyance. "It hardly matters what we think or want. If we left him behind, he would follow. Besides, this way, if Commander Gryton wants to try for Shadowlight a second time, he'll have to go through an entire military camp on high alert to get him." Gran ducked under a low-hanging branch, and then looked back, "Strange as it might seem, this is the safest place for our young friend. That's why Darkness and Gregory agreed to send him here. Even his mother agrees."

Well, that decided it. Anything that old battle axe agreed with, Anna had to automatically oppose.

"Darkness will be with us every step of the way. He won't allow his son to be harmed by the humans even if he does get caught.

Anna still wasn't reassured. Darkness didn't have the best track record as far as she was concerned.

And one fully grown gargoyle, no matter how skilled and experienced, wasn't a match for what they were walking into.

He just wasn't.

"Oh, stop worrying," Gran hissed at last, "and have some faith for once."

"Fine, ask me again in a few hours. I've got lots of faith."
Faith that their asses would be in cages.

The first checkpoint was twenty feet ahead.

Darkness, Vivian, and Shadowlight hung back another twenty feet behind her, still firmly cloaked in shadows. For the moment Anna was, too. Shadowlight was awaiting her signal to drop the shielding magic cloaking her.

He'd promised to keep a physical barrier in place, encircling her body in case anyone got trigger happy. Anna appreciated the added layer of protection but was more worried for the young gargoyle.

Suddenly appearing in the middle of a base that seemed to be both edgy and on high alert did seem like an excellent way to get shot.

She glanced around one more time, hoping to see someone from her unit. She'd much prefer to be taken in by one of her own. It might minimize the manhandling, and Major Resnick always seemed able to get the gears turning faster.

If she could convince him of the fae's good intentions, maybe he would champion her cause.

Unfortunately, there wasn't one familiar face in her immediate vicinity.

At least she had gargoyle back up. They'd promised to pull her out if it looked like she couldn't convince the other humans.

Ah hell.

What really bothered her was the fact that the people

she'd once relied upon could now no longer be trusted to have her back. That tore her up inside.

"Let's get this over with." She waved to Shadowlight, their agreed upon signal. A slight tingle and what felt a bit like water flowing over her exposed skin was the only warning before the shadow magic cloaking her vanished. A shout of alarm from the nearest soldier caused a riot of activity, and suddenly two dozen guns were pointed at her.

With her hands held above her head, she shouted her name over a chorus of commands to get on the ground.

"I have an important message for Major Resnick. I need to speak with Major Resnick."

There was more shouting of 'get on the ground.'

With a sigh, she dropped to her knees.

This was going to be one long damned day.

After much shouting of orders, marching at gunpoint, and a few painful prods to redirect her in the direction they wanted her to go, Anna finally arrived at her present location. A nice roomy cage with transparent walls made of some impenetrable compound.

She'd been ordered to tie herself to the only piece of furniture, a metal bunk situated in the center of the cage. Its four stout legs were screwed into the cage's floor. Zip tying her ankles to the bench legs was easy enough, but how the hell was she supposed to tie both hands behind her back?

So, she'd asked.

In the end, she tied them in the front and used her teeth to secure the tie. It was stupid. But she also admired how they'd learned not to touch anything they found in the forest. For all they knew, she might have been a Riven. But she wasn't. Damn it! Now she sat in a brightly lit cage, tied hand and foot, while several soldiers and a number of scientists looked on.

Great. She imagined more persons of importance were watching her from behind the windows of the second-floor offices and other viewing rooms which circled the arena floor.

Above her head, lying belly down upon the roof of her clear prison, Shadowlight had taken up the best position to watch the goings-on below. She had to continually remind herself to not look up and give his position away.

There were two other cages on the floor with hers. One was intact. The other looked like it had shared a dance with a wrecking ball. Darkness and Gran sat on the ceiling of the intact cage. Anna forced her eyes away from their direction too.

"If you won't send Major Resnick, I'll just start shouting my message until I lose my voice."

No response.

"I am Corporal Anna Mackenzie. The night of the town-wide masquerade I was attacked by creatures called the Riven. They are straight out of your worst nightmare."

Still no response from her audience, so she continued. "Their bite is part contagion and part venom. Once you're bitten, you start to transform into one of them. They are as evil as it comes. Like a rabid animal, but one that retains enough intelligence to be calculating. I was bitten by one of these little monsters several times. The only reason I'm not one of them is that there was something else in the forest that night hunting them."

More silence. No, wait, there was a familiar thump of booted footsteps coming from outside in the hall. The person halted. She heard the whispering of voices. A crackle of a radio.

She continued her report to the room even though her attention was on whoever was coming down that hall. "The one hunting the Riven found and saved me instead."

More whispering just outside the room's main double doors.

There was a slight squeak of a door opening, a change in the air currents, and then the sound of several more boots joining the first set. Major Resnick came into view accompanied by some other upper brass.

Well, maybe she'd gotten someone's attention after all.

"And does this he have a name?" Major Resnick asked.

Anna nodded, "He goes by the name Shadowlight. As you can guess, he's not from around here. Neither are the Riven."

"Does this...Shadowlight...come from the same place as these Riven?"

"Yes, but they are natural enemies. Here's the kicker." Anna cleared her throat wondering if she was about to kiss goodbye to whatever credibility she might still have but figured she might as well release the big white elephant into the room.

"They are not of Earth. They are from the Magic Realm."

There, I just kissed away any credibility, Anna thought with dry humor.

Resnick's nostrils flared slightly, but that was it. He held his silence for several moments.

No one else said a word, though, the scientists standing near the back of the room were tapping away on their tablets.

"This Shadowlight told you this? And you just believed him?"

"Well yes. Here's the thing. He's a gargoyle. He has the wings, tail, and horns to back up his claim. Oh, and his blood is toxic to the Riven. Gargoyles serve the Light, and the Riven, the opposite." She laughed at Resnick's expression. "That takes some getting used to, sir. Magic. Not a hoax. Not space aliens. Two warring factions from another realm and we're just catching some of the fallout. It's only going to get worse."

She was going to be hoarse long before she was done talking.

CHAPTER THIRTY-FOUR

Shadowlight watched from his perch and yawned for the fourth time. All they did was talk.

And talk.

Talk in loud voices. Talk in hushed voices. Talk in tiny whispers between each other when they didn't want Anna to hear. Talk on radios or other devices to yet other humans in other rooms.

They talked but did not listen. Were they deaf?

Anna sounded tired and hoarse. He couldn't blame her. They asked the same things repeatedly as if they didn't have the intelligence to remember the answers the first ten times.

His father said they did it to wear down the human and to try to catch her in a lie, but it wasn't working because she'd told them nothing but the truth. A truth they didn't want to hear.

Shadowlight stood and stretched, circling the dimensions of the cage's roof, looking for the impossible: a more comfortable position.

Anna pretended to stretch her shoulders and neck, using the move to hide her real purpose: to send a dagger-sharp look his way.

He sighed and flopped his haunches back down on the surface, flicking the tip of his tail so Anna would know he was getting tired of being invisible and doing nothing.

Hunger was starting to gnaw at his belly. It had been several hours since he'd last eaten, and his body had burned through many of its reserves during healing.

His father looked bored as well. Gran might have been bored had she not been weaving the spells to keep the humans calm and willing to talk.

He frowned. Gran's spells were working too well. The humans were going to talk each other to death.

"So, this gargoyle you call Shadowlight healed you with his blood to rid you of this so-called Riven's taint. How do we know one is any better than the other? Or that this Shadowlight wasn't just some construct created by your delirious mind to make sense of what was happening to you?"

It was the male scientist by the name of Fleming who made that last remark. He was the most doubtful, having trouble accepting magic was real. He wanted to blame all the events on something called aliens. As if magic was a figment of a weak mind.

"Have you any proof to back up your claims?"

"What?" Anna barked out a harsh laugh. "The claws and teeth aren't enough?"

"They are anomalies certainly. But magic? No. I'm sure there is a better explanation."

"What about the sidhe and the sprite you captured and then lost. The kid told me about that."

"An as yet undiscovered species."

"Oh, come on," Anna hissed. "They are not originally from this world. They came from the Magic Realm long ago."

"There is no such thing as magic."

Another scientist and two of the military advisors who had been part of an earlier discussion looked like they were ready to start another back and forth debate.

Shadowlight was sure he'd perish if he had to listen to another one of their long-winded debates.

"Human," he called down to the greatest doubter, the scientist with the grey-peppered hair. "What will it take to make you realize Anna has spoken nothing but the truth?" Shadowlight dropped his cloaking magic and tilted his head as he waited for the human's response.

As Lillian would have said, they did not disappoint.

There was a wave of noise and motion, and every gun was suddenly pointed at him instead of Anna in the cage.

Over it all, he could hear Anna swearing and shouting.

"Hold. Hold fire! He's bulletproof. They'll ricochet. He's protected by magic. Don't fire."

Shadowlight merely held his position and let the humans sort themselves out. The room grew still once more, with the scientists and other persons of importance shoved to the back of the room while more soldiers with guns came forward. Shadowlight was mildly surprised none of the humans had used their projectile weapons upon him yet.

Which was good, since Anna might be right. Once his magic deflected the bullets, there was no telling where they'd end up—possibly in a human. That wouldn't be good for what Gran called negotiations.

The one called Resnick had held his position a few feet in

front of the cage. It was very brave or foolhardy, as he was within easy jumping distance of Shadowlight's location.

His tail flicked playfully at the thought.

"Don't you dare!" Anna hollered at him from below, her voice muffled by the thick cage walls. "You'll start a firefight for sure."

"Aw, humans are no fun."

"These humans aren't, no. What they are is 'twitchy as hell' and understandably so. Don't you dare move." Anna transferred her gaze from him to other humans out in the room. "I know he's big and scary, and far from harmless, but he's just a kid. He's only eight years old."

The one called Resnick made a series of hand gestures.

"Hey! Whoa, wait." Anna shouted, "Think of this as peace talks. No shooting or tranquilizing the delegates."

Resnick glared at Anna.

"The kid isn't alone. If you do something drastic to the kid, his dad is going to do something drastic back, sir!"

Shadowlight noticed a few pairs of eyes drifted away from him to scan for other threats, but they always returned to him every few seconds. To his left, Gran and Darkness were shifting, likely preparing to do something to draw attention away from him.

A voice rose from several places at once, and he decided it came from one of the communication devices.

"Subdue and capture the specimen."

Gran shot up, her magic flaring around her. "Oh, for the love of Light. Boys and their guns." She muttered a few choice words as she stepped off the top of the cage and dropped the eight-foot distance to the ground like she was stepping off her back patio. She landed gracefully and brought her staff to the ground as her concealment spell vanished.

Magic flashed outward from her staff, flying across the room faster than the eye could follow. By the exclamations the soldiers made as their weapons vanished, they might now be a little less skeptical about the existence of magic.

"Peace. I mean you no harm." Gran walked over to Anna's cage and tapped on the front. It disappeared on the second rap, and then Anna's zip-ties vanished. "However, cages and guns are no way to begin an alliance."

She made her way toward a side door. "A conference room is a much nicer place to talk. I just happen to know there is a spacious one through that door, up a flight of stairs, and a short walk down a hall." Two soldiers approached her, knives at the ready.

"Really, boys?" Gran asked them in a pleasant tone. "Need another demonstration?"

Shadowlight hopped down from his perch and walked up behind Anna where she was attempting to reason with three soldiers trying to corner her.

The soldiers backed off at his approach, deciding Anna wasn't an easy snatch-and-grab.

By this time, Gran had convinced her two soldiers to go elsewhere. Though Shadowlight realized it might not have been Gran's threat which drove them off. Everyone still in the room was evacuating.

Gran laughed. "Good to know I can still clear a room."

"This was pointless," Darkness hissed from the shadows near Shadowlight's right side. "The humans are too blinded by their fear and prejudices to be of any use."

"Oh, my tall, winged friend," Gran said and gestured to

the lab at large. "This was just the start. I'm still softening them up. They will be more reasonable after they get over their shock."

Anna made a choking sound, which might have been a cough, he wasn't sure. "When they get over their shock, they are going to come at us with everything they have."

Shadowlight heard his father's growl.

"Ah, my dear doubters, you will see." With that, Gran led the way to the conference room.

Anna sat in a big comfortable meeting room chair—one of the ones that rolled. She rocked the chair from side to side as she chanted 'we're all going to die' under her breath.

No one else seemed to believe her.

Gran sat in the chair across from her. Darkness stalked the room's outer walls, and Shadowlight played with the other chairs, pushing them around the table. By the cant of his widespread ears, he was clearly delighted by rolling chairs.

"Shadowlight, come here." Anna caught herself about to pat her thigh and froze. Gran, however, missed nothing and grinned at her near social gaffe.

"Nice catch," Gran whispered in a conspirator's tone.

Shadowlight galloped over to her and pushed two of the chairs closer together. He then proceeded to sprawl across both seats.

"That's not going to...," Gran started to say just as both chairs rolled in opposite directions, and Shadowlight landed on the floor with a disgruntled huff. "...end well."

Anna folded her arms on the table and dropped her head

down on them. "They're not just going to shoot us dead. Oh no. We're all going to get dissected, and then frozen or pickled or something."

"Frozen?" Shadowlight asked, sounding entirely unconcerned.

"Or maybe they'll use gas, less damage to the bodies that way. No, wait, some politician is going to be pissing in his pants and order a missile strike. Yeah, air strikes for us."

"Oh, hush," Gran said, "Lillian and Gregory are on drone duty, and the unicorn and pooka are ready as well. As masters of deception themselves, they are astute at sensing and locating human devices that, shall we say, don't want to be found."

"The who and the what? And is that your roundabout way of saying some of your gang can detect tech hidden by stealth technologies?"

"Never mind dear, just remember we have our own air and ground forces capable of taking out nasty things. The drones are unmanned, which will make them fun target practice for some of the other fae if this escalates into something hostile."

"You're all crazy. I thought it was just the kid because he's a kid. Nope, you're all..." Anna halted mid-sentence and turned toward the meeting room's north door.

Darkness was already there, and Shadowlight took up a protective stance next to Anna's shoulder.

Gran turned her chair toward the sound of footsteps.

Anna was holding her breath. It was a bad habit she'd been relapsing into these last few days.

A knock came, firm and sharp—an actual knock, not the sharp crack of a door being kicked in by a heavy boot.

"Enter," Gran called, "if you're ready to listen."

Major Resnick eased the door open, one hand pressed against it, the other palm up, and then he advanced into the room. Darkness retreated to the southeast corner. To make the Major feel more at ease?

It was a nice thought but wasted. Nothing was going to put her CO at ease. Well, maybe the business end of one of his tranquilizer darts.

"I'm here to relay messages to my superiors." His eyes scanned the gargoyles.

"Well, that's a start." Gran gestured at the chair closest to Major Resnick. "Why don't you have a seat?"

The chair she'd suggested was at the far end of the table, about as far from the two gargoyles as he could get and still be sitting at the table.

Resnick raised an eyebrow at Shadowlight and then directed his next questions at Anna. "You sure it's safe? That one looks like he thinks I'm going to take away his favorite bone."

Anna tracked up to Shadowlight and studied his expression. "Oh, that's a gargoyle version of a smile. He likes you. I think," Anna added a shrug to the end of her statement.

Shadowlight's grin grew wider. "I like the brave."

Major Resnick coughed into his fist. "You'll like the military then. Our ranks are filled with many brave men and women."

"Good," Gran piped up, "I'm hoping you and Shadowlight will hit it off."

Major Resnick arched an eyebrow again. Anna decided her CO was going to sprain a facial muscle before the day was over.

CHAPTER THIRTY-FIVE

Resnick was sure his face must have frozen in an expression of disbelief some hours ago. The 'negotiations' got off to a rough start, but once Vivian started talking, it was hard to dislike the woman who was merely known to most of the town as Gran.

Doubt, distrust, and question her motives? Most certainly. But dislike? That was harder. The more she talked, the more things snapped into place. Events, impossibilities science couldn't explain—those she shed light on in a way to make them plausible if not palatable.

The stuff about other realms, armies, demigods, and swords that could create Armageddon-level shit that could crush the world—that was bound to give him nightmares for life.

And this Commander Gryton? Him, they'd run into once already, and he'd left ten dead men in his wake.

It all sounded so impossible and fanciful he worried his superiors wouldn't believe it even though they were listening in.

But they did believe.

At least enough to agree to listen to Gran's plan to hunt and track this Commander Gryton. The first test of the fledgling alliance was when Gran and Darkness were asked to go with the senior advisors to further outline the plan to track this Gryton in detail. While that was going on, the scientists would begin their study of Corporal Mackenzie.

To his surprise, Gran agreed to his terms. Then the magic-wielders surprised everyone a second time by asking Shadowlight be allowed to stay with Anna, saying a war council was no place for children.

Anna and Shadowlight had both been put out to be called children. However, both agreed to aid the scientists. Just as Vivian and Darkness—the big, mean-looking gargoyle—had been about to leave in the company of a unit of soldiers and an assortment of other brass, she'd come over to him and thanked him for babysitting her two young charges.

Yeah, he didn't miss how Gran had lumped Corporal Mackenzie in with her group.

But perhaps the biggest shocker of the day was when Darkness had come over and told his overgrown kid to behave and obey Major Resnick.

When Resnick had openly questioned why they trusted him, the gargoyle had grunted in humor and left it to Gran to explain. She'd informed him gargoyles could read a person's intent. In other words, gargoyles could smell a lie or a dishonest thought a mile away.

That sounded a lot like being able to read minds.

"Corporal Mackenzie," Resnick called over his shoulder as he held the door for them, "if you and.... Shadowlight will follow me, I know a few scientists beside themselves with excitement at the thought of talking to you." Outside, several of his men were waiting to act as escort.

"Talk, sir?" the Corporal asked with a hint of sarcasm. "If only."

The gargoyle bounded over to them with lightning fast speed and sniffed at Resnick. Having that much power and natural weaponry within inches of his exposed neck made Resnick's pulse increase and his fingers itch for a gun.

Shadowlight shifted and leaned against Resnick's right shoulder, jamming him against the door frame as the gargoyle's muzzle came around to sniff along the underside of his jaw. Sweat trickled down Resnick's back.

His men trained their weapons on the gargoyle.

Shadowlight flashed his fangs at the other soldiers and a deep growl issued from his throat.

"Whoa! He's just taking in Resnick's scent."

"Easy!" He cautioned his men. "I'm good."

Resnick remained unmoving as the gargoyle continued to inhale.

"He's just getting my scent like the corporal said." He rolled his eyes in her direction and mumbled, "Right?"

"Yes, sir." She paused, seemed to think something over, and then chuckled. "Beware, though, they seemed to be rather social and will use every opening to get in a good lick."

Now that gave new meaning to the term 'take a licking.' He raised a hand and slowly pushed the large muzzle away from his throat and then directed his next words at the young gargoyle. "You will not make any more of those sudden leaps at any of my personnel. Neither will you invade anyone's personal space. There will be boundaries put in place for your protection."

And for everyone else's protection, because there was no way the bigger gargoyle was going to remain nice if something happened to his kid.

Shadowlight gave a deep, huffing cough. Resnick wasn't sure if it was in annoyance or humor. Though he thought it might be humor.

Babysitting detail was sure going to be interesting.

CHAPTER THIRTY-SIX

*L*illian stood shoulder to shoulder with Gregory as they gazed up into her hamadryad. "Do you really think this is going to work?"

Gregory wasn't one hundred percent sure if she had directed her question at him or the tree. Since the tree couldn't verbalize words, he figured Lillian had directed her question at him.

Gregory turned more fully to her and nuzzled her shoulder.

"Yes. Commander Gryton would have come here initially on a recovery mission to save face with the Battle Goddess. If he'd been able to capture River and Darkness, or Shadowlight and the human, he could have returned to his goddess and likely retained his position, or at least his head.

But he failed in his attempt. Now we know he's here. He is injured and knows he's being hunted. It's no longer a mission to save face. Now it is pure survival. His best bet for continued existence is to return to the Magic Realm. If he takes what he knows about this place to the Battle Goddess, he may keep his head."

"That's a lot of guesswork and speculation. What if he goes after Shadowlight again?"

"Commander Gryton won't chance it—at least not until he's healed. Once we close our net around him and force his hand, he will come to the hamadryad. He'll have no choice."

"Something isn't right," Lillian said and started to pace. "Why didn't we know he was here?"

"Perhaps...," Gregory touched the tattoo on his neck, "these prevented us."

"Yes. Maybe. I don't know." Lillian paced a circle around the base of the tree.

Gregory was drawing breath to soothe her, or at least try to reassure her, when she spun around on her tree.

"Why didn't you warn us?" Her question was aimed at the tree.

He cocked an ear at the tree but kept his attention on Lillian. "A hamadryad does not concern herself with mortal drama—it is but a blink of time to one of them. Besides, they do not communicate in complex thought."

"You're wrong. This one communicates. She isn't a normal hamadryad. She is the Sorceress. You can't tell me she didn't know Gryton was here in the Mortal Realm. He had to have used the bridge the two hamadryads formed to travel here." Lillian rounded the tree and came toward him, her expression troubled. "Why would she hide that from us? I'm telling you something isn't right."

He cast a thoughtful glance between Lillian and her

hamadryad. He wanted to dismiss her concern. There was no way the Sorceress would intentionally hide Gryton's presence. Yet Lillian was also correct. Why hadn't the tree warned them in some way? While a hamadryad would not directly interfere with mortal drama as he'd said, she would still protect and warn her dryad of any and all dangers. Gryton was certainly a danger. One the Sorceress could not have missed.

Trailing his gaze slowly up the tree, the first hint of doubt crept into Gregory's heart. What if the Battle Goddess had found a way to corrupt the tree?

His emotions churned and rolled, nearly a physical sensation.

No. It was not possible. The hamadryad was untouched by evil.

Still deep in his internal debate, Gregory was taken somewhat off guard by the arrival of a newcomer in the glade. The last thing he wanted to do was hold a conversation with one of the fae.

The sidhe paused at the maze's south exit, glanced around the base of the tree, spotted them in the shadows of her wide branches and then made his stiff, slow way over to Gregory's side. The signs of his time among the humans were still evident upon Whitethorn's being.

A hint of foreign chemicals, what Lillian called drugs, still clung to the sidhe lord and his wrists showed the deep blue-black of bruises.

But it was good to see him back on his feet. Gregory reached out and gripped the sidhe's shoulders. "It gladdens me to see you recovering."

"I wished to thank you and your lady, as well as the other

gargoyles, for saving the sprite and me from the humans." He sighed and then gestured toward one of the picnic tables Gran had left in the maze. "If you have a moment."

He and Lillian nodded and followed the sidhe.

Once Whitethorn was perched on the bench, he eyed them both with a frown. "You rely too heavily on your magic to protect and hide you." He gestured at his own body armor. "I think it wise to have a few more layers of protection given how advanced the humans have become. They know we exist, and while they may be temporary allies, they could very well start hunting us again with little warning. If I hadn't put so much faith in my magic, I might not have become their prisoner. As you already know, my metalsmiths have been working on body armor for you both, I have asked the other gargoyles to be measured and fitted as well. When finished, it will help protect against magic, bullets, and tranquilizer darts."

Whitethorn held up his hand when Gregory made to comment. "I know you will be concerned about noise and mobility, but my master metalsmiths assure me what they have designed will impress. When you have a moment, they would like to fit them to you both and then meet with Darkness and Shadowlight as well."

Gregory nodded agreement. The more layers between Lillian and harm the better.

Lillian folded her arms under her breasts. "Shadowlight won't be near anymore fighting, but if it helps keep him safe, then yes, make sure he is fitted as well." Her stance was one he was coming to know meant he might as well just agree to it now because the argument was already won—by her.

Gregory nodded to Whitethorn and then added, "How soon do you need us?"

"At your earliest convenience."

Gregory nodded a second time, sensing they might need extra protection sooner rather than later.

CHAPTER THIRTY-SEVEN

Displeasure at his own folly raced through Gryton's blood. He'd allowed himself to fall into a trap even the child gargoyle, Shadowlight, would have seen.

He sprinted up a slight incline and then over the ridge to an easier trail once again. As he leaped over a fallen trunk, he glanced behind.

Human soldiers with their strange, handheld lights pursued him. Stranger still was their sidhe scout guiding them when they lost his trail.

They were still a league distant and fell farther behind as he outpaced them. It was the same as the last three patrols he'd encountered.

He'd killed the first group, which, he reflected sourly, was probably what allowed the second group to reach his position. There had only been enough time for him to injure a number of that patrol before a third had arrived at the site, drawn by the noise.

Survival instincts had spurred him into motion then,

escape more important than victory. It wasn't until this newest patrol had picked up his trail that he realized there was an ambush, and he'd already stepped right into it.

A contingency he hadn't foreseen had occurred. The fae had aligned themselves with the humans of this world and had somehow convinced the humans to hunt him instead.

His magic flared in warning seconds before he heard a high-pitched whine and a loud blast of sound as something leaving a fiery tail in its wake cut through the forest in his direction. He darted to the right as the tree to his immediate left blew apart.

Behind him, the forest exploded with heat, fire, and noise. A wave of force from the explosion knocked him to the ground. He rolled to his knees and summoned fire, sending it back the way the humans' weapon had come.

His magic flew true, and then came shouts of warning followed by screams of pain. He didn't stay to see how many his magic would claim. Lunging to his feet, he began to run.

There was only one direction.

He knew it as surely as his enemies did.

But it was the only way to escape this godless realm.

The hamadryad was his only chance of survival and if he hadn't misread her emotions—and he didn't think he had— she held enough maternal instinct for him that she might aid him. If she wouldn't help him willingly, then she would aid him unwillingly.

As for his father—the Gargoyle Protector had never failed to send his enemies to the Spirit Realm for judgment.

Gryton's lips peeled back from his fangs. They would soon see if father or son was stronger, he supposed.

This realm was not the battlefield he would have chosen

for such a contest, but perhaps it was for the best.

The Gargoyle Protector was limited by this Realm and may not yet have come to terms with how best to fight without the full command of his power.

From the moment of his birth, Gryton had been limited. He'd spent centuries learning to use and not be used by his magic. He knew how to fight and win against impossible odds.

Though, he still felt his magic's mad, mindless hunger to feed upon everything around him, always there to remind him of his misbegotten heritage.

A monstrous abomination that never should have been birthed upon the three Realms.

But he had been born.

And he planned to defy fate and the Divine Ones for many more centuries to come.

More weapons fire cut through the forest just steps behind, impacting the trees and undergrowth still shaking in his wake.

Gryton put on a burst of speed and then rolled and slid down another embankment and followed a stream for a few paces until another game trail presented itself.

He would live to see his enemies fall.

He'd just have to escape this forsaken realm first.

"Well, I'll be damned," Anna whispered as she tracked the small flares of light suspended over a spell map depicting life-like forests, streams, hills, valleys, and roads in a hundred and fifty-kilometer radius around ground zero.

Ground zero, the hamadryad, was depicted on the floating map as a three-inch-high tree.

The map shimmered and shifted, homing in on the action.

"Fuck me," Major Resnick mumbled under his breath as he studied the map, disbelief still evident in his eyes.

She doubted if she was supposed to hear, but her new gargoyle senses were still evolving. No one else other than Shadowlight would have heard her CO anyway.

So yeah. This shit was happening. Their teams were out there, herding a demigod in the direction they wanted.

A destination with three gargoyles, an assortment of fae, and an entire squadron just waiting for the evil overlord to poke his nose out of hiding. Oh, yeah.

She wished she could be there to see his helmeted head getting blown off his armor-clad shoulders.

Yet, as much as she wanted to see him dead, she was equally glad to be here, keeping Shadowlight out of trouble and as far from that monster as possible.

Darkness had talked the young gargoyle into staying here, away from the fight. When she'd asked Gran how he'd managed that, she'd grinned and said Shadowlight had a more important job. Protecting his pet human in case Gryton somehow discovered the tracking spell and followed it back to HQ.

Anna knew a lie when she smelled one. She was just glad the kid hadn't sniffed it out yet.

"It wasn't a lie," Shadowlight said as he sidled up next to her and looked over the map. "Gran spoke the truth about Gryton being able to track the spell back to this location. Though he won't come back this way. There are too many humans here, and they can now see past Gryton's own personal shielding spells thanks to my father's work."

The kid was correct—his father had been busy weaving dampening spells all over the base.

Shadowlight butted her in the stomach, looking for a head scratch. "Gryton would, as you say, be taken out before he could harm us."

Anna grunted and studied the map that the tracking spell was linked to in a new light.

Well, damn. So much for feeling the kid was safe from harm. Now the reason for all the guards in the room took on a new light. She'd just thought they were there to 'guard' her, the kid, and Gran and to ensure the other gargoyles and fae behaved.

Anna glanced back around the room, seeing it with new eyes.

All non-essential personnel had been removed—even the scientists had been ordered away, much to their loud and strident denials. Besides the ever-watchful guards, only a handful of the command staff was present. It made sense.

They were relaying intel to a secondary command site elsewhere.

She and Shadowlight were still present only because no one could forcibly move the half ton of gargoyle against his will.

Around the outside walls were the screens showing real-time data, satellite and drone feeds, radar, troop placements—everything trackable was being tracked using both magical and mundane means.

"Gryton isn't trying to evade left or right. He's moving in a straight line." Gran pointed at the markers on the map, and then looked up at Major Resnick. "He knows he's fallen into our net. Now he's only interested in escape using the hamadryad. Keep your men out of his path. He'll kill them before they have a chance to inflict serious harm on him. Leave him to us."

Anna could see Colonel Tremblay having trouble following Gran's suggestion. After a long hesitation, he ordered the teams to keep their distance and allow Specter Team to execute.

Anna grinned at the name given to the gargoyles.

"I want a team name," Shadowlight said. "Why don't we have a name? We're a good team. We almost beat Gryton when he attacked us."

"That's not how I remember it going down."

"He wanted to take you both alive," Gran said in all seriousness and then added, "You're T-team," She grinned, "As in toddler team."

"Nah, more like Pre-School One." Anna turned serious again as another green blob floating above the map flared and went dark. Her fists tightened in silent rage. It marked the present position of a team just forty feet to the northwest of Gryton's current location.

The darkening of the tracking spells couldn't tell the watchers how many in each team had been killed. It only signaled a powerful wave of magic had just rolled over that unit's location.

Human tech didn't fare any better under the intense magical attacks.

Colonel Tremblay ordered more teams to assist.

Anna just hoped there was more than bodies to assist when they got there.

CHAPTER THIRTY-EIGHT

From her position underneath the boughs of her hamadryad, Lillian watched and waited.

And waited some more.

Dropping to all fours, she paced around the tree's perimeter, the weight of her new armor and swords shifted slightly as she moved, but as promised, they made no noise. At first, the change in her balance had felt strange to her, but she'd grown used to it quickly enough.

When her feet made to wander even as her mind was, Gregory huffed out a warning growl. She tilted her head in acknowledgment and stalked back to the tree's base.

Gregory had commanded her to wait at the hamadryad's base, saying the tree would protect her from Commander Gryton.

Lillian wasn't so sure. What she felt from the tree was vague, confusing, but it didn't feel like a warning or alarm. She'd already told him of her concerns more than once, and he denied them flat out. She was debating revisiting that conversation again. If there was even a slim chance her hamadryad and Gryton were working together, it was just too important to ignore.

"Gregory," she called to his mind. *"Link with me. You need to feel my tree's emotions."*

He turned an ear back in her direction but didn't move from his spot next to the stone pillar marking the north entrance to the maze. Darkness was guarding the south entrance. They both claimed Gryton would likely navigate the labyrinth instead of going through it or over it since the cedar maze had a taste for blood and magic, thanks to the leshii.

If they got through the next few hours, she planned to thank Greenborrow for planting and designing the maze all those years ago.

Long after Lillian had given up on getting a response from Gregory, he answered her earlier inquiry. *"The hamadryad is alert, sensing our battle readiness, but she is not concerned. She does not consider Gryton a dire threat to us and trusts me to be able to dispatch him."*

Lillian decided Gregory was a little rusty on hamadryad speech. *"I think you might be a little overconfident there."*

"That is why we have Darkness, Greenborrow, River, two dozen fae archers, and many more human snipers."

Lillian didn't correct him on any of it, not even the snipers. The soldiers, while they did carry big guns and looked like they knew how to use them, weren't snipers. Then again, maybe the snipers were far enough off she couldn't sense them.

That was all well and good, but the hamadryad might not consider Gryton a threat because she had brought him here for some purpose.

Lillian liked her tree better before she started thinking and waving all her magic around.

She could feel the steady current of magic as it flowed away from the tree and on out into the Mortal Realm. Not for the first time she wondered if the tree was planning on converting the Mortal Realm into a second Magic Realm.

"As much as I didn't like having command of all that power, I think I still preferred me being the Sorceress instead of you," she mumbled to her tree. "At least that way, when everything goes sideways, I'll know who to blame." But now?

Perhaps sensing her agitation or understanding her words, the hamadryad's branches shuddered, and three of the closest boughs reached out to touch her on the shoulder.

It was a pat of reassurance.

She wasn't reassured.

All will be as it should be.

Lillian jerked back in surprise. *Ha, and Gregory says hamadryads can't talk—bullshit.*

The hamadryad retracted her branches, and Lillian was still mulling over the words when the tree added something else.

The bright warmth has come.

That one took her off guard for a second before she deciphered the meaning.

Gregory had said Gryton was a fire elemental, beyond that no one seemed to know what he was.

But bright warmth might refer to the heat of a fire.

"Gregory! Gryton is coming. I think he's already within the maze." Then as an afterthought, she shouted a final order at him. "Do anything you must to kill Gryton."

Lillian's words of warning and final order spurred Gregory into a higher level of battle readiness.

Shadows and the intense power from the Magic Realm swirled around him in a robust half-seen current. The abundance of raw power was waiting for him to shape it into whatever spells he would require.

In truth, he didn't know what Gryton was, or what it would take to stop him.

He just hoped magic from the Spirit Realm wasn't required. Lillian's fears about that power might be warranted. To call upon it a second time would probably kill him. The scars were still visible against his dark skin from his last near-fatal attempt.

There was a slight click and then a short sound of static from the humans' radios, and then silence again.

But it was enough to signal Gryton had been spotted.

Gran had said that was how the humans would know when Gryton was almost upon them.

Stretching his senses out beyond the glade's center, he scanned for the commander within the maze's corridors. As he'd expected, there was no sign of his opponent.

Lips curling back from his teeth, he growled softly. Darkness heard and answered from his position at the other end of the glade.

Whitethorn had demanded to be present though Gregory thought it might just be to guard against any human treachery.

The other's distrust and tension crawled across his skin, and Gregory's wings shuddered at the prickly sensation. Jaws agape slightly, he tasted the breeze, seeking information on his enemy. Nothing.

His ears tracked every little sound, every little shift the humans and fae made—though the humans were louder. Each heartbeat, each breath, each rustle of the leaves, he looked for what didn't belong.

Still nothing.

He sent another wave of magic outward, seeking his prey's thoughts, hunting intentions as he would any target. It had never failed him before.

Why could he not sense their enemy when the hamadryad already had?

It made no sense.

Then with a sudden dreadful understanding, he knew why he couldn't sense Gryton. The slave collar had another master besides Lillian.

Gryton had created them, he might be able to use it to hide his presence. Panic threatened to steal Gregory's confidence, but he forced the useless flood of emotions back. Reason returned. If Gryton had the power to command him as Lillian could, his opponent wouldn't risk a fight here, nor would he have attempted to use Shadowlight as bait. He'd simply have commanded Gregory to take Lillian and return with her to the Battle Goddess's temple.

That gave him a tiny bit of comfort. Lillian started toward

him again. He glowered at her, and she halted but didn't return to her spot. At least she was still within the protection of the hamadryad's branches.

His gaze was just sliding away from Lillian when Darkness burst into motion, leaping toward the maze entrance he was guarding.

Shadows raced ten feet before him and collided with a wall of fire. A second wave of the fiery power exploded outward from the maze's opening to meet the gargoyle's magical attack.

Bright light seared Gregory's eyes when the two opposing forces met.

His vision was still obscured by dark spots, but he was already summoning a spear of magic to penetrate his enemy's shields.

A loud explosion of sound abused his ears as the human soldiers nearest Gryton's position found a target.

A shard of fire broke away from the wall and raced toward the humans. Gregory was faster. A wall of his own power deflected Gryton's away from the human soldiers and into the green cedar walls beside them.

The cedars burst into flame. Gregory didn't have time to worry about the maze, but raced toward it, calling more shadow magic to mix with the smoke and flames. When it was a sufficient churning mass to hide his energy spears, he sent it ahead as he raced toward Gryton.

Gregory circled to the right, avoiding Gryton's shifting wall of flames and sent a spear of power at his enemy. Swatting the spear aside at the last moment, Commander Gryton lunged to the side and nearly into Darkness's drawn sword.

Gryton deflected the point and sidestepped away from the gargoyle and took several steps into the glade before a rain of arrows and bullets diverted him back toward Darkness.

Gregory leaped toward the enemy fire elemental just as he lashed out.

A massive ball of fire and molten heat smashed into the ground five body-lengths to Gregory's left, shaking the ground hard enough to lift Gregory off his feet. He tumbled sideways through the air until he collided with the tall cedar walls of the maze. Their springy growth softened his landing, but it took a few precious seconds to free himself. Each second, he expected to feel Gryton's punishing fire upon his skin.

Finally, free of his green prison, he dropped to the ground and sought out Gryton. His enemy was only twenty feet away, still close to the maze's south entrance. Darkness was doggedly hounding him with sharp little bits of shadow magic, preventing him from getting closer to the hamadryad.

The other gargoyle was not without injury. One wing membrane was split and blackened by fire, and he was favoring his left foreleg. Other oozing burnt patches criss-crossed his hide.

Gryton was not without his injuries either. One of the fae had managed to land an arrow. The shaft had gone straight through Gryton's thigh where the armor was missing from the previous attack on Shadowlight.

It had probably been the fae's last act in this life. A glance behind confirmed what his other senses had already told him.

Many of the fae and human soldiers had been killed,

Gryton's formidable power having incinerated all the magical protections he and Darkness had erected.

Gregory stalked Gryton, calling on more magic from the Magic Realm, but fearing it wouldn't be enough to stop this fire elemental.

The hamadryad was also summoning power. This from the Spirit Realm, he felt its renewing chill against his skin. That raw power might be the only thing capable of extinguishing Gryton's fiery magic. At least Lillian was safe, protected by the Sorceress.

He thanked the hamadryad silently, and then reassured of Lillian's safety, he turned his full attention back to the lethal enemy who must be destroyed at all cost.

Gryton was not some low-level servant of the Battle Goddess. He had to be one of the last surviving fire demons from the ancient time.

Gregory had thought he and the Sorceress had eradicated ones such as him long ago. They must have missed one, or he had been hiding behind the Battle Goddess's power all this time.

Either way, it was past time Gryton returned to the Spirit Realm.

Gregory and Darkness lunged at the same time, sending their magics out ahead of them. Their combined power hit Gryton squarely in the chest. The elemental roared in pain and rage, then lashed out with another wave of burning power. Gregory returned the magic blast for blast.

But what would have vaporized almost any other enemy had little effect on this one. Worse, Gregory could feel himself weakening faster than his enemy.

It had to be the tattoo draining some of his magic away harmlessly, so it wasn't reaching Gryton with full strength.

Gregory was pondering this new problem when Darkness raced past him and shouted, "Protect my children!"

"Stop!"

But Darkness had already raced into the river of Gregory's magic and together, their combined power was enough for Darkness to slip past Gryton's defensive shields. Gregory lunged after him, clearing the swirling mist, fire, and smoke in time to see Darkness impale himself upon Gryton's sword.

The visor of Gryton's helmet was up, and Gregory saw his enemy's startled expression.

Darkness snatched at Gryton's wrist, locking them together and Gregory realized what the other gargoyle was trying to do.

Chilled power from the Spirit Realm rushed toward them, turning Darkness's skin to stone, as his soul prepared to depart.

All gargoyles returned to Lord Death upon their own demise, and Darkness was planning on taking Gryton with him.

If Gryton was an ancient fire demon as Gregory speculated, Darkness's sacrifice might not be sufficient to drag their enemy along with him.

Lillian screamed her father's name as she started toward them.

Darkness spun out hundreds of filaments of his shadow magic, attempting to tie the other male to him, to hold onto Gryton with more than physical strength, but he was losing the battle.

Jerking with desperate strength, Gryton freed himself.

Drawing his own sword, Gregory attacked. In a blur of speed, he drove his sword's point forward, but the commander's second blade deflected his own. In retaliation, he used his blade-tipped tail to slash at Gryton's unprotected face. The fire elemental proved to be just a hair faster.

Drawing his second sword from its scabbard, Gregory sent the deadly sharp tip slicing toward Gryton's neck.

The commander caught the sword, the force of the blow cutting deep.

Fire and blood welled up from between Gryton's hands where he held Gregory's sword trapped. Moments later, an intense wave of molten heat rushed up the length of Gregory's sword, vaporizing both blade and hilt.

Pain lanced up his arm and shoulder, but he drove into Gryton, grappling with him and forcing him back, away from the hamadryad one step at a time.

"Let me go, and no one else need die this day," Gryton rasped. "I only want away from this cursed land before it brings about the death of us all."

Ah. That was truth. Gripping his enemy by the throat, Gregory felt something of Gryton's thoughts, emotions, and power.

He was a fire elemental, but not a fire demon of the ancient world. He was something else, something newer—young compared to Gregory's vast age.

And half-trained as he was, Gryton was ruled by his power—he didn't control it.

Could he be crossing swords with the Battle Goddess's son?

How had such a thing come about? If so, how had she hidden him for so long?

Gryton's power surged again, greater this time than before. Only Gregory's talons, where they had pierced through the commander's armor, held his enemy locked in place and prevented him from being tossed aside by the blast wave.

The power raced past him, out into the glade where it caught Lillian as she ran to his aid. The force lifted her off her feet and tossed her back toward her tree where she hit the ground and rolled with the limpness of death or unconsciousness.

He slammed his weight into Gryton, forcing him to his knees.

Lillian wasn't dead. He would have known instantly if she was, but still, he worried for her.

Without his spirit magic, he knew he couldn't defeat Gryton, not quickly, certainly not fast enough to prevent other friends, allies, and family from dying.

But Darkness had shown him the way.

With a last look where Lillian lay, the mother of his yet unborn child, alive and beautiful in her gargoyle form, he closed his eyes and called to a power greater than himself.

It answered his call with a joyful rush. His scars flared to life and began to glow as the trapped power looked for the easiest route of escape.

Gregory locked his jaws against the first wave of pain as his body struggled to hold itself together even as more magic flowed into him from the Spirit Realm.

Lillian had ordered him to do whatever was required to win, and she hadn't realized her mistake, and now she was unconscious, unable to stop him, for which he was grateful.

Gryton kicked and twisted, but Gregory held fast as the cold power of the Spirit Realm built within him.

He sent his mind seeking Lillian's, to find her coming back to consciousness. It was too late to stop him from destroying himself and Gryton along with him, even if she issued another order. *"Beloved, I am sorry. I saw no other way to save you and our child. I want more than anything to be there, but I must go for a while. Know I will return to you, even though it will be many years. Good-bye."*

Lillian jerked and rolled to her feet. "No! Gregory, no!"

Something else answered Lillian's desperate call, and he felt the ground shaking and rolling under him. The force of a sudden violent surge tore his enemy from his clasp.

Gregory cursed and tried to go after him, but the ground heaved again as hundreds of thin reddish ropes coiled around his body. Tiny filaments sprouted from them and crawled along his skin.

Roots.

They were roots.

The hamadryad shuddered, her branches quaking as if a hurricane was bearing down on them. The ground heaved again.

One of Lillian's endearing but naïve questions from an earlier conversation came back to him in a rush. She'd asked if the tree was going to relocate and walk back to the Magic Realm or some such. He'd brushed away her question as silly.

Now, he wasn't so sure.

He wondered if the last thing he was going to see in this life was the marvel of a fifty-foot tree taking her first few steps.

He'd seen many strange things.

A walking tree wasn't one of them.

His disbelieving thoughts snapped back into sharp focus when a thousand tiny roots prodded at his scars. Their questing tips sank in, digging deep, past skin and into muscle and bone.

He roared in pain as the tree began to feed.

CHAPTER THIRTY-NINE

*L*illian staggered to her feet and felt Gregory's mind merge with hers, to say goodbye. She screamed her denial and started toward him, but her hamadryad reacted faster. She could only watch in horror as more roots shifted below the ground.

The roots got there first. Lillian arrived at his side just as he roared in agony.

Tiny filaments dug into his body. She felt what he felt at that moment. Blood and power leaked out a thousand tiny punctures.

Horror and helplessness filled Lillian, and she drew her dagger and reached for the nearest root.

No harm. Heal our beloved, her hamadryad whispered into her thoughts.

Lillian's hand froze halfway to her target as she realized what her eyes were seeing.

The lattice-like webbing of a shielding spell glowed pale between the reddish roots covering him. Skin or armor, the roots didn't care and dug into each equally. The tree fed upon his blood, but she was also drawing off the excess magic trying to tear itself free of Gregory's body.

The hamadryad was preventing Gregory from being torn apart.

Still, it had to be unbearably painful, and Lillian paced a circle around him. At least he seemed to have passed out.

Gryton had staggered off several steps, heading in the direction of her hamadryad. Lillian narrowed her eyes and then sought out her mother.

She was bent over next to Darkness's stone form, and a new lump grew in Lillian's throat. River rose from beside her mate, tears leaving tracks down her face.

Her father—Lillian had never really known him, they'd only had days together.

It was not fair.

It was not just.

Well, by God and the Divine Ones, she'd just make her own damn justice.

River met Lillian's eyes and then gave a nod in wordless agreement. With a swirl of long skirts and the hollow ring of twin swords being drawn, River darted after the retreating form of Gryton.

Lillian followed, her own swords ringing loud to her heightened gargoyle senses.

River's sharp steel swept out in a deadly arc toward Gryton's neck. He whirled and blocked, twisting his upper body enough to force River's swords down and away.

He kicked at her, but she danced away and then darted back just as fast.

Swords clashed in a blur of bright silver light and the ring of honed blades. River slashed at Gryton. He snarled as the dryad's sword cut a four-inch gash just above where the arrow had hit. In retaliation, he gave River her own red, gaping wound on her right arm. She came at him again, their sword hilts locking together for a moment. He took advantage of the opening to deliver a crippling blow to her shoulder with his armored elbow. There was a sickening crack, and River lost her grip on one sword.

The injury barely slowed her, and she continued to harry Gryton with her remaining sword.

Lillian stepped in, taking up the rhythm of the fight. It was apparent she was outclassed, but her interference was enough to prevent Gryton from winning the battle.

The battle continued for longer than Lillian would have liked, somewhere behind her Gregory was still fighting for his life. At least Gryton was weakening. Perhaps River sensed it too because her attack turned vicious, Gryton barely managed to block in time.

"Let me go," he said suddenly, directing his statement at River. "You know what will happen if I lose control of my magic here."

"Perhaps I would have cared before you killed my mate," River thrust her sword's point at him, catching him in the side, penetrating his armor. "Now I will send you back to the Battle Goddess a piece at a time. What should I send back first? Your head?"

"If you force my hand, we'll all die here in this forsaken land."

Lillian decided a change in tactic was in order and dropped to all fours and rammed Gryton in the back, her horns ground against his armor and found a seam, stabbing deep, up under where a rib would have been on a human. Just as quickly, she dropped and rolled, coming up several feet away from him.

She remembered what his blood had done to one of Gregory's swords.

Gryton stumbled sideways, and she thought the bastard was finally going down for the count, but it was just a maneuver to avoid River and her lethal blade.

But Gryton was desperate now. She could smell the stink of fear and exhaustion upon him even over the hot, dry smell of fire.

When River closed in on Gryton for the kill, he roared, and a wave of heat blasted out from his location. River was closer, and it rammed into her with the force of a train.

Lillian darted behind one of the small standing stones circling her tree. The shelter was enough to save her from mortal injury, but she could already smell the burnt flesh of her exposed wings.

They didn't hurt, which was probably really bad.

"You should have let me go," Gryton said as he limped into her field of vision. "We'll die together. I suppose there is some symmetry in that. Mayhap the Divine Ones are laughing at us all." He'd lost his sword somewhere, but no longer really needed it.

A film of fire crawled across every inch of his armor and danced in the breeze of its own making.

CHAPTER FORTY

Anna stood shoulder to shoulder with Gran and watched the map. She was still somewhat surprised she and Shadowlight were allowed in the war room.

Still, she imagined Gran and her magic had a lot to do with the whole calm atmosphere thing.

But even Gran's magic couldn't keep everyone calm when all the little floating lights above the map marking the maze's center blinked out.

The tension increased a few more notches, and Anna eyed the others in the room as they continued their assignments as calmly as if it was a training exercise. Colonel Tremblay gave the order to signal all other teams to move in and engage.

As a group, the senior officers turned their attention from the map to the live feeds, which showed the real-time view of the glade, as seen by a number of helmet cams and an aerial drone circling the area.

Anna trailed behind Shadowlight as he came to stand next to one of the screens. He was silent, staring at the screen with an unhappy expression. It was worry, harder to read on a gargoyle, sure, but worry all the same.

Having the kid watch the flickering lights on the magic-enhanced map was one thing. Having him watch live feeds as his family faced off against a formidable enemy, was something else.

"Shadowlight shouldn't be watching this," she directed her statement at Gran because there was no way she was going to interrupt her superiors. She was still too uneasy about the concept of her continued freedom.

The older woman frowned. "No. Likely not."

"I'm staying." The note of finality in his tone shared qualities with a concrete wall reinforced with rebar.

There was no way an eight-year-old should sound so damned confident of himself. "I don't think…"

"I've seen worse."

"Well, you bloody well shouldn't have," Anna countered.

"Fighting the Riven and Gryton has shown me true evil doesn't care if one is a child or an adult. We can all still die."

Anna felt ill. "Good Lord, kid. When all this is over, we're so going to sit and watch some Saturday morning cartoons, and you're just going to be a kid."

Everyone was looking at them now.

Major Resnick was giving her his best 'shut the fuck up' look while Gran just looked thoughtful. Colonel Tremblay's intense stare was enough to make her come to attention and seal her mouth firmly shut. His eyes remained on her for a second more and then returned to the screens.

Well, damn it. Shadowlight was just a kid. He should get to be one.

Then all hell broke loose on screen, and there was no time to worry or argue.

She watched in helpless fury as Tin Man went about the business of systematically exterminating every human and fae present in the glade.

It wasn't that fast, of course, but after several minutes of battle, there were few left to face him. It came down to just the two male gargoyles. Even they were having trouble.

"Father!" Shadowlight cried out in horror when Darkness fell.

With the absolute certainty of hindsight, Anna knew she should have made the kid leave, somehow.

Shadowlight darted toward the door. Gran called to him as Colonel Tremblay issued more orders, other officers relaying them on down the chain of command.

"Wait, kid!" Anna shouted above the noise. "I'm coming too."

She heard Colonel Tremblay order a strike package as she raced toward Shadowlight. Like hell, she thought, knowing what she was about to do next could only end in a court-martial, but the kid's family was there, and they might still be alive.

Shadowlight paused at the door, half in and half out, long enough for her to reach his side. He dipped a wing in invitation, and she realized he intended for her to ride on his back. Well, he was the size of a large pony, so why not.

"Mackenzie, halt!" Major Resnick shouted.

"One minute," she said to Shadowlight when she noticed Major Resnick rushing up to her. He shoved a gun and some ammo into her hands, and then stuffed a few more things into a pack and handed it to her too.

"Go kill that bastard for me," Major Resnick bit out. "He's killed way too many of my men. He doesn't get to live."

Anna glanced at the pack and saw the grenades and gave Resnick a wolfish grin.

"Just hold him off until we can send reinforcements." Resnick patted her on the arm. "And don't get killed. Your father would never forgive me."

Anna nodded and then slung a leg over an impatient Shadowlight.

Then the gargoyle was off and running, and Anna was holding on for dear life. Outside, she realized Shadowlight wasn't planning on running the whole way. He spread his wings and leaped up into the air. Her shout of surprise was stolen by the wind, and then she was too busy not falling off to scream in terror.

CHAPTER FORTY-ONE

After that last powerful blast wave of fiery magic, Lillian gave herself a shake, rolled to her feet, and prepared to face Gryton and death standing up. The hand not clutching her only remaining sword strayed to her belly. Her mind raced for a way to save herself and her unborn child.

But Gregory and Darkness were down. River was unconscious and covered in terrible burns. Lillian could smell the burnt flesh scent from here. Her hamadryad was busy healing Gregory, River, and Darkness, too, she sensed. Though what her tree could do for her father, she didn't know. Gryton had all but gutted him.

She'd heard his heart stop, but he had turned to stone.

Was he still alive?

She wished she knew more about gargoyles. But she didn't and there wasn't time to worry.

The remaining humans and fae were dead, dying, or no better off than her mother.

She raised her blade for a final defense against Gryton.

Although, by the growing intensity of the fire surrounding him, it wouldn't be a sword fight.

"You. Destroyed. My. Maze," roared a voice almost deep enough to rattle Lillian's teeth in her skull. She glanced to the left in time to see a ten-foot-tall troll-like Greenborrow slam Gryton with a massive spike-studded club.

The much altered Greenborrow continued past Lillian in pursuit of his prey. He landed a second hit, caught Gryton just under the chin and flipped him on over onto his back.

"Those were my little ones! I planted them. This is my forest!" Another punishing blow punctuated his statement, and Gryton flew back another fifteen feet.

Gryton hissed something Lillian didn't understand as he got his feet under him again. He was moving much slower than before, but still moving. Those blows should have killed Gryton. He should have been dead several times over. Lillian began to worry Gryton couldn't be killed.

No, he could be killed. Gregory had been going to sacrifice himself to do it—that meant Gryton could be killed. They just had to figure out how.

"And you were welcome to the forest, leshii," Gryton hissed out. "I care nothing for this realm. All I have ever wanted is to return home. But you and your people, and that meddling hamadryad would not allow me to leave." He directed the last bit at Lillian. "Now this world will burn along with me."

Gryton raised his hand to the level of his shoulders and then opened his fist, palm out toward the leshii. Fire raced down Gryton's arms and leaped across the distance. Greenborrow moved faster than Lillian thought someone of his size could, but he didn't clear the fiery wave completely, and it caught him just below the elbow.

It reduced the club and the lower part of Greenborrow's arm to ash. The only reason Greenborrow might not die of the wound, Lillian saw, was because it had been cauterized by the same fire which had taken his arm.

Lillian bared her fangs and flexed her talons.

Gryton was raising his other hand to blast the leshii with a second wave of power when Lillian lunged forward.

She was coming to realize she probably wasn't walking away from this fight when a loud war cry split the air.

"Heads up asshole. Incoming," Corporal Mackenzie snatched the pin out of the grenade she was holding and tossed it at Gryton. "Catch that, Tin Man."

It landed a meter from Gryton's feet as Shadowlight bolted past.

Her little brother and the human circled around just as the grenade blew, sending Gryton and a cloud of dirt flying. Had Gryton been even remotely mortal, he would have died about ten or fifteen blows back, but he just crawled back to his feet, his hellfire burning more hotly than before.

Anna and Shadowlight came around for another volley. The human landed two more grenades almost as close as the first one.

Gryton stumbled back and away as Anna lobbed another grenade at him.

Again, and again, the two courted death to herd Gryton back toward the tree where the hamadryad was reaching for him with outstretched branches.

Seeing an opening, Lillian called shadow magic to her aid. She shaped it into little dagger-like shards as she'd seen her mother do. Once she had several hovering in the air, she raced forward, rejoining the fight. Her tiny biting shadows harassed Gryton. They were not lethal, but she summoned more and more of them until they resembled a swarm of bees attacking the commander.

Closing in on his location, she increased her speed and then rammed him hard enough to send him back the last few feet and within the hamadryad's reach.

Branches slammed him into the ground where more of the reddish roots sought entrance into Gryton's armor.

A storm of magic boiled up where molten fire met cold spirit magic.

Thunder rumbled. The earth shook. Lillian lost her footing and went down. Shadowlight and the human went sprawling on the opposite side of the glade just as more soldiers arrived on the scene.

They froze at the sight of the tree wrapping Commander Gryton in layers of roots and power.

Lillian wasn't sure if the tree was trying to crush the life out of him or if she was draining him of power as she had Gregory.

Whatever the hamadryad was doing, it was a massive spell growing in size and power as Lillian watched.

The very air vibrated to the flow of power. The flames, which had earlier been crawling across Gryton's armor, were now hissing and flickering like a guttering candle. Well, at least, the parts of him she could see under the mound of fibrous roots.

On the other side of the glade, Shadowlight and Anna scrambled to their feet. The human soldier had an assault rifle pointed at Gryton, and Shadowlight was inching closer as well. Both looked uncertain what to do with the hamadryad still draining Gryton.

Lillian tightened her fist around the one sword she'd managed to hold on to. Taking one step and then another in the enemy's direction, she switched her hold to a two-handed one.

She might not know what her hamadryad was doing to Gryton, but she knew what needed doing. The power in the air intensified the closer she got to his location. Layers of magic thickened in the air, increasing in resistance with each step.

Lillian was almost upon her prey when she felt her hamadryad's thoughts merge with hers.

Gryton is needed.

"Like hell."

She raised her sword above her head, willing herself to plunge the blade down and separate his damned head from his shoulders. Surely all her gargoyle strength would be enough to end him.

She just had to do it.

One swift downward thrust and then it would be over, a threat neutralized. Justice served.

Closing her eyes, she shifted her weight and then thrust the blade down. Gargoyle strength and the magical blade cut through the layers of resistance protecting Gryton.

Bright light seared her eyes even with them closed tight, and still, she forced the blade down until its tip buried itself in the spongy loam of her glade.

She didn't have to open her eyes to know Gryton was gone.

Gone.

Not dead.

Her damned meddling hamadryad.

"Where is he?"

The hamadryad didn't respond, at least not in thoughts or emotions Lillian could understand, but more power washed outward from the tree. A soothing flow of magic took away the throb of burns, the ache of cuts, and the thousand tiny abuses of a battered body.

Even her damaged wings were healed, but it did nothing for her emotional stress.

Gryton was gone, out of her reach. She didn't know where. Yet, she doubted it was back to the Magic Realm. The hamadryad had alluded to needing him. So, she'd probably stashed him somewhere out of the way.

The Spirit Realm would have been nice.

Lillian sighed and calmed her thoughts. Raging about an escaped enemy would do nothing to aid the survivors.

Immediate danger past, or at least out of her reach, she turned and took in the damage, her heart in her throat.

Gregory was an unmoving lump, and her father was cold stone. The fluctuating waves of power coming from her hamadryad prevented Lillian from sensing anything else.

Conflicted, Lillian turned a slow circle, stretching her magic and senses to see if they still lived.

The lump of roots shifted, and Gregory fought his way onto his forearms, his ears shifting this way and that as he searched for her.

Relief and adrenaline spurred her into running. She skidded to a stop next to him as he fought to free himself from the hamadryad's roots.

"Lillian?"

He turned his head and sniffed.

"Shhh, I'm here. We won." Then she saw the blood seeping from under his closed lids. By the Goddess, he was blinded. "Oh, my poor gargoyle." She reached for his face, but there were so many wounds she didn't know where to touch him without causing more pain. She settled for stroking his horns.

"I will heal." He brushed his muzzle along her arm, leaving a streak of blood behind. "Are you hurt?"

"No," she said in a rush, "I was, but it was not as bad as you, and my hamadryad already healed me."

"I owe her my life."

"The tattoo almost killed you. I'm so sorry."

"It was my choice. Not your fault." Gregory tried to get his feet under him, but the roots still held him locked in their embrace. He slumped back and rolled onto his side. "Perhaps I will rest here a little while longer."

"Why haven't you turned to stone to heal?"

He nuzzled her hand and licked at her fingers. "The Sorceress is still healing me. I know my wounds look fierce, and they are, but she is healing them far more quickly than I could during my stone sleep."

"If you say so."

"She's healing me from the inside and then working her way outward." Gregory sighed and then allowed his head to rest on the ground. "It will be some hours yet before I am healed enough to leave under my own power. You'll have to stay here. I see the tattoos still exist."

"Of course I'm staying. I would stay even if the tattoo didn't make it a requirement." Lillian huffed angrily and then lay down next to Gregory. She might have offered to go aid the other survivors, but no one else was near enough to satisfy the tattoo's need for closeness.

From her position next to Gregory, she watched as more soldiers and fae made their way out of the maze and into the meadow. They scanned the area for signs of danger, and then slowly approached the survivors—though the humans were as uncertain of what help they could be as Lillian herself was.

Every survivor was covered in masses of fibrous roots, being healed by the hamadryad.

Corporal Mackenzie and Shadowlight were patrolling between River and Darkness. River was still alive. Lillian could hear her slow heartbeat and see the slight rise and fall of her breast with each breath.

Darkness was slumped on the grass, still a cold, unmoving statue. However, the fine mesh of roots growing over his stone skin gave Lillian hope he might return to them one day. She doubted her hamadryad would otherwise be lavishing attention on him. Shadowlight must have seen Gregory stirring, for he abandoned his parents to come over to Gregory and Lillian. Anna trailed behind him, as if the human wasn't willing to let the youth out of her sight.

Her little brother sniffed Gregory over and gave a little whine, but he didn't say anything aloud. However, his eyes asked a great pleading question.

"Gregory," she asked, not really wanting to give him something else to worry or feel guilty over, but both she and Shadowlight needed to know. "Can our father heal from what Gryton did to him?"

"Gryton is more formidable than I had…. expected. But Darkness is old and powerful, too. All gargoyles have a choice when they are mortally injured. Return to the Lord of the

Underworld in spirit form and then be reborn or sleep the stone sleep. I am sorry. Either way will take him out of your lives for many years. He is stone, so he chose to stay with his family. Even if he cannot be a flesh and blood father to either of you, he is here in spirit. Your father loves you both very much."

"I was not sure if he did love me because of what the Battle Goddess made me into," Shadowlight confessed. "Thank you for telling me this."

Anna came forward and patted Shadowlight awkwardly on one shoulder but remained silent.

"He loves you both more than his own life," Gregory answered.

Lillian continued to sit and guard her beloved long after Shadowlight, followed by the ever-watchful Anna, had returned to his pacing between River and Darkness.

Gran arrived at some point in the company of yet more soldiers. Lillian recognized Major Resnick. If there were more brass with him, she didn't recognize them.

Resnick and Gran worked to keep the peace and coordinate the two different factions. By some miracle, and maybe it was divine intervention, the fae and the humans held to the earlier alliance. It may have helped that the hamadryad was healing both human and fae survivors, showing no preference between the two.

Lillian was far too tired to care. She rested her muzzle on her forearms and closed her eyes. She didn't sleep deeply though, still not trusting the uneasy peace, and her ears tracked every sound in the glade.

CHAPTER FORTY-TWO

Several hours later, Lillian had awakened in dryad form after having fallen asleep even after telling herself she wouldn't. She never knew if it was a dream, or simply the act of sleep itself which triggered her to shift from gargoyle back to dryad form. That was a question to ask Gregory another time.

Gran had told her the scientists were practically tripping over each other to get her reverse shift on tape.

Lillian frowned at her reflection in the bathroom mirror.

Yeah, she was sure there was going to be scientists and military and complex politics in her future. Luckily, Gran was dealing with that mess for the moment.

For the rest of this night, all she had to face was a long, hot bubble bath, where she planned to soak away the day's worries along with the aches of her abused body. Her hand strayed to her belly, still marveling at the life which grew there.

Gregory had checked her over as soon as he was healed

and back on his feet and proclaimed their child was still a strong life force within her.

The relief which had washed over her had left her weak-kneed and ridiculously happy. That mellow warmth had stayed with her all the way back to the house and up the stairs. It had even survived watching Gregory strip and step into the shower where the powerful showerheads washed away the layers of dried blood and loam to show her the raised ridges of pale scar tissue crisscrossing his body.

Her beautiful gargoyle looked like someone had cut him up and sewn him back together.

"They'll fade again in a few days," Gregory said as he stepped out of the shower.

"Do they still hurt?"

Of course they did, she scolded herself. How could they not?

Gregory shrugged. "They still ache a little. The warmth of the shower helped."

He turned to the vanity and hunted through the drawers for a comb to tame the wild mess of his mane.

Her eyes slid sideways to her bubble bath and then back to Gregory. The heat of the water would do him good. It was a big Jacuzzi-type tub. She went over and sat on one of the steps leading up to it, and then eyed Gregory's large form again.

"Come here." She patted the step next to her.

"There are certainly more comfortable places to sit," he said with an accompanying flick of his tail.

"How comfortable is it to rest on your wings? Do you think you could fit?" she gestured at the tub again. "The heat would do you good."

He looked like he was going to shake his head, so she decided to sweeten the deal. "I'll groom your mane for you while you soak."

Gregory huffed softly and then walked over to the tub. He discarded the towels he'd already wrapped around his hips and stepped into the water without a word. Lillian turned her head to the side so he wouldn't see her grin.

When he relaxed back into the water, she scooted behind his head, and equipped with a comb, began work on his mane. She'd only taken three sweeps at the task when Gregory reached behind him and stroked her leg where it was draped over the side into the water.

Wordlessly, he reached for the other leg and then arranged them both, so they draped over his shoulders and then allowed the heels to rest against his pectorals. She sighed when he started to rub them in a skillful massage.

"Foot massage in payment for untangling this mess," Lillian tapped the comb playfully against one of his horns. "Sounds about right to me."

He rumbled out a wordless agreement as he worked.

As much as she enjoyed the foot rub and grooming his mane, only a part of Lillian's attention was on the tasks at hand. When she closed her eyes, what played over and over on the backs of her lids was seeing Gregory about to be torn apart by a magic that was his birthright. He'd been going to sacrifice himself to save the rest of them.

It was noble and brave, but she didn't want him to die for her.

She wanted him to live to raise their child.

She wanted him as her mate, wanted them to live a long and happy lifetime together.

And she'd come far too close to losing him.

Lillian leaned down and pressed a kiss to first one horn and then the other. Gregory paused in his massage and tilted his face back to study her. Then decided, she pulled her feet from his grasp and turned sideways so she could stand and come around the side.

He was still looking up at her questioningly, though he had to know what she was thinking. Untying her robe, she shrugged it off her shoulders. Underneath she was naked. Gregory inhaled, his lips parting to better take in her scent.

Leaning forward, she braced her hands against his shoulders and placed kisses along the side of his face and neck. He rumbled and returned the favor, wrapping his hands around her hips to help her balance.

There was a ripple in the suds, and then his tail emerged from the depths and slid along her right leg from ankle to hip and back again before it coiled around the calf to anchor her in place. Not that she felt the least bit like running away. Gregory rumbled again and dragged her closer until she was in danger of losing her balance and falling into the tub with him.

"Hmmm, love, that would likely be painful for all parties."

The way his brow furrowed was almost comical. "Strange little dryad, I have no plans to let you come to harm anytime soon."

He hoisted her down into the tub with him. Lillian squealed, but it quickly changed to a surprised gasp as Gregory settled her in his lap. She tried to keep some of her weight supported in her arms so she wouldn't knee him too badly somewhere sensitive. "I hadn't intended for this to...I mean I know you're dead tired. I don't expect you to..."

Gregory laughed, shaking her entire body. "Nor had I intended anything more than playfulness. In truth, I'm not sure if I'll be able to...perform as required. However, I very much like the direction this is taking. Let's see if we can make this work."

He kissed her again, shifting her closer. The position wedged her knees to either side of his hips, and it left little up to the imagination, and she leaned forward to kiss him in return. When he finally cupped her breasts, she sighed out his name and allowed herself to relax against him. Even if neither of them was at their best, it could only be good between them.

He slowly rocked against her, the solid heat of him hotter than the bathwater. "I can't guarantee stamina, but I'm more than willing to brave an attempt," he rumbled in her ear.

"I love you," she said in between kisses and nips as she caressed him.

Gregory rumbled his own deep-throated words of love, and then there was no more talking for a long time, only soft kisses, groans, and laughter. And lots of splashing.

CHAPTER FORTY-THREE

A heavy-handed knocking roused Lillian enough to lift her head off Gregory's well-muscled chest. Whoever was on the other side of the door better have a damned good reason.

"If the Lord of the Underworld and the Lady of Battles are not, at this very moment, fighting to the death on the front lawn," Gregory growled at the door. "I'm going to eat someone."

There was a stretch of silence, and then shuffling outside the door. Lillian heard Gran's voice scolding someone. "Get out of my way."

"Sure," Jason whispered back. "Better you than me. Gregory didn't sound too happy about being disturbed."

The door handle wiggled, but the door didn't open. Lillian had wised up and started locking it. Gregory had laughed at her last night.

She arched a brow at him. "See? Told you. Not even

twenty-four hours of peace. My bet is the scientists want us to pee in a cup."

"Humans are strange."

"And gargoyles aren't?"

The knocking came again. Harder. Gran this time.

"Get out here, or you two are going to miss all the action. The hamadryad is up to something."

Gregory lunged out of bed so fast it bounced. Lillian jumped to her feet as well.

He was already tying on his beaded loincloth. Lillian was just a step behind him when she pulled on the first thing that came to hand—a sundress.

What had Gran sounding so flustered? More importantly, what was her hamadryad up to now? Had she returned Gryton?

She raced after Gregory as they made their way downstairs and out the back door. He dropped to all fours and soon outdistanced Lillian. In dryad form, she couldn't keep up with him, and he was so focused on his destination, he was ignoring the warning flares from the tattoos.

Well, hell. Even breaking into a sprint, Lillian barely kept the tip of his tail in sight. She raced after him, calling his name, but he ignored her. By the time she cleared the maze and crossed the distance to her tree, Gregory was already there. He reared up to stand on two legs, his wings mantled out behind him in shocked surprise.

Lillian joined him, wishing she'd thought to grab a sword or some other weapon.

Inching out around his wings, she peered at her tree, not sure what she was expecting to see. But the gaping, bloody crevasse in the hamadryad's trunk wasn't it. The greater surprise was the slim line of a leg emerging from the trunk. It was pale, and blood covered, but human-looking. The rest of the body followed suit, extracting itself—no herself, for the body was female—from the hamadryad's embrace.

Lillian might as well have been a statue. All she could do was stand and stare at the woman, too shocked to do anything else.

The woman held up a hand and studied her arm, wiggling the fingers and then glanced down at the rest of her nude, blood-smeared body. She compressed her lips at the sight of the blood, or maybe it was the nudity part. Lillian had no idea, but with a wave of one hand, the bloody residue of her birth disappeared.

Now the stranger was merely naked. It didn't seem to bother her overly much as she took a couple of wobbling steps from the base of the tree. Lillian noted how the stranger grasped one of the branches, using it to steady her first few steps. Her newborn-like lack of coordination didn't look like it was going to stop her from achieving her goal, which to Lillian's unsettling realization was Gregory.

The destination shouldn't have been a surprise. Lillian had always been drawn to Gregory's presence even when he'd been a stone statue in Gran's garden. So, it made perfect sense this stranger would be equally drawn to him.

Lillian's own throat had closed off to the point where swallowing past the lump in her throat was nearly as impossible as unclenching her locked jaw. All she could do was watch in a kind of dreadful fascination as the stranger made it halfway to Gregory.

He merely watched her approach, outwardly calm, but his tail flicked with excitement and his wings tremored with each beat of his great heart. If he'd been a dog, he would have been thumping his tail and wiggling with happiness at first sight of his beloved owner.

Lillian's heart dropped to her toes, and she broke out in a clammy sweat, seeing more than her happy future with Gregory evaporate as her clone held out her hand and gestured him forward.

So, the hamadryad had found a solution to the problem of the tattoos.

Gregory had said she would. Yet, Lillian didn't think even he had guessed the tree would do this. The fae standing around seemed equally shocked.

"Durnathyne, my Hunting Shadow, my other half, I have missed you," the clone said in Lillian's own voice.

"My Sorceress," Gregory answered, emotion thickening his voice as he swooped into a deep old-world bow.

The other fae took their cue from Gregory and bowed to the Sorceress.

When Gregory straightened, he gave a little shudder and then dropped to all fours and bounded over to Lillian's twin.

"Beloved," he said as he gathered her to him, sheltering her in his vast wings. "Forgive me, had I known, I would have been here sooner."

"There is nothing to forgive."

The Sorceress turned her gaze to Lillian, a hint of pity showed in her eyes.

Lillian didn't bow, and she damn sure wasn't going to let this one see her tears. Instead, she returned her replacement's pitying regard with her own steely gaze, and said, "Welcome to the Mortal Realm, Sorceress. It takes some getting used to, I'm told."

And so too would this, Lillian thought.

But she'd survived everything else fate and the Divine Ones had thrown at her. She'd damn well survive this also.

THE END

Lillian, Gregory, Shadowlight and Corporal Anna Mackenzie's adventures will continue in
Sorceress at War.

Hey before you go, can I interest you in signing up for my author newsletter?
You get my free starter library as a gift for joining.

http://lisablackwood.com/join-the-newsletter-here/

Did you enjoy Sorceress Hunting?

If you have a moment and wouldn't mind leaving a review, that would be greatly appreciated.

Reviews help other readers to decide if a book is something they would like.

It doesn't need to be long. Even a few words is tremendously helpful.

None of this would have been possible without, you, my readers. You're awesome! Thank You!

Bye for now,
Lisa Blackwood

ABOUT THE AUTHOR

Lisa Blackwood is the author of the bestselling Gargoyle and Sorceress urban fantasy series. Her work has also landed on the Wall Street Journal and the USA Today Bestseller lists as part of the Dominion Rising Anthology. When she's not reading and writing, she also enjoys gardening and spending time with her horse and her dogs.

At present, she grudgingly lives in a small town in Southern Ontario, though she would much rather live deep in a dark forest, surrounded by majestic old-growth trees. Since she cannot live her fantasy, she decided to write fantasy instead.

BOOKS BY LISA BLACKWOOD

Gargoyle & Sorceress

Dawn of the Sorceress

Sorceress Awakening

Sorceress Rising

Sorceress Hunting

Sorceress at War

Sorceress Enraged

Legacy of the Sorceress

Sorcery & Firedrakes

Scion of the Sorceress

Sorceress Eternal

In Deception's Shadow Series (Epic Fantasy Romance)

Betrayal's Price

Herd Mistress

Maiden's Wolf

Death's Queen

The Prince's Gryphon (forthcoming)

Ishtar's Legacy Series (Epic Fantasy Romance)

Ishtar's Blade

The Blade's Beginning (short story)

Blade's Honor

Blade's Destiny

The Blade's Shadow

First Queen of the Gryphons

The King of the Anunnaki (forthcoming)

The Anunnaki's Blade (forthcoming)

Huntress vs Huntsman (Epic Fantasy Romance)

Master of the Hunt

Night Huntress

Dragon Archer

Soul Mage (forthcoming)